THE ISLAND

A Selection of Recent Titles by M.J. Trow

The Grand & Batchelor Series

THE BLUE AND THE GREY *
THE CIRCLE *
THE ANGEL *
THE ISLAND *

The Kit Marlowe Series

DARK ENTRY *
SILENT COURT *
WITCH HAMMER *
SCORPIONS' NEST *
CRIMSON ROSE *
TRAITOR'S STORM *
SECRET WORLD *
ELEVENTH HOUR *

The Inspector Lestrade Series

LESTRADE AND THE KISS OF HORUS
LESTRADE AND THE DEVIL'S OWN
LESTRADE AND THE GIANT RAT OF SUMATRA

The Peter Maxwell Series

MAXWELL'S ISLAND
MAXWELL'S CROSSING
MAXWELL'S RETURN
MAXWELL'S ACADEMY

* *available from Severn House*

THE ISLAND

A Grand and Batchelor Victorian Mystery

M. J. Trow

CRÈME de la CRIME

This first world edition published 2017
in Great Britain and the USA by
Crème de la Crime, an imprint of
SEVERN HOUSE PUBLISHERS LTD of
19 Cedar Road, Sutton, Surrey, England, SM2 5DA.
Trade paperback edition first published
in Great Britain and the USA 2018 by
SEVERN HOUSE PUBLISHERS LTD

British Library Cataloguing in Publication Data
A CIP catalogue record for this title is available from the British Library.

ISBN-13: 978-1-78029-102-4 (cased)
ISBN-13: 978-1-78029-510-7 (trade paper)
ISBN-13: 978-1-78010-924-4 (e-book)

All Severn House titles are printed on acid-free paper.

Severn House Publishers support the Forest Stewardship Council™ [FSC™],
the leading international forest certification organisation.
All our titles that are printed on FSC certified paper carry the FSC logo.

Typeset by Palimpsest Book Production Ltd.,
Falkirk, Stirlingshire, Scotland.
Printed and bound in Great Britain by
TJ International, Padstow, Cornwall.

The quarter-moon did little to light Summer Street that night in Boston. Like most cities the world over, Boston rarely slept but on a November night in the warehouse district, it could be said at first glance to be dozing comfortably. There were people around, but few enough not to disturb the feral dogs and cats that wandered the sidewalks, scavenging the rubbish left outside the buildings. For every pile of cotton waste there was a pile of pig bones, so pickings were good, if a little sporadic.

Humans were outnumbered many times over by the dogs and cats, racoons and rats which scuttered over the cart-rutted roads. Every now and then, the *Boston Herald* would have a story about someone seeing a bear wandering across the Common, but there had been no really reliable sightings for years. Old Bostonians regretted that; they liked to think of themselves as still having that old pioneering spirit on the freedom trail behind the Minutemen. But for anyone with business in the deserted financial district at night, it was good to know that the worst that could happen to them would be coming face to face with a mangy dog or cat.

Boston didn't like to think of its problem of the ladies of dubious repute who prowled the streets after dark *as* a problem. Mayors and councillors for decades had denied they existed at all. The police rounded them up from time to time, treated them to a night or two in the cells, but otherwise they were free to ply their trade as long as they didn't do it in the road and frighten the horses. The business district might be deserted by honest citizens at night, but it had its very own population of women and the men they served, in the shadows, out of the light of the moon or the occasional police bullseye. They were a scuffle in the darkness, a cry in the shadow, but largely invisible, a miasma as real as the one which rose on cold nights such as this from the Charles River, across town.

It was early for there to be much trade going on, so a few of the ladies had gathered together for warmth in the doorway of the cotton warehouse at Number 82. They were giggling together as women will when discussing men's shortcomings and one of them in particular had a gift for mimicry which was unbeatable. Suddenly, one of them, a newcomer, hushed them.

'Ssh!' She held up a finger. 'What was that?'

'Ah, you're hearing the rats, honey,' one of the others scoffed. 'You'll get used enough to them when one runs over your skirts when you are with a gentleman guest.'

The listening one shook her head. 'No,' she said. 'I can hear something. Listen.'

They all cocked their heads in elaborate attitudes of attention. The woman was clearly hearing things. Then, one by one, they heard it too. The crackle of fire, somewhere nearby. They all instinctively moved out of the warehouse doorway. Cotton waste was notoriously flammable and could smoulder for hours before bursting suddenly into an inferno.

'Look!' Someone pointed across the road. Behind the huge, blank windows, a blossom of fire was glowing and as they stood there transfixed, another window, then another and another, sprang to orange, flickering life.

'Run!' Suddenly there were people everywhere. A janitor dashed out of the burning building, calling for help as he ran. The shoulders of his thick jacket were smouldering and there was ash in his hair.

'Help!'

'Fire! Fire!'

Rats poured out of the buildings the length of the street. Women and their gentlemen guests appeared from every doorway. The newcomer in their trade looked around her in amazement. Who would have thought that there were so many, so silently hidden. The street was like a market day, back in her home town far away, full of milling souls. A man brushed past her, knocking her to the ground.

'Out of my way, bitch!' he snarled at her, eyes flashing, and he was gone, as a wall of flame suddenly shot up ahead of him and he seemed to disappear into it. With the flames growing, pouring out of the windows like arms, reaching for her with their hot fingers, she scrambled upright, took to her heels and ran for her life.

ONE

The smell of bacon hit James Batchelor like a warm blanket as he pushed open the door of the house behind the Strand. The sounds of Mrs Rackstraw's voice raised in discordant song wafted with it up from the basement kitchen and he smiled to himself as he hung his hat on the stand in the hall. It was good to be home. He hated the all-night jobs, and not just because they usually meant a cold and lonely vigil waiting for an errant husband or wife to show their true colours. He hated them too because he felt left out of the real world, the world where eight hours in a nice warm bed was preceded by a milky drink, preferably laced with something comforting and then, with morning, the curtains would be pulled aside by willing hands to reveal a golden London morning, the sun gilding the dome of St Paul's and a cup of tea steaming on the nightstand. He was feeling grubby and grumpy, bacon notwithstanding. The next all-night job was Matthew Grand's and no error.

The morning room was awash with sunlight, streaming like golden syrup across a table littered with breakfast detritus. The toast was mere crumbs, the coffee pot had an empty look. Batchelor sat down opposite his partner and shook it experimentally.

Grand looked up from his letters and smiled. 'James,' he said, as though it were just moments ago since they had last been speaking, 'did you sleep well?' He glanced at the clock. 'Bit late for you, isn't it? I believe Mrs Rackstraw has kept breakfast for you, though.'

Batchelor flared his nostrils. 'I have been out all night, as a matter of fact,' he said, sharply.

Grand raised an eyebrow. 'Have you, indeed? Well, you're a dark horse and no mistake. May I ask the lady's name?' He gave a little man-of-the-world chuckle and sat back, waiting.

Batchelor could feel his throat tighten with annoyance.

Matthew Grand was a good detective and a dear friend, but when it came to remembering what was going on outside his own head, he fell very far short of perfection. 'The Duchess of Chilcott,' he said, keeping his voice level.

Grand slapped the table and guffawed. 'James!' he shouted in delight. 'Moving up in the world!' He stopped then, frowning. 'But . . . surely . . . she's got to be fifty if she's a day.'

The door crashed back as Mrs Rackstraw shoved it open with a solid hip. She was bearing a tray laden with bacon, eggs, toast and a fresh pot of coffee. She put the whole lot down in front of Batchelor and put the back of a work-roughened hand on his forehead. 'You're as cold as ice, Mr James,' she said. 'But that's March for you. I'll get the girl to fill you a nice hot bath. I'll let you know when it's ready.' With an accusing look at Grand, she slammed out of the room again.

'Cold?' Grand asked. 'Does the Duchess prefer her tumbles al fresco, James?'

'No.' Batchelor let him wait while he chewed a giant mouthful of bacon, egg and toast. 'No, she does not, as a matter of fact. She prefers a feather bed with all the trimmings. Happily, she prefers it to be situated in the gardener's cottage, which has a handy apple tree growing outside. So I was able to lodge myself in the branches and watch for her arrival and her subsequent . . . activities. I only fell out twice, so it was not a bad night, all things being equal.'

'You were up a tree . . . Oh!' Grand slapped himself on the forehead. 'The Duchess of *Chilcott*! The *case*!'

His mouth full, Batchelor merely nodded.

'So, you have proof for the Duke, do you?'

'Not proof as such. There was no possibility of getting the camera up the tree and she was away like a greyhound once she had had her fun, so I missed it. The gardener, however, was most amenable. The Duchess isn't quite fifty, but he is only eighteen and is ready to move on to something a little less . . .'

'Feudal?'

'Good word. Yes. The Duke has promised him he can keep his job if he testifies. All in all, we can write this one up as finished.'

'Well done, James. I'll invoice the Duke later.'

'He's paid,' Batchelor said, digging in a pocket and dragging out a wad of rolled banknotes. 'He says he is going to deal with it from hereon in. I wouldn't like to be in the Duchess's shoes, that's for sure.'

'Well, that's a comfort,' Grand remarked suavely, reaching over and counting the money. 'Hmm. A bonus. You must have delivered the goods.'

'Well . . .' Batchelor found himself blushing. 'The Duchess has some rather esoteric tastes. The gardener had no problem describing them either. Sort of thing you find in the shadier bookshops down Villiers Street.' He blotted his forehead with a handkerchief. 'All in all, I will be happy not to look through any bedroom windows for a while.'

Grand beamed. 'I'm glad to hear you say that, James,' he said, waving some letters at him. 'I think it's time we took a little vacation.'

'Do you?' Batchelor knew that Grand was not as dependent on the earnings of the agency as he was, but even so, holidays were something that happened to other people.

'Yes. I have some letters here from the folks at home,' Grand said. 'And an invitation to my sister's wedding.'

'Martha's getting married? That's nice.' Batchelor had never met Grand's family, but felt he knew them all. The patrician father, who had never been able to understand Grand's choice of profession. The doting mother, torn between her only son and her husband. The little sister, who spun from one romance to another, her heart broken irrevocably on a regular basis. And now, she was getting married. Batchelor wondered what the odds were against it ever actually coming about.

'Well, I can't see it happening, myself,' Grand said. 'To be fair, she's never gotten this close to the altar before, so perhaps she really has found the right man this time. In fact,' he ruffled through the papers by his crumby plate, 'she says so here, look.' He pointed. There, in his sister's looping hand, Batchelor could clearly see the words 'The One'.

'We're not really going to go all that way, though, are we?' Batchelor asked. 'For a wedding?'

'I wouldn't as a rule,' Grand said. 'But it is my little sister. And . . . I won't lie to you, James. Sometimes I do miss my mom.'

Batchelor was touched. He had always known that Grand and his mother were close. The letters came weekly, full of news and family titbits of gossip. But it seemed strange, therefore, that Grand had seemed to have no inkling of the forthcoming wedding. As if he had read his mind, Grand spoke again.

'And anyway, I want to know why this wedding has come out of the blue. It wouldn't be out of the question for my father to have arranged this for the sake of his business. Martha and I were always commodities in his eyes, pieces of real estate, really. I got away, so Martha has to earn the keep of two.'

'But he seems to be The One,' Batchelor pointed out.

Grand smiled mirthlessly. 'Martha could easily be persuaded that he is The One,' he said. 'Don't forget how many "Ones" she has had over the last few years, ever since she came out?'

Batchelor chuckled. 'I stopped counting at ten,' he said.

'Exactly so. So . . . a little holiday?'

'Can we afford it?' Batchelor didn't like to say out and out that he couldn't.

'I don't know about *we*,' Grand said. 'But *I* can. Let me treat you for once, James. After all,' he smiled at his friend and partner, 'you *have* been up a tree watching a Duchess do what a Duchess does all night. You deserve a rest.'

'And we have been busy,' Batchelor said, persuading himself.

'But it's gone a lot quieter,' Grand agreed. 'We've just got a couple of domestic things pending and we can always farm those out.'

'It isn't as if the Yard has asked for our help lately,' Batchelor said. 'Dolly Williamson seems to be coping without us.'

'He'll be back.' Grand reached over and helped himself to the last slice of Batchelor's toast. 'But he'll have to wait.'

'When are we leaving?' Batchelor had caught the excitement of the pending trip.

'This morning,' Grand said, pushing back his chair and swallowing the toast. 'On the boat train from Waterloo.'

'This morning? Impossible! I must pack!' Batchelor said, jumping up.

'All done,' Grand said, making for the door. 'Have a quick bath, change your linen and we're off!'

Mrs Rackstraw, listening behind the door, rubbed her hands

together. She hadn't thought it would be this easy. Her niece and her three children, homeless this last month after her wastrel husband had done a runner, would fit very nicely into the house without the gentlemen in residence. It would give her family time to gather their scattered wits and find somewhere else to live. She had sent a message as soon as she knew that Grand had bought the passages.

'But wait!'

She held her breath. Mr James, always trying to put a spoke in the wheel.

'What, James?'

She stepped away from the door and pretended to polish the hat-stand. It wouldn't do to be found eavesdropping again, however much the mahogany gleamed.

'What if someone really needs us? What if someone comes, with a case, and we're not here?'

'They'll have to wait. London's been here a while, I guess. It'll be here when we get back.'

She could tell that Mr Matthew had turned to the other man. She smiled like something better suited to basking on a rock at the dawn of time. When Mr Matthew wanted something, not many people could resist.

'Come on, James, old man. Think of poor little Martha. Forced into a marriage with an unsuitable bounder.' How could an American sound so much like a Penny Dreadful?

Mrs Rackstraw nodded to herself. Talking English English. That always clinched the deal.

'Well . . .'

'You know we must, James.' The handle turned and Mrs Rackstraw flew across the hall and carried on her polishing at the far corner. 'We *owe* it to poor little Martha.'

'Well, if you put it that way . . .'

And the deal was done.

The sun was dappling the filing cabinets by the time Superintendent Williamson reached his office. Whitehall Place had never looked so crowded, the Black Marias lined up with the ostlers harnessing the horses and the clash and carry that every morning brought. Williamson threw his hat in the approximate direction of the stand and, as if on cue, there was Jonas, hair carefully Macassared, a mug of tea in each hand.

'Good morning, sir. Cup that cheers?'

'Morning, Jonas. Thanks. Any news?'

'Nothing yet, sir. Well . . . apparently the Duchess of Chilcott fell in the lake early this morning. The housekeeper sent a runner to the Yard, but there's nothing for us there. Just some daffy rich tart wandering lonely as a cloud or summat.'

Williamson chuckled. He had heard the rumours. He looked at the man, slightly hazy now through the steam of the mug. 'You shouldn't be here, Fred. It's not every day a man becomes a father, if you catch my drift.'

'Ah, I've been here before, sir. My Emily's never in a hurry. It was the same with little Fred. And little Emily, come to think of it.'

'What's this one to be called?' Williamson asked. The Jonas parents were not over-endowed with imagination, and this third child would tax them to the limit, he was sure.

'Well, if it's a boy, we'd like to call him Adolphus.'

Williamson looked over the rim of his tea mug. 'That's ridiculous, Jonas,' he said. 'People will call him "Dolly". And that's no way for a grown man to be known.' He winked at the sergeant, who never knew whether he should take his guv'nor seriously or not. Yes, everybody called Superintendent Adolphus Williamson 'Dolly'. But they only ever did it behind his back.

'And if it's a girl?' Williamson asked. 'What then?'

'Oh, it's not going to be a girl, sir. My Emily has a sixth sense about these things. She's been right so far. And I've got a team of runners on hand to get news to me when anything breaks, in a manner of speaking.'

'Right, then.' Williamson put the mug down and sat in his swivel chair, one of the few luxuries he allowed himself at Scotland Yard. 'To cases. What have we got?'

Sergeant Jonas hauled a ledger off the desk and flicked to the relevant page. 'Another insurance office raided, sir. Early hours.'

'Where?'

'Bow Street.'

Williamson nodded. 'That's C Division's problem. What else?'

'Body parts. Sir. Battersea.'

'Can you be specific as to parts?'

'Doctor wasn't sure, sir. Torso and one leg, he thought. Left, to be precise. But it could be a goat.'

Williamson blinked. 'Who's the surgeon?' he asked.

'Er . . .' Jonas scanned the ledger. 'Grimshaw, sir. B Division.'

The superintendent nodded. 'Ah, no surprises there, then. Fanny Grimshaw was last in the line when they gave out the medical certificates. Anyhow, it's a Thames issue. I wouldn't deprive the Bluebottles of their bit of fun. Anything else?'

'Well, there's the Carberry business, sir, ongoing.'

Williamson sighed. 'Isn't it, though? Refresh my memory, Jonas; when did old man Carberry call last?'

'Three days ago, sir. Tuesday.'

'Really? You amaze me. I thought the man camped out in the vestibule. How annoyed was he, in the scheme of things?'

'Very, I'd say, sir. Used language that fair made some of the lads blush, I can tell you.'

'Recapitulate for me, there's a good detective sergeant.'

Jonas cleared his throat. 'Peter Arbuthnot Carberry, aged thirty-one, found dead in Regent's Park on the fourteenth inst. Head bashed in. Single powerful blow to the cranium. Wallet still in pocket. Watch still on chain. Chain still fixed to waistcoat.'

Williamson raised an eyebrow. 'Clothing disarranged?' he asked.

Jonas checked his notes. 'Inspector Oates says "no", sir.'

'Good enough for me.' The superintendent knew his men. If Oates said 'no' then 'no' it was. 'So, no robbery. Nothing unnatural. Signs of a struggle?'

'No, sir. I don't think the late Mister Carberry knew what hit him.'

'Enemies, then?' Williamson was leaning back in his chair, resting his clasped hands over his waistcoat and closing his eyes. He had been down roads like this before, more times than Jonas had had hot dinners. There was a sense of the mechanical about it.

'According to everybody Mr Oates has spoken to, sir, the deceased was some sort of saint. He was a model boss in the haberdashery trade; went to church of a Sunday – or chapel, I should say; Calvinistic Methodist; gave to charity; devoted husband and father.'

Williamson shook his head. 'I just love these, don't you, Jonas? There's no earthly reason why this man should be dead, but he's already pushing up the daisies in Kensal Green and we haven't got the first clue who put him there. Time to shelve it, don't you think? Usual assurances to family – no stone unturned, every avenue pursued, clichés by the thousand. Whereas actually—'

'Filing system, basement,' Jonas nodded. 'Third level.'

Williamson nodded. The third level of Scotland Yard's basement was the Abyss. Lowly constables crept in there with a candle for company, left the case notes and got out before the dank darkness consumed them. The third level was the rats' domain; better leave it alone.

'Er . . . the only problem, sir . . .' Jonas felt he had to raise it.

'. . . is that old man Carberry owns a sizeable chunk of London and moves in circles so far above us that he might as well be in heaven with his late grandson; yes, I know. The Home Secretary calls him Tommy and in the days when we still had a Queen, he was a regular visitor at the Palace. However . . .' Williamson leaned forward, stirring his tea with the blunt end of his pen.

Jonas couldn't help but smile. He knew that look on the guv'nor's face. It was the look of a man about to pass the buck.

'Grand and Batchelor.'

'Sir?' Jonas sat upright. He knew those names – every copper in Scotland Yard did – but he hadn't expected to hear them in quite this context.

'Get a bobby . . . no, better; go yourself. You know their offices, along the Strand?'

'Yes, sir, but surely . . .'

Dolly Williamson could freeze any detective sergeant with his basilisk stare and Jonas stopped in mid-sentence.

'I know, Fred,' he said, quietly. 'Grand and Batchelor are amateurs, with none of our technical expertise. They work for the grubbiest of reasons – money. But, although I'd tear out my own tongue rather than admit it, either to them or in public, they happen to be rather good at what they do. Tell them there's a case of national importance. Do not, repeat, do not tell them we're stumped. On no account are you to mention the name of Carberry. Clear?'

'As a bell, sir.'

'Good. Don't worry, Sergeant. On paper and as far as the world knows, *we'll* still be handling the case. And if Messrs Grand and Batchelor come up with the goods, *we* will take the credit. It's the way of the world.'

'Do you think they'll do it, sir?' Jonas asked. 'I mean, what's in it for them?'

Williamson settled back again, with a complacent air. 'They're private detectives, sergeant; enquiry agents, I believe they call themselves. They'll have been trailing errant husbands and looking for lost cats for months. I'm giving them a juicy unsolved murder on a plate. Man, they'll be more grateful than they know.'

As usual, the Strand's traffic was chaotic that morning. A dray horse had gone down on Wellington Street and the language, even by the standards of London's cabbies, was particularly choice. Fred Jonas, of course, knew a short cut, so he hopped out of the growler and took to the pavement, straight into the arms of Jesus. General Booth's angels rarely came this far west since the godlessness of the Mile End Waste kept them pretty busy; yet here they were, all black taffeta and tambourines, their shrill voices rising to the smut-laden rooftops and the Lord above them.

Jonas tipped his hat but otherwise kept a close grip on his wallet and his loose change. He ducked down Catherine Street towards the river where the black lighters drifted in the tide and the pale spring sunshine sparkled on the dark water. He turned left, through Angel Court and down the cobbled alley that ran between the offices of the greatest city in the world. All the way from Whitehall Place, he'd been trying to remember the number of Messrs Grand and Agents and he finally settled on 46. Since the shingle there, gleaming brass in the late morning, read Wetherby and Sons, Notaries Public, he changed his mind and tried 48.

He took the stairs two at a time and rapped on the glass of the door. The place looked deserted. Bugger. But all was not lost. He knew where the pair lived, further east and he retraced his steps.

He was still retracing them when Grand and Batchelor clambered on to their growler in a flurry of suitcases and portmanteaus and disappeared around the corner.

'Scarf.' Batchelor clicked his fingers and stepped down again from the rocking gig.

Grand rolled his eyes heavenwards. 'You won't need it, James,' he called. 'Maine in the spring is delightful.'

But Batchelor didn't hear him. He nipped down the mews at the back of the house and went in through the kitchen. Mrs Rackstraw, humming happily to herself as she gathered the ingredients together for a welcoming cake for tea, almost died of fright to see one of her young men suddenly back again.

'Something wrong, Mr Batchelor?' she asked, through lips tight with the stress of it all.

'My scarf, Mrs R.,' he said. 'The blue paisley.'

'Oh, you won't be needing that, sir,' she soothed, with the air of a woman expecting her homeless family at any moment. Batchelor ignored her, dashing up the stairs. It was a trifle, really, the scarf, but the haste of this departure had unnerved him more than a little. Everybody seemed just too keen for them to go. It was almost as if . . .

'There's somebody at the door, Mrs R.,' she heard Batchelor call from upstairs.

There was. A large dark shape beyond the glass. And the shape had rung the bell. Mrs Rackstraw hauled up her voluminous skirts and scuttled down the corridor. No one in her imminently expected family loomed as large as that beyond the glass, but even so.

'Yes?' she scowled, keeping her voice low.

'Detective-Sergeant Jonas,' Jonas said. 'Scotland Yard.' He edged out the silver-crowned tipstaff from his inside pocket by way of identification. 'Looking for Mr Grand.'

'Missed him, I'm afraid,' she said, and leaned her weight against the door.

Jonas was faster. Years of doorstepping people who didn't

want to talk to him had given him lightning reflexes. His size tens stopped the mahogany in its tracks. 'Batchelor, then,' he smiled. 'I'll settle for Batchelor.'

'Him an' all,' she said, trying to stare the sergeant down. 'Gone.'

'Who is it, Mrs R.?' Batchelor called down from upstairs.

'They've gone away.' Mrs Rackstraw was suddenly hard of hearing. 'Like I said, you've missed 'em.'

Jonas was not about to take that for an answer. 'Then who . . .?' he pointed up the stairs from where the voice had come.

'Mr Jonas, Mr Jonas!' A squeaky voice shattered the moment and a grubby urchin stood on Grand and Batchelor's front step. 'Message from Constable Barret, sir. 'E says you're to come quick!'

'Barret?' he said to the lad. 'Big bloke? Ginger hair?'

'No, sir,' the boy frowned. 'Little bloke. Sort of brown. His hair, that is. Not him. He give me a message.'

'What message?'

The lad screwed up his freckled face to remember it. 'He says, "Beggin' your pardon, Sarge, it's Mrs Jonas's time." Or summat like that. Oh, and he give me half a crown, too.'

'Did he?' Jonas said, noting the boy's outstretched hand. 'Well, that was generous, wasn't it?' He glanced up at Mrs Rackstraw, still quietly trying to dislodge his foot. 'I'll be back,' he said, his life – and his wife – whirling before him. 'Tell Grand and Batchelor I'll be back. It's urgent.'

She slammed the door, hearing the departing footsteps of the detective and the plaintive whining of the lad. 'Constable Barret said you was good for another half-crown.'

There was a thunder of boots on the stairs. 'Got it, Mrs R.' Batchelor was waving his scarf as he made for the back door. 'Who was that?'

'Some beggar,' Mrs Rackstraw told him. 'Brought his kid with him. I hate that, don't you? When they use their kids to get money. There ought to be a law.'

'Indeed there ought,' Batchelor called back. Suddenly, he stopped. 'Will you be all right, Mrs R.?' he asked. 'All alone in this great big place?'

Mrs Rackstraw put on her bravest smile. 'Oh, I'll manage, sir, really I will.'

TWO

The docks at Southampton had not been conducive to chatting and Batchelor didn't get a chance to share something with Grand until they were in their laughingly called stateroom, in which a cat would be totally safe from being swung. But at last, as they lay in their bunks on board the *Frisia*, tucked in by a steward who would brook no argument and who would rule their lives for the next eleven days, he had his moment.

'Matthew,' he said, over the creak of the pitch-pine lining of the cabin, 'you do know I don't travel well, don't you?'

From above his head, he heard Grand chuckle. 'I haven't forgotten the last time, no,' he said. 'Why do you think you are on the bottom bunk?'

Batchelor was silent for a moment. 'I don't think I was that bad, was I?'

'I doubt you remember that much,' Grand remarked. 'As I recall, you lived almost entirely on beef tea, rum and sal volatile. You did come into dinner that one time, but you didn't stay long. Pity, the devilled kidneys were just peachy. Yours were particularly good.'

The silence from the lower bunk was almost deafening. Batchelor had heard this story before and he still didn't believe it.

'You sat next to the granddaughter of the Duchess of wherever. You must remember them; they had fallen on hard times and they were off to seek her fortune in the West. I told her the silver was all played out in the Comstock lodes, but she wasn't having any.'

Still nothing from down below.

'She had a face like a boot. That was the granddaughter. The grandmother doesn't bear thinking about. I hope they found some mining town which was still short of womenfolk, or I think they were doomed to disappointment. You gave her a thrill, though, James, didn't you?'

'Did I?' The voice was tight with menace. If the floor would hold still for a minute, Grand would be sorry for bringing the story up.

'You were not too bad for the soup, though you did get that dumpling down her décolletage. The trouble came when you passed out during the entrée and followed the dumpling. It was a good job we had cleared the coast of Ireland, or they would have put us off in Cork.'

'I have no memory of it,' Batchelor said and closed his mouth with a snap.

Grand chuckled again. 'Don't be snappy,' he said. 'We've a ways to go and we don't need to fall out just yet. Let me tell you about my family. It's best you know the worst before you meet them, I think.'

'I know about your parents and Martha.' Batchelor wasn't ready to be friends yet.

'They're not even the half of it,' Grand said. 'My mother comes from a family of eight girls, though I doubt they'll all come to the wedding. Four of them are dead anyway and one is in Wisconsin, so as good as. Auntie Mimi is as mad as a rattler and doesn't travel. Mom is the next to youngest. Her baby sister, Auntie Nell, she'll be there. You'll like her.' Again, the chuckle. 'And she'll like you. She likes 'em young, does Auntie Nell. But don't turn your back on her and you'll be fine.'

Batchelor made a mental note.

'Pa comes from a smaller family. Just him and Uncle Josiah left now. I gather there many children born and died between the two, but that was how it was back then. Only Philip, Pa and Josiah made it to manhood. Uncle Phil died in the war. Uncle Josiah is older than Pa by a good few years and doesn't wear it well – I guess the hooch will do that to a man. Mom has asked me to look him up in Boston on our way to the wedding. He will never make it on his own otherwise.'

'Does he know we're coming?' Batchelor's voice was slurring with sleep.

'No. Well, I say no. There's no point in telling Uncle Josiah anything in advance. He's got the long-term memory of a May bug, but he'll be happy enough to see me when we get there. I'm his favourite nephew.'

Batchelor did some mental arithmetic. 'How many does he have?'

'Just me, these days. But I would be his favourite, anyway, don't you think? I well remember the time when he came to stay over, we used to go fishing in the creek. That's at the country house, of course, not the town house. Lord, yes . . .' But Grand's reminiscences fell on deaf ears. James Batchelor was asleep.

'Tell me again, Matthew.' James Batchelor leaned back in the First Class Pullman. He couldn't see anything out of the window, what with the New York fog, the locomotive's steam and the condensation running down the glass.

'Just think of it like this.' Grand was patience itself, holding up his right hand. 'This,' he pointed to the palm, 'is New York. Sort of London, through a funny glass.'

Batchelor nodded. He had been to New York before, but he hadn't remembered it being so built up, with tall towers every-where and buildings of a depressing shade of brown everywhere he looked.

'Cornelius Vanderbilt's railroad lines are my fingers. We're taking this one.'

'Your pinkie,' Batchelor said, to prove to his colleague that he understood.

Grand looked at him oddly. 'Whatever,' he said. 'My little finger is the Jersey City and Albany Line, running through . . . and the conductor will correct me if I'm wrong, Jersey City, Stamford, Bridgeport and New Haven. We'll have to change there to cut across to Norwich, Cranston and Quincy before we hit Boston.'

'Ah.' Batchelor smiled. He was getting his bearings now. 'The Tea Party.'

'As you say,' Grand smiled too, but for a different reason. 'We're going to pick up Uncle Josiah there.'

'Josiah,' Batchelor repeated. 'He's the drunk?' Batchelor's memory of Grand's cabin stories on the *Frisia* was hazy, crowded as it was with the rolling ocean and the salt spume spray.

'That's the cuss,' Grand nodded. 'He'd never find his way north by himself. Sometimes he finds it hard enough to find his ass with both hands. That's where we come in.'

'So there are still Grands in Boston?' Batchelor was trying to find somewhere to put his portmanteau. Even a First Class compartment on a Pullman left a lot to be desired.

'I think Josiah's the last of the line,' Grand said. 'Everybody else moved down to Washington way before the war. Except Ira, of course.'

'Ira?' Batchelor frowned. 'I don't think I remember him.'

'Nobody does. I didn't mention him on the boat because he's probably no longer with us.'

'Cousin?'

Grand nodded. 'Philip's boy. Ran away to sea in . . . fifty-nine, I think it was. I was still at school. Ira's a good couple of years older than me. Last we heard, he was on a whaler out of New Bedford.'

'So . . . if he *is* still with us, will he be at the wedding?'

'Hell, no. Nobody – and I mean nobody – has heard from him since before the war. And, believe me, we've got enough black sheep and skeletons without Ira joining the fold.'

'Or the closet.' Batchelor could be irritatingly pedantic at times.

'Or, as you say, the closet.' Grand shook out his *New York Times* and retired behind it. 'Tammany Hall under fire' screamed the headlines. It was all Greek to James Batchelor.

The door swung open with a rattle of latches and a scream of hinges.

'Good morning, gentlemen,' an English voice said. 'Any room in here?'

'I'm afraid not,' Grand said automatically spreading his newspaper even wider to indicate the lack of space.

'My God!' Batchelor sat upright, open-mouthed.

'Something troubling you, young man?' the Englishman asked. 'I assume you *have* seen an astrakhan collar before.'

'Aren't you . . . aren't you Edward Latham?'

The Englishman raised an eyebrow. 'And if I am?'

'Sir,' Batchelor said. 'If you are, please allow me to shake you by the hand. You are legend where newsmen gather.'

'I am legend where anyone gathers,' Latham said. 'Who are you?'

'Oh, you won't have heard of me. I'm James Batchelor.'

'You're right,' Latham said. 'I haven't.'

'I used to write for the *Telegraph*.'

'Oh, bad luck.'

'Matthew, this is Edward Latham, of *The Times*.'

Nothing.

'*The* Edward Latham.'

Still nothing.

'The *New York Times* at the moment, dear boy,' Latham said, tapping Grand's paper. 'Edward Delane made me an offer I couldn't refuse.'

'Mr Latham is a god,' Batchelor enthused. 'Covered the Mutiny in Fifty-Seven, your Civil War of course. And the Franco-Prussian business.'

'Keeps me off the streets,' Latham smiled, his head swelling further with every puff that Batchelor gave him.

'Fascinating,' said Grand. 'But I'm afraid there's still no room in here.'

'Oh, but surely, we can . . .' Batchelor was already squeezing himself into one corner, trying to create space.

'Tell me, Mr Latham,' Grand said. 'How many cases are you carrying?'

The doyen of newspapermen glanced back at the porters struggling along the platform. 'Er . . . I don't know . . . eight or so. On my way to some Godforsaken place to cover some Godawful society wedding.' He closed to Batchelor. 'It's not all about cutting-edge journalism,' he murmured. 'But then, as a *Telegraph* man, you'd know all about that. Not to worry. You, there,' he pointed at a porter who was almost invisible behind a steamer truck. 'Get along or we won't leave until tomorrow. I'm going to have to have a word with the Commodore about his bloody railways. Well, come on, man. What did that nice Mr Lincoln give you people freedom for if you can't carry a case?' And he vanished into the fog.

'My God.' Batchelor sat back again, his eyes bright with

excitement, hero-worship seeping from every pore. 'I can't believe it. It's like . . . it's like . . .'

'It's likely we'll meet him again,' Grand said, putting aside his paper, tilting his hat over his eyes and folding his arms.

'Why do you say that?' Batchelor asked.

'Stands to reason.' Grand didn't move. 'He's going to cover a society wedding at some Godforsaken place that can't be far from here; not on this line. How many society weddings can there be between here and a hard place?'

'That's amazing,' Batchelor said, tilting his hat back on his head and loosening his tie. 'Just amazing.'

'Isn't it, though?' Grand murmured, sleep starting to claim him already. 'Tell me again; what is it you do for a living?'

But Batchelor's quite colourful reply was drowned out by a shrill whistle and a loud voice yelling, 'All aboard for New Haven, calling at Jersey City, Stamford, Bridgeport and New Haven.'

'There you are,' Grand's lips barely moved. 'Told you so.'

Uncle Josiah wasn't at Boston and Lowell Station; but then Matthew Grand had not expected him to be. He slipped a porter a few bucks and obtained in return a list of hostelries within a tight radius from Summer Street to the Common. The pair left their luggage at the station and began the search. The Elephant didn't know him. He had been banned from the Paul Revere months ago. The Minuteman regularly entertained any number of gentlemen who *might* be Josiah Grand, but he wasn't there that day.

'Don't these pubs ever close?' Batchelor felt obliged to ask as they entered the umpteenth. His feet were killing him and this was a man who wore out shoe leather for a living.

'Bars, James, bars,' Grand reminded him. 'And no, they don't. Get me a beer, will you, while I check my list again.'

Batchelor called over a waiter. 'What's the best in the house?' he asked.

'Val Blatz, sir. Unless it's spirits you're after.'

'Are you Irish?' Batchelor asked. The detective was torn. He had an Englishman's aversion to Irishmen, but he was far from home and the man's accent was a breath of Spitalfields and points east. He decided to be civil.

'I am, sir. Offaly born and bred.'

Grand was a little surprised. The Irishmen he knew weren't usually so self-deprecating. 'Worked here long?' he asked.

'A little over three years, sir. There was nothing for me back home, so.'

'So?' Grand frowned.

'So I came over in steerage. There's more bloody Irish in Boston than ever there was in Offaly.'

'We're looking for someone,' Grand teased a bill from his wallet.

'Who might that be?' the waiter asked.

'Name of . . .' The door crashed back and an old soak stood there, crimson-faced and bloodshot-eyed. 'Never mind.'

'Ah, that'll be Josiah Grand,' the waiter beamed. 'And sure, there he is,' and with the speed of a bullet, he had whisked the dollar bill from Grand's hand and had gone in search of the Val Blatz.

'Uncle Josiah!' Grand stood up and moved centrally to the man so as to engage his vision.

'Do I know you, sir?' The old man looked the younger one up and down with one eye, the other searching for a waiter with his usual.

'You should, Uncle,' Grand said. 'I'm your nephew, Matthew.'

For a moment, the old man swayed, frowning and shaking his head, trying to focus on the here and now while dredging whatever was left of his memory. Then, his face brightened into a smile. 'Little Mattie!' he crowed, grabbing Grand's hand with both of his. 'How's the army?'

Grand sat him down. 'I resigned my commission, Uncle,' he said. 'A long time ago.'

'What? You never made general?'

Grand shook his head.

Uncle Josiah did too. 'How'd your papa take that? Must've broken the old feller's heart. And your mama? I don't even want to think about that.'

'Uncle, I only joined up because of the war,' Grand reminded him. 'Like a lot of cusses. Soldiering isn't in my blood. I was going to follow Pa into the bank.'

Josiah was appalled anew. 'What? You never made general manager?'

'No. I live in England now, Uncle. London. Remember? I wrote you.'

'London, huh?' Josiah was looking for the waiter with both eyes now and, as they wandered rheumily over the room, had found Batchelor. 'Who's this?'

'My associate,' Grand said. 'James Batchelor. James, I'd like you to meet Josiah Grand.'

'Sir.' Batchelor extended a hand.

Josiah scowled at him, took his hand briefly and leaned across to Grand. 'You know this cuss is a Goddamned Limey, don't you?'

'Yes,' Grand sighed. 'They tend to be in England.'

'Ah, Paddy me boy,' Josiah's eyes lit up at the waiter's arrival.

'Seamus, sir,' the waiter smiled, setting down his tray.

'You got that right,' Josiah said.

'I took it upon myself to bring your usual tipple, Mr Grand. I hope I did right.'

'In your calling, dear boy,' the old man held the glass aloft and looked into its amber contents, 'how could you not?' He sipped, sighed, closed his eyes and leaned back, apparently asleep. Suddenly, he was awake again, sitting bolt upright. 'So, Mattie,' he said, straightening his watch-chain and rubbing his eyes. 'What brings you to . . . er . . . Boston?' He looked around for confirmation of his location but, finding nothing, forgot all about it.

'The wedding, Uncle,' Grand sighed. This was worse than he had feared. The last time he had seen Josiah was eleven years ago, when the younger man was a lieutenant in the Third Cavalry of the Potomac. The old man had been quite lucid, then; at least he knew his blue from his grey. 'You know, Martha, your niece.'

Josiah frowned. 'Of course I know Martha's my niece. I may be the wrong side of sixty, feller, but I've still got some lead in my pencil. Who are you again?' He closed one eye and looked at the Englishman doubtfully.

'Batchelor, sir,' Batchelor said, wiping the froth from his moustache.

'Right,' Josiah said. 'And you make sure you stay that way, sonny. Women, huh, Mattie! They've been the downfall of us men right from the get-go. Ever since Eve. Who'd you say was getting married?'

'Martha, Uncle,' Grand sighed. 'Your niece. My sister.'

'I know, I know.' Josiah mopped up the tiny globule of drink he had spilled with his handkerchief and looked at the damp spot regretfully, deciding at the last minute that, in deference to company, he would not suck it to get the precious fluid as he otherwise would have done. A memory surfaced and spluttered at the surface of his brain. 'She's marrying that Linsey-Woolsey feller.'

'Chauncey-Wolsey,' Grand corrected him.

'Like I said. Getting married in Exeter.'

'Rye.' Grand corrected him again.

'Don't mind if I do. Paddy!' And the old boy's hand was in the air, desperately trying to click his fingers.

THREE

'**M**artha!' The woman descending from the carriage in a positive froufrou of furs and frills screamed above the yell of gulls wheeling in the sky above the Grand house on the hill. 'Martha! I can't believe I'm here for your *wedding*! I never did think I'd see the day!'

No one looking at the two as they ran into each other's arms would have dreamed that they were born just two months apart. One was a woman, the other still a girl, with hair unbraided down her back and a clean and open face. She was beautiful, with creamy skin dusted with freckles across the nose, and a mouth which, though a little petulant, was rosy without the help of cosmetics. The newcomer held the girl at arm's length.

'Why, Martha!' she said. 'You look as if you belong in the schoolroom. You're about to be married; you shouldn't be wearing your hair down like this. And . . .' she peered closer.

'Are those freckles on your nose? Have you been out in the sun without a parasol? Whatever is your mama thinking?'

Martha laughed and put her arm through her friend's, leading her into the house. 'Mom doesn't even own a parasol, let alone think of my freckles.' She dropped her voice. 'She lives here almost year-round these days,' she said. 'Pa goes to Washington or New York to see to business and sometimes he's gone for weeks. I can't say we miss him much. He and Mom haven't . . . well, let's say they haven't seen eye to eye for years now.'

'Mom? Pa? Martha Grand! You sound like something from a dime novel. Mama and Papa, that's what we were taught in school. Jeremy would never tolerate my using words like "Mom".'

Martha's face fell into a scowl. Her friend had once been a harum-scarum to beat the band and now here she was, trussed up like the Thanksgiving turkey and talking about parasols. It was this aspect of marriage that had always made Martha back away at the last minute. But she knew that her Hamilton would never try and change her. He loved her just the way she was, freckles and all. But Mrs Jemima Zzerbe was still speaking.

'Jeremy says it is too, *too* easy to fall into lax ways of speech.' She lowered her eyelids and leaned nearer. 'He says that coarse speech and behaviour will bring this country to the brink of another war, if we're not careful. Jeremy won't even . . . disrobe . . . in front of me. He says that too much coarseness . . .'

Martha laughed and gave her friend a pinch. 'Come, Mima,' she said. 'You can't tell me you have never seen Jeremy . . . disrobed. How do you . . .?'

Jemima bridled. 'Martha Grand, wash out your mouth this moment! I am here as your matron of honour and I promised Jeremy I would answer any questions you may have about . . .' she primmed her mouth and swallowed hard, '. . . about what is to come, but I will not have lewdness. No, I will not.'

'But Mima,' Martha said, 'I haven't said anything lewd, have I? I just wondered how you and Jeremy . . . but let's wait till later for that. Perhaps you don't want to speak of lovemaking while we are still only in the hall!'

'I don't want to speak of it at all!' Jemima's furs and lace were all of a tremble. 'There is more to marriage than *that*, you know.'

'Oh, I know,' Martha said. Her mother spent hours telling her about how to keep accounts, how to stop the servants getting above themselves, how to order the food, how to receive visitors. What Martha wanted to talk about was seemingly out of bounds. Her mother blushed. Mima quivered. Martha's head was full of Hamilton's naked body pressed to hers in the dark nights when he crept to her room. How his . . . 'Sorry.' She gave herself a shake. 'I wandered off for a moment there. Nerves.'

Jemima squeezed her hand. 'Of course,' she said. 'Of course you're nervous. But it lasts just a minute and hardly hurts at all.' She looked over her shoulder at the figure struggling in through the door, laden with boxes and bags. 'Alice,' she called. 'Be careful with those bags. My gowns will be crushed and then you will be up all night pressing them and we don't want that, do we?' She turned to Martha and laughed, a trill up and down the scale, as taught by her singing master. 'She is so cranky if she doesn't get her five hours' sleep.'

Martha peered closer at the woman outlined against the sun. 'Is that Alice? She looks . . . bigger.'

Jemima was puzzled for a moment, then smiled. 'No, it isn't *Alice*. Not Alice from when we were girls.'

Martha still thought of herself as a girl but didn't interrupt.

'No, that Alice died. Consumption. Something like that. No, this is . . .' She called over her shoulder again. 'What's your name, Alice? Your real name, you know.' She turned again to Martha. 'I can never remember it. Foreign, you see.'

'Magdalena, madam.' The voice was soft and low. 'Magda.'

'That's it. Anyway, I was used to calling for Alice, so that's what I call this one. It's easier for everyone.'

Martha, catching a glimpse of the woman's face, was not so sure.

'Is your old nurse still here? What was her name?'

Martha could hardly believe it. When she and Jemima were children they were hardly ever apart. If they weren't in Jemima's house, playing under the great kitchen table, begging scraps from the cook, they were racing around the Grands' enormous yard, climbing trees and coming in filthy for nursery teas presided over by beloved Annie. Annie, who had never stopped loving either Martha or Matthew, her charges since their births. Martha knew that the first thing Annie would say when she saw Mattie was that he was too thin. She would then flick a speck of lint from his shoulder. But the love in her eyes would be there, just as it had always been. She found herself not liking this new Jemima very much. 'Annie,' she said. 'Her name is Annie. And yes, she is still here. But she doesn't work now, of course.'

Jemima pulled back and made a disbelieving face. 'Why is she here, then?' she asked, nonplussed. 'Surely, she's not here for the *wedding*! The help at your *wedding*!'

Martha wanted to tell this stranger beside her that she wouldn't get married without Annie there. That her mother, her father, even her beloved brother, meant no more than a hill of beans when it came to being loved despite their faults. That Annie had always been there for her and while there was breath in her body always would be. When she moved with Hamilton to their little house in Boston, with its dear little yard and its rooms in the roof already earmarked for the nursery, then Annie would be coming too. And that only Annie knew quite how soon the nursery would be needed. But again, she chose the short answer. 'She is on a pension from Pa. She has made my wedding gown. She had been making the lace for it since I was about twelve. There's enough for a dozen gowns, but she has managed to cram it all on to this one.' She forced a laugh.

Jemima was again rather shocked. 'You will need lace for your nightgowns,' she said, censoriously. 'I have at least ten yards on each of mine, trimming the neck and cuffs. A wife has to remain decent, you know.'

They started up the stairs, Alice-Magda puffing in the rear. Martha had decided to pretend that she liked Jemima, otherwise she would be screaming before night fell. But it was going to be hard. Very hard. And especially as Hamilton had decided, for decency's sake, to stay in nearby Exeter until the wedding, seeing her at the wedding supper the night before the ceremony and not before. She would let Jemima braid her hair, paint her face discreetly and give her a talk about lying back with her eyes shut and her teeth clenched. But only Annie would be allowed to lace her gently into her wedding gown. Only Annie would be allowed to place her old, loving hand on her stomach, to quieten Hamilton's child quickening within.

James Batchelor craned his neck round to take in the house as they approached it from the road. It spread, white and gleaming, across the flat land carved from the hill, sweeping down to the water's edge. Its windows were wide like a child's eyes, the door stood open and a carrier's cart was parked near the entrance to the stable yard. Behind the house and outbuildings, a mixed forest of conifer and newly budding beech and maple swept up the hillside in a dense mass. From a distance, it looked like moss, thick and soft enough to lie on, but from nearer to, it became a forbidding place, the sun only just managing to gild the trees which leaned over on the cliff to the north. A neat little brougham was moving away down the other curve of the drive, the two bays tittupping on their oiled hoofs. All looked bustle and business and Batchelor was confused.

'I thought we were going to the small house,' he said, turning back to his companions behind him.

Josiah laughed a phlegmy chuckle.

'This *is* the small house,' Grand told him. 'The *big* house is one arc of Pacific Circle in Washington.'

'And don't forget,' Uncle Josiah chimed in, 'the *medium* house in Boston. That's just half of a side of Haymarket Square; Andrew lets me live there and it suits me. Ten bedrooms are plenty for a poor old man like me, living out his last lonely years.'

Grand looked at him wryly. 'Uncle Josiah,' he said, 'as I see it, your years are far from lonely. You know every barkeep in Boston, and I don't imagine you spend many nights alone unless you choose to.' He turned to Batchelor. 'Please don't take this old reprobate at face value, James. He is a favourite of most of the . . . shall we say "unattached" ladies, Uncle?'

Josiah nodded, chuckling evilly. He had had his moments and he wasn't going to tell his nephew and this Limey that only his memories kept him warm these nights. The sap didn't rise much these days, Josiah reasoned, because of the hooch. It was all about equilibrium.

'The unattached ladies in Boston. Despite appearances and his living scot-free in his brother's house . . .'

'*Your* house, Mattie, by rights,' Josiah pointed out.

Grand shrugged. 'In *my* house, he is worth a dollar or two and it seems a shame to let it go to waste.'

'You should hope they don't get me, Mattie,' Uncle Josiah said as the trap came to a halt. 'It will all be yours when I go, as you well know.'

Grand clapped the old man on the shoulder. 'You'll outlive us all, Uncle Josiah,' he said.

'It's true pickling does make things last longer, but I'm not sure that applies to livers.' Uncle Josiah was not a miserable drunk, you could at least say that for him. 'Where's m'hat?'

'You gave it to the carman at the station.' Batchelor came out of the reverie into which the house had thrown him. 'You wore his cap all the way to Exeter.'

'I did?' He was puzzled and looked aimlessly around. 'So where is it?'

'Where's what?' Grand had jumped down and was unloading the luggage from the rear.

'The cap.'

'You threw it away. As I recall, you asked us how a greasy, smelly old thing like that had got into the trap with us and you chucked it out of the window.' Batchelor had been impressed by the old man's aim; he had got a passer-by squarely on the back of the head with the flying headgear.

Uncle Josiah was unfazed. He knew that he and his brother had the same size head; it was only what was inside that differed. He would go to the funeral – or whatever it might be – suitably headgeared, and no mistake.

Grand and Batchelor stood on the steps surrounded by boxes, grips and trunks. There were parcels from milliners, dressmakers and makers of unknown furbelows which had miraculously multiplied at the Boston house for transport to Rye. Uncle Josiah scrambled down and looked at the two men standing there with mild incomprehension.

'You fellers know how to travel light, I see,' he said with an attempt at irony.

As at least half of the trunks were his, the two enquiry agents thought that was a bit much, but forbore to answer.

Suddenly, there was a commotion in the doorway behind

them and they turned as best they could without falling into the boxes and crushing an essential frill.

'Mattie! Mattie!' Martha Grand rushed down the steps and leapt into her brother's arms, ignoring the luggage at his feet. 'Oof, Martha!' Grand complained. 'You've put on a pound or two, I think.' But he hugged her close all the same and she clung to him, her face buried in his neck. 'Don't *cry*, Martha,' he laughed. 'I'm really here, don't you fret. And look, I've brought James to see you. James Batchelor,' he looked over his shoulder, 'please meet Miss Martha Grand, soon to be Mrs Hamilton Chauncey-Wolsey.'

Martha slid down and stood beside her brother, her arm around his waist in case he disappeared again. It had been lonely standing up to their parents on her own. She extended a languid hand. 'I'm charmed to meet you, Mr Batchelor,' she said. 'If Mattie ever wrote, I would say I have heard so much about you, but, as I am sure you know, he is only a moderate letter-writer, to put it at its best.'

Batchelor smiled. The likeness between the two as they stood there entwined was startling. They had the same dark golden hair with a little wave just above the temple, the same candid blue eyes. Had Grand had recourse to the New England sun instead of the London murk, he would have had the same scattering of freckles, too. Only the mouths were different, set above the same determined chin. Martha's was pretty enough, but showed a temper; Grand's was good-natured and his usual smile had left its mark on the corners. Batchelor extended his hand to meet hers and bent to kiss it. 'Delighted to meet you, Miss Grand,' he said. 'And because Matthew doesn't need to write to me, but merely chats across the breakfast table, I *have* heard so much about you.'

She dimpled prettily and looked up at Grand. 'Mattie,' she said, 'he's just *darling*! Tell me, Mr Batchelor,' she turned back to him. 'Do you have a wife at home? A sweetheart, perhaps?'

Batchelor blushed. 'No. Umm . . . pressure of work, you know.'

'Well, Mr Batchelor,' she said, 'I won't let you leave here without at least a sweetheart. And as for you, Mattie,' she poked him in the ribs, 'I just despair, I really do.'

'We've had our moments, Martha,' Grand said, kissing the top of her head. 'But now you really must let us get inside. And wouldn't you like to go and say hello to Uncle Josiah? He's looking a tad disgruntled.'

Disgruntled hardly covered it. Uncle Josiah had had to pay the cab and was not happy. Although, as Grand had pointed out, he was worth a dollar or two; even a cent spent on anything non-alcoholic was a cent thrown away, in his book. But a few kisses and pats from his only niece soon soothed him and she led him away into the house to find her parents.

Grand watched her go, wittering to the old man about nothing in particular and with her arm twined in his. 'She's good, you know,' he said to Batchelor. 'I sometimes think she's wasted on our family. She would have made a great businesswoman, if our father had allowed it. Poor girl; I hope she's made the right choice this time.'

Batchelor laughed and picked up as many parcels as he could manage. 'If she hasn't, she has only herself to blame. If I remember rightly, she has gone through enough false starts to know what she's looking for by now.'

'True, true.' Grand picked up the remaining parcels.

'Sirs, sirs.' A voice from the top of the steps stopped them in their tracks. 'Please, leave that to me.'

Grand was startled. 'And you are?'

'Hart, sir. The butler.'

'What happened to . . .?'

'Pensioned off, sir.' The man was smooth and fast-talking, with a slight accent that neither Grand nor Batchelor could trace. 'He had become a little . . . unreliable.'

'Poor old chap,' Grand said to Batchelor. 'Unreliable is only the half of it. Why, before I even left home, he had a habit of climbing into bed with all kinds of unsuspecting guests. A visiting bishop was the last one I remember . . .' He chuckled to himself. 'I still remember the screams. I didn't know the bishop had that kind of vocal range.' He turned to the butler, standing respectfully on the top step. 'We can manage, Hart, really. Just point us to where these need to go.'

'I believe Annie is in charge of parcels, sir,' Hart said,

inclining slightly from the waist. 'One of the maids will take them up to her.'

'Annie? Is she here?' Grand's smile became a beam. 'In that case, we really will take these parcels in, Hart.' He turned to Batchelor. 'Our old nurse, James. I can't believe she's here. Come on,' and he added the last parcel to his armful and led the way inside.

Hart looked sourly at the two. This wedding was trying his patience already and now he had these two to contend with. They had brought no help with them and although they had taken the parcels willingly enough, they had left the trunks for him to cope with and he just couldn't do it by himself. He turned into the hall and pushed open the green baize door. 'Boy!' He didn't care which one came and he had not bothered to learn their names. Boot boys were a dime a dozen, when all was said and done. 'Boy! Take these trunks upstairs and make it snappy. Mr Matthew Grand, Mr Josiah Grand and Mr James Batchelor.'

He let the door swing to. If they got it wrong, he could vent some of his annoyance on them. If they got it right, by some outside chance, then it was one job less to deal with. He stood in the hall listening for running feet from the house's nether regions and, when he was assured that at least one boot boy was on the way, he turned on his heel and went into the drawing room. There had been no bell from there for a while so hopefully he would find it empty. Mechanically, he checked the fire and wiped a few invisible specks of dust from the over-mantel, then turned to the window. A few moments in the window alcove looking out on to the Isles of Shoals always calmed him when he felt like cuffing a subordinate upside the head, and he was in need of those few moments now.

Upstairs, Matthew Grand was elbowing open a door on the upper landing. His feet had drawn him there without his brain needing to help at all; he had made this journey a thousand times, bearing newts, grazed knees or a broken heart and the result was always the same; loving words and a toffee. James Batchelor was along for the ride. He had never had a nurse. His mother had always been too busy keeping the family from descending from genteel poverty into just plain old poverty and his father had been a dark and gloomy presence, mainly asleep in front of the kitchen's meagre fire, keeping most of the heat from the children.

Grand peered round the door and was rewarded by a cry of welcome. 'Master Mattie!' The little woman who had been sitting sewing by the window jumped up and scuttled over, pulling him in. Despite her years, she was unbent and her eyes sparkled. Her hair, still more brown than grey, was caught up in a soft bun at the nape of her neck and she wore rimless glasses on the end of her nose for embroidery purposes only; her sight was still as sharp as it had been all those years ago when she could spy out any of Grand's little indiscretions at a mile.

He piled the parcels on the table and hugged her, lifting her off her feet. 'Annie,' he said, 'you haven't changed a bit!'

'Master Mattie,' she said, flicking a speck of lint off his shoulder, 'you're thin. Have you been eating properly? That London food has no goodness in it, I'll be bound.' She looked past him and raked Batchelor with an eagle eye. 'Who's this?'

'Annie,' Grand said, letting her go and turning to his colleague, 'I would like you to meet James Batchelor. I wrote you.'

She cast her eyes up.

'I wrote you a while ago and told you all about him. We have a business together.'

'Two letters in seven years don't seem like half enough,' she said, 'but it's good to make your acquaintance, Mr Batchelor. Perhaps now you've met us all, you can write instead of Master Mattie, here.' She had a sudden thought. She realized that he came from the heathen hell that was London; who knew what went on there? 'You *can* write, can you?'

'I was a journalist, ma'am,' Batchelor said, by way of explanation.

Annie shrugged. That didn't mean much, in the scheme of things. 'Like Sam,' she said and Grand nodded. 'Well, Mr Batchelor, I'll leave it in your hands, then. Have you seen Martha?' she asked Grand. Her mind was like a moth, fluttering hither and yon.

'Just now, as we arrived. She looks well. Happy. She may be carrying the extra pound or two, but it suits her.'

The old nurse looked him up and down. Perhaps this private investigator thing wasn't so much nonsense after all; it wasn't every man would notice Martha's condition, but now was not the time to discuss it, not with a stranger in the room. 'She's happy enough, yes,' she said. 'Young Mr Hamilton seems to be happy too, and that's a lot to give thanks for.'

'I was going to ask about him,' Grand said. 'You've met him, of course. What do you think of him?'

Annie pursed her lips and frowned for a moment, choosing her words. 'Handsome,' she said at last. 'Handsome, I'll say that for him.'

'And that's it?' Grand said. 'Handsome?'

She pursed her lips again and nodded. 'Handsome, yes. I'd say he is.' She shut her mouth with a snap and Grand knew he would learn no more.

'Have you seen your pa yet? Your ma?'

'Not yet.' Grand sounded like a naughty schoolboy and Batchelor smothered a smile.

'Then get yourself down those stairs and see them right now, Matthew Crockett Grand, and say hello. You're too old to behave like a spoiled brat.' She held out an arm to Batchelor. 'You stay here, young man,' she said. 'This is something Master Mattie is going to do on his own. You can stay here and tell me all about London. Do you boys eat regular? You don't fend for yourself, I hope. What kind of help d'you all have?'

Batchelor settled himself beside her on the sofa. He would have to edit as he went; if he told Annie about Mrs Rackstraw without changing some of the details, the old girl would be packing up to come back with them. So he started with the wonders of her pastry and after that, everything fell smoothly into place.

Liza Grand had forced herself to do some stumpwork just to keep her mind off things. As a mother, she had imagined the coming days so often; yet they had never come. Martha was forever finding Mr Right, only to discover in a flood of tears that he was Mr Wrong after all. Now she had nailed her colours to Hamilton Chauncey-Wolsey's mast. Liza wasn't convinced. But Andrew seemed to be.

She looked across the room at him. Andrew was like his son through a strange mirror, the blond hair turned white now with the cares of the years. In Boston, where the Lowells spoke only to Cabots, and the Cabots spoke only to God, God spoke only to the Grands. And that took some effort on Andrew Grand's part. He had made his money in property and was sitting on a sizeable fortune. True, he had lost a little in the war – who hadn't? But most of all, he had lost his son. He would never admit that to anyone, least of all to Liza. But Liza knew. Wives and mothers do. When Mattie was little, his father was too busy making his pile. When Mattie was riding the Wilderness with the Army of the Potomac, his father was too busy protecting that pile, flitting from Washington to New York and back with the thunder of distant gunfire in his ears. And then the boy had gone mad and moved to London, spying on people for a living. Maybe it was the war. Maybe it was his mother – too soft on the boy. Maybe – and only in the darkness did Andrew Grand consider this – maybe he had been too hard.

Either way, both of them were on their feet as the door opened.

'Mattie!' Liza shouted, her stumpwork forgotten, her arms open wide.

'Matthew,' Andrew nodded. And he hadn't moved.

FOUR

Batchelor escaped from Annie after an interrogation that would have made Dolly Williamson green with envy. She now knew everything, from Grand's diet to whether he wore wool next to his skin. Every romantic interlude had been probed and graded on a scale of inappropriateness – no one, Batchelor learned, was good enough for Master Mattie – and the financial standing of the agency had been taken out and shaken till its pips squeaked. He was now in the small drawing room at the rear of the house, although he could not quite see why it was called 'small', as their entire house in London could have been put down in it and room to spare. Hart had brought him coffee and, as there was no alcohol on offer, he knew he was not likely to be interrupted by Uncle Josiah. Female twitterings from a room across the landing from his bedroom had given him Martha's whereabouts, and so he relaxed back on the overstuffed Spanish couch and closed his eyes. The Grand family took some getting used to.

'Asleep, James?' Grand came into the room on a whirlwind of pent-up energy. Dealings with his father usually left him like that, but he had kept it under wraps for the sake of his mother.

'Just resting my eyes,' Batchelor murmured.

'Well, don't. We need to talk.'

'About?' Batchelor could have drifted away quite happily in the warm sun streaming in through the window. Travelling always took its toll and the huge amounts of countryside he had journeyed through had exhausted his city soul.

'Hamilton.'

'Hamilton?' Batchelor grunted. 'Which one is he, again?'

Grand kicked Batchelor's foot. 'Wake up. Concentrate. Hamilton is my sister's intended. It's not hard to keep track, you know. And you are an enquiry agent, when all is said and done.'

Batchelor raised a tired eyelid, sighed and sat up straight. 'All right,' he said, giving himself a little shake. 'What's up?'

'Annie said he was handsome.'

'Well, that's no bad thing, surely. No one wants ugly people marrying their sister, I should have thought.'

'No, no, don't you see? That's *all* she said. Handsome. Not kind. Not clever. Not anything else, just handsome.'

Batchelor thought for a moment. He had just been all but disembowelled by Annie in her search for detail, so he saw the point. 'I see what you mean. Handsome is all she can say that's good about him.'

'Right. Yes. If there was one thing she always dinned into us when we were whippersnappers was if you can't say something good about someone, say nothing at all. And she's saying nothing at all.'

'You're sure you're not just being . . . well, overprotective?'

'Hell, no. Martha can take care of herself, I know that. But . . . it niggles me. What can be wrong with him that Annie won't talk of?'

'We know he hasn't got the metaphorical eye in the centre of his forehead at least,' Batchelor offered. 'Perhaps *Annie* is being overprotective.' He didn't tell Grand how much she now knew about his winter underwear.

'She worries, I know that,' Grand said, gnawing his lip. 'But I will allow I'll feel happier when I've met the cuss.' He shivered. 'Is it me, or is it cold in here?'

Batchelor had to admit that when he moved out of the sunbeam he had been basking in, it had got a bit chilly. New England nights bore no resemblance to New England days and the cold that came with the darkness was stealing up from the water to wrap the house in its embrace. Grand leaned over and put a match to the fire. The cedar chippings caught at once and the fire crackled into life. Batchelor watched entranced. Mrs Rackstraw often took half an hour of muttering and cursing to get the slacky London coal to catch.

'That's a neat trick,' he said, pointing to the flames. 'Why don't our fires light that well?'

Grand shrugged. He had never really given it that much thought. Laying and lighting fires had always been something for someone else to do, in his experience. He rang the bell beside the fire. 'I think it's time for some brandy to go with that coffee, don't you?' he asked.

Batchelor looked startled. He had already learnt it was unwise to mention an alcoholic beverage unless you wanted Uncle Josiah to appear forthwith.

Grand read his mind. 'Josiah is in with my father,' he said. 'Even he has to accept that he is a Grand sometimes. They are discussing the family trusts. Josiah is a signatory, though not a very active one. But now Martha is getting married, they need to do some business.'

Hart appeared, with a tray of brandy and glassware. He knew these two would be making work and he had made a guess to save his legs. 'Sirs,' he said, depositing the tray on the low table beside Batchelor. 'Will there be anything else?'

'I don't think so, Hart,' Grand said. 'There has been quite a lot of carriage traffic outside; was it Mr Chauncey-Wolsey, by any chance?'

'No, sir. Mr Chauncey-Wolsey is lodging in Exeter until the nuptials, I believe. His sister is arriving today and he was meeting her at the station. He has been . . . staying here, of course, until this week. But, with the wedding . . .'

'Of course.' Grand nodded to the butler, who withdrew silently. Grand turned to Batchelor. 'Lodging *here*! That doesn't sound like something my father would allow.'

'Perhaps he didn't,' Batchelor said. 'Perhaps that's why he's now lodging in Exeter.'

'We will make an enquiry agent of you after all, James,' Grand said, pouring them both a drink. 'I wonder if that's what Annie meant. Perhaps he tried a little . . .'

'Window shopping,' Batchelor said, swirling his brandy in the glass. 'Squeezing the fruit to test if it's ripe.'

'Do you mind?' Grand said, outrage in every pore. Then he laughed. 'That is rather a good analogy, though. Once a journalist, always a journalist, eh?'

Suddenly, the door crashed back and a wild-haired man stood there, eyes sparkling under the thatch of his brows and a huge moustache hiding his upper lip.

'What's a man have to do to get a smoke around here?'

Grand was on his feet, laughing. 'Sam, you old river pilot! How long's it been?'

'Too long, you blue-coated sonofabitch,' and the newcomer shook Grand's hand before hugging him to his chest.

'James,' Grand was still laughing, 'I'd like you to meet Uncle Sam.'

Batchelor's face had already frozen and he stood staring stupidly at the latest Grand to arrive. 'Uncle Sam?' he repeated, as though he had heard the words for the first time.

'Are you still coming out with that nonsense, Matthew?' Sam laughed.

'But you're . . .' Batchelor was still blinking, even as he gripped the man's hand. 'You're . . . you're Mark Twain, surely?'

'Surely,' said Sam, grinning. 'Samuel Clemens would be a better description.'

'When you said "Uncle Sam",' Batchelor had not let go of the man's hand yet, but he was looking askance at Grand, 'I always assumed you meant the American government.'

'Nearest I've come to that,' Clemens said, 'was when I worked as old Bill Stewart's secretary. He was a senator for Nevada, or so he kept telling me. You are . . .?'

'Flabbergasted, annoyed and honoured all at once,' Batchelor said. 'Er . . . James Batchelor.'

'Ah, Matthew's associate. The private detective, huh?'

'Enquiry agent,' Batchelor corrected him. 'May I say, Mr Twain, what a great honour . . .'

Clemens pawed the air with his free hand. 'My lecture audiences call me "Mr Twain", James. My friends call me Sam. Er . . . any chance of my hand back any time soon?'

Batchelor dropped it at once. 'I'm sorry,' he said. 'It's just . . . well . . . it's not every day you get to meet the author of *The Innocents Abroad* – as a matter of fact, I feel a little bit like that myself at the moment.'

Everybody laughed as Grand passed a brandy and a cigar to Clemens. They all sat down.

'May I say . . . er . . . Sam, how much I enjoyed "The Celebrated Jumping Frog of Calaveras County"?'

'That's kind.' Clemens lit up, his face flaring briefly before disappearing in smoke. 'I hope you'll like *Tom Blankenship* just as much.'

'Tom Blankenship?' Batchelor was intrigued.

'The Adventures of.' Clemens leaned back, sending smoke rings to the ceiling. ''Course, I won't call it that. Tom was an old boyhood friend of mine, back in the day, but I don't know how he'd take to having his name in print. I'll call it something else . . . oh, I don't know . . . Huckleberry Finn; how's that?'

'Huckleberry Finn,' Batchelor marvelled. 'Superb!'

Clemens laughed. 'Well, it won't be any time soon. I've got another river story in mind first. *Tom Sawyer*, I'm thinking.'

'Brilliant!' Batchelor all but clapped.

'I heard about the baby, Sam,' Grand said, his face solemn. 'Sorry.'

Clemens suddenly got up and strode to the fireplace. He put his glass on the high mantelpiece and looked down at the drifting smoke. 'Diphtheria took him, little Langdon,' he said. 'He had the most beautiful blue eyes . . .' His voice tailed away and for a moment there was silence. 'But I've got a new angel now,' the writer said, smiling. He began to prowl around the room. 'Little Susy. Living spit of her mother.'

'How *is* Olivia?' Grand was glad to have the slight change of subject.

'Livy's just fine. Actually, that's not strictly true. She gets the vapours now and then and she took Langdon's loss pretty hard. She wanted to come for this here bash, but I told her "No". She should rest.'

'I'd like to meet her some day,' Grand said. 'And little Susy.'

'Count on it, dear boy. If you fellows have time, come back to Hartford with me once we've thrown some shoes and rice. It'll make a change for her. In the meantime, either of you met the groom-to-be?'

Grand shook his head. 'We've heard he's handsome,' he said.

Clemens nodded wisely. 'That's important,' he said. 'If a man's going to have a brother-in-law, he ought to be handsome.'

He caught Grand's look and both of them burst out laughing. Clemens fished his watch from his vest pocket and gulped down his brandy. 'I've got to get out of these clothes, fellas,' he said. 'Been on the road for more hours than I care to count. Matthew. James. I'll see you at dinner.' And he swept out.

'I'd forgotten about that,' Grand said.

'What?' Batchelor asked.

'Sam's annoying habit of walking round a room while he's talking to you. It drives Ma into a conniption fit. He always was as mad as a hatter.'

'I still can't believe it,' Batchelor said. 'Your uncle is Mark Twain, one of America's greatest writers after Nathaniel Hawthorne, Herman Melville and Harriet Beecher Stowe and you don't mention it! Is he really your uncle? He doesn't seem much older than you.'

'Everybody in the family calls him that. He's actually a cousin, somewhat removed. Don't ask me how it works – it's to do with Great-Grandpa and some kind of feud; the family's full of them. I'll have to remind Sam later that he once fought for the South.'

'He did?'

'Well, when I say "fought for", that's a little strong. He spent a couple of months in the Home Guard outfit in Hannibal, Missouri. Then he got the silver bug in the Comstock and opted out. Don't mess with him, though. The man can swear for America and he's no stranger to the duelling piste.'

'A swordsman?'

'Pistol shot. And pretty deadly, by all accounts.'

'Thanks,' Batchelor said. 'I'll remember that. So, Matthew,' he leaned back in his chair, 'which of Uncle Sam's writings do you admire the most?'

'Don't know.' Grand shrugged. 'Never read him.'

When breakfast was over the next day, Batchelor excused himself and went for a walk. The Grands and their entourage had been delightful, but they were bubbling over with the forthcoming festivities and the staff were tripping over each other hanging up bunting, frills and furbelows to further order. Hart stood in the middle of them, barking orders and snipping comments. By the time Josiah was reaching for his third brandy in Andrew's library, Batchelor was striding out along the beach.

The grim, grey rocks gave way to smaller pebbles that were less threatening to the ankle and they in turn gave way to sand, pale and flat under the running tide. Far ahead, black rocks jutted out to sea, and there the surf pounded, spraying the sky in its fury. The gulls wheeled high above it all, watching the solitary figure making his way north, their cries a melancholy counterpoint to the sea's boom.

Then, suddenly, Batchelor was not solitary any more. A dark shape crouched at the water's edge, prodding something that rolled over with the incoming tide. It was a man, scruffy in his clothing, with unwashed hair hanging lank and days' old stubble blurring his features. He had an axe in his hand.

Against his better judgement, Batchelor tipped his hat and said, 'Good morning.' Then he looked more closely and instantly recoiled. 'My God, what's that?'

The man squinted at him, shielding his eyes from the weak sun that dazzled on the water. 'You're not from round here, are you?' he said. The words were guttural, harsh.

'Er . . . no.' Batchelor was still staring at the black thing moving with each incoming ripple.

The man kicked it. 'That's a seal. Or he was. Killer whale will have got him. Look – half his body's gone.'

It had. Batchelor had never seen a seal before, not even in the zoological gardens or the circus. He could make out the animal's nose, the stiff bristles of the whiskers and one ragged flipper.

'Good thing it's this time of year,' the man grunted, 'or you'd smell this half a mile off. It'd be thick with flies. Aach!' He spat into the sand, but it was not aimed at the dead seal or even Batchelor's feet. He had caught sight of someone walking quickly towards them from the dunes. He muttered something incomprehensible before scowling and turning away, hoisting his axe on to his shoulder and trudging towards the north.

'Oh, the poor thing.' The woman in white had reached Batchelor now and was looking down at the seal. She was about Batchelor's age, statuesque in her day dress, with her chestnut hair piled high. The cloak she wore flapped in the wind and she had a staff in one hand and a basket in the other.

Batchelor tipped his hat again, with rather more enthusiasm this time. 'Good morning,' he said. 'It's a seal. Killed by a whale, I should imagine.'

She narrowed her eyes at him. 'Should you?' she half smiled. 'You're not from round here, are you?'

'Er . . . no, no indeed. James Batchelor. I'm from England.'

'Ah, the Old Country. How delightful.' She was smiling fully now. 'I'm Celia Thaxter. I run Appledore House.'

Batchelor had no idea what that was, but smiled politely anyway and shook her proffered hand.

'Yonder.' Celia pointed to the middle distance. 'That's Appledore Island, one of nine in our Isles of Shoals.'

'We have an Appledore at home,' Batchelor told her on a wave of homesickness. 'It's in Kent. But it's not an island. When you say run . . .'

'It's a hotel,' she told him. 'Look, do you mind if we walk on? I can't bear looking at this poor creature.'

'Of course.' And off they went.

'Where did you acquire your knowledge of seals, Mr Batchelor?' she asked him. 'Not to mention whales.'

Batchelor laughed. The woman had found him out already. 'From that man I was talking to before you arrived,' he confessed.

Celia's face darkened. 'Oh, him.'

'Not a friend of yours?' Batchelor guessed.

'Not a friend of anybody's, I shouldn't imagine,' she said. 'His name's Wagner. He's an odd-job man; collects driftwood and the like and rows between the islands. He put the surl into surly.'

'That's rather good,' Batchelor said, pausing far enough from the water's edge so that he didn't get his feet wet.

'What is?'

'That *bon mot*, just then. "Surl into surly".'

Celia blushed. 'I like to think of myself as something of a writer,' she said.

'Me too,' Batchelor beamed.

'Really?' She looked at him. 'I had you down as an artist. They come here in droves every summer to paint the islands, the lighthouses, my garden. It is a *little* early in the season, though.'

'Well, I'm here for a wedding,' Batchelor told her.

'Martha Grand's?' She caught his arm, instantly regretted her forwardness and withdrew her hand.

'That's right. It's all rather complicated. I'm a friend of Matthew Grand, Martha's brother.'

'Matthew Grand.' Celia stood rock still, as though a Sanctus bell was sounding somewhere, in her head or along the bay. 'I haven't seen him for years. I remember every summer he came to Rye.'

'You do?' Batchelor's investigator's nose twitched.

Celia, suddenly flustered, made light of it. 'Well, some of them,' she said. 'He used to pull my pigtails.'

'Hmm,' Batchelor nodded sagely. 'That certainly sounds like the behaviour of a captain in the Third Cavalry of the Potomac.'

'Oh, Lord,' Celia laughed. 'He won't remember me. I've been invited to the wedding too.'

'Excellent,' Batchelor said. 'It'll be like old times for you both.'

But Celia wasn't smiling. She was staring, head down, at the sand.

Batchelor gave her a moment with her memories. 'So,' he said brightly, when he thought she had had long enough, 'you've lived here all your life, Miss Thaxter?'

'Most of it,' she said. 'My father keeps the lighthouse on Appledore. There. Look.' She pointed out to sea.

Batchelor looked. A white tower glowed clear, above the jut of black rocks, against which the surf crashed like distant gunfire. At its tip, the light flashed every half-minute, barely visible in the brightness of the morning. 'You should see it at night,' Celia said. 'I used to think, when I was a girl, that there were people walking around up there, in the light chamber. Oh, it's just the reflections of the glass, of course, the lenses. I know,' she complained, 'I've polished them often enough. But when you're here on the beach. Or out there, on the water . . . you'd swear . . .'

They had stopped walking and were both staring at the light-house, with its steady, silent signal of safety to those in peril on the sea. She looked up at him.

'You know this place is haunted, don't you?' she said.

Batchelor could still see the carcase of the seal bobbing at the water's edge and the black guillemots bickering with each other as they tore at its bloated flesh. He felt the hairs crawl on the back of his neck.

Celia was walking on. 'Pannamy, the Indians called it,' she said, 'before the whites settled here. The Laconia Company, Mr Batchelor, from your country. Way back in 1623.'

'Good year.' Batchelor shook himself free from the image of the mangled corpse the tide had rolled in and the silent people forever trapped in the lighthouse light.

'They settled at Odiorne Point, just around the headland. They had fish aplenty, of course, and timber. Their God sustained them. At least, he did until 1691.'

'What happened then?'

'There was an Indian attack; the Micmac tribe. Way up there,' she pointed inland, 'through the woods. They wiped out the families of Goodman Brackett and Goodman Read. Dashed the babies' brains out on the rocks along the coast aways.'

'Do you believe that?' Batchelor asked. His granny had told

him similar stories when the gypsies came calling and people had refused to buy their lucky white heather.

'I can show you the very rocks,' Celia said, straight-faced. 'Stained with their blood to this day.'

They walked on in silence. Then she laughed and said, 'You'll think us all mad, Mr Batchelor. All this talk of ghosts and death. We're here for a wedding, after all.'

'We are,' Batchelor smiled, glad to be on a different track. 'We are.'

'So, you're a writer,' she quizzed him.

'Not any more, not for a living,' he said. 'I used to be a journalist, with the usual plans to write the great British novel. I have at least twenty Chapter Ones in my desk at home. Now, I am an enquiry agent.'

'A what?'

'A private detective.'

Celia stopped and clapped her hands. 'How exciting,' she said. 'I don't think I've ever met a detective before.'

Batchelor could hear Grand's voice in his ear – 'You still haven't' – but he let it go. 'Ah, we're a dying breed, Miss Thaxter. A dying breed.'

'Have you worked on any famous cases?' she asked, her eyes bright. 'Any murders I would know about?'

Batchelor thought for a moment and then shook his head. 'I don't believe our work has been reported here,' he said. 'Important cases, oh, yes, many important cases, but . . . well, nothing the Americans would be interested in.'

'Mr Batchelor,' she said, and held on to his arm again, not letting go. 'I have a small picnic in my basket here. Why don't we go up the beach and find a nice sheltered place under the bank and share it while you tell me about your cases? For example, have you had anything to do with royalty? Dukes, Duchesses, that kind of thing . . .?'

She looked so eager and the wind was a little chill down by the water; it had been a while since breakfast. Batchelor took her arm and let her lead him to a good spot, where the pines stood solid, the ground thick with the ancient carpet of their needles. 'Well,' he began, 'I was recently involved in a very complex case with a certain . . .' he looked her in the eye with a roguish twinkle, 'let's call her Lady C. Her husband had reason to believe . . .'

Wagner, hiding among the rocks, heard the Englishman's voice diminish as they walked away from him. Foreigners! And he spat.

FIVE

B atchelor was just putting the final touches to his toilet when Grand poked his head around the door.

'Where have you been all day?' he asked, stepping over to help his friend tie his bow tie, a skill the journalist had never really mastered.

'I met a fascinating woman on the beach . . .'

'Oh, ho!' Grand finished the tie with a pat. 'Tell me more.'

'She knows you,' Batchelor hedged. 'Celia Thaxter.'

'Oh?' Grand's eyebrows rose. 'She's using Thaxter again, is she? That's interesting.'

Down in the distant hall, a gong boomed.

'What do you mean by that?' Batchelor asked, hanging on to Grand's lapel.

'Nothing. Really, nothing.' Grand tugged away towards the door. 'Listen. It's the gong. Mother was adamant we shouldn't be late.'

'Again?' Batchelor said.

'Well, be fair,' Grand said. 'We haven't *been* late yet, but—'

'No, I mean, Celia's using Thaxter *again*, you said.'

'Oh, James, I'm just . . . gossiping. You must take no notice. But come on, do – there's the gong again. I must say, that Hart is a bit of a stickler. Have you noticed – every corner you turn, he seems to be there. But, no, of course . . . you were on the beach all day with Celia.'

'Not all day,' Batchelor said grumpily, letting himself be led down the stairs.

'No,' Grand said, thoughtfully. 'I should think all day of Celia would be a little wearing, one way or another.'

'She was telling me, she's from Appledore.'

'And Smuttynose.'

For a moment, Batchelor stood still, thinking his ears were playing him tricks. Then he burst out laughing. 'Where?' he managed to get out at last.

'Smuttynose,' Grand said, straight-faced. 'It's another one in the Isles of Shoals. Bit more remote than Appledore. If memory serves, Celia was born there . . . What *is* the matter with you, James?'

Batchelor was still laughing so much it hurt, his shoulders heaving and tears running down his cheeks. 'Sorry,' he said, trying to pull himself together. 'It's just . . . Smuttynose. It's rather tickled my funny bone.'

'So I see.' Grand wasn't even smiling. 'And this is from a man who lives in a country with place names like Huish Episcopi!'

'Yes, all right.' Batchelor's fit of hysterics subsided. 'Point taken.' There was a pause. 'Still,' he said. 'Smuttynose!' And it started all over again.

Grand thought it best to change the subject slightly; he turned and gave Batchelor one of his widest smiles, usually a precursor to something Batchelor would live to regret. 'As for Celia, she's a lovely, lovely woman, James. Now, let's go into dinner and get my sister wed.'

'Or not.'

'Or not?' Grand was now talking out of the corner of his mouth. 'What makes you say that?'

'Well,' Batchelor said, looking around, 'don't forget, all Annie had to say of the groom was that he was handsome. If that proves to be his one good point, perhaps you might want to . . . have a word?'

'A word?'

'Something like . . . it would have to be more than one word, probably, but . . . "Go"? That should make it clear.'

The two were approached by a maid, dressed in a crisp apron and cap, who took Grand's arm firmly and led him round to the head of the table, where he was placed two places to the left of centre. Other guests were being dragooned into place and Batchelor found himself standing beside a well-preserved woman who looked short-sightedly at his name, written in flowing script on a card in front of his plate.

'Mr Botched?' she said, doubtfully.

'Batchelor,' he said, smiling. 'And you are . . .?' He peered at her plate. 'Miss Helene Waterford.' He held out a hand. 'How do you do?'

'You're English,' she accused him.

'I am indeed.' Was he going to have to explain his nationality to everyone he met? At least she hadn't told him he wasn't from round here.

'You're not from round here,' she said. 'I could tell that as soon as I saw that tie.' She flicked it contemptuously. 'No American would tie a tie like that. But I shouldn't judge. I'm not from round here either. I'm from Boston.'

'Lovely city,' Batchelor said politely.

'You know it?' Her face lit up.

'We caught a train from there yesterday. We picked up Mr Josiah Grand, I don't know if you know him . . .'

'That old reprobate! I should know him. He's my brother-in-law.'

Batchelor did some quick calculations. He came to a horrified conclusion just as he looked up and saw Grand's raised eyebrow. Yes. This was Aunt Nell, who would have him for breakfast. He pulled out her chair and seated her comfortably, remembering Grand's injunction not to turn his back.

'Such a gentleman,' she purred. 'You must be, now I come to think, Mattie's partner in crime, if you don't mind the phrase. You must tell me all about it. I would imagine you have some tales to tell, do you not? Some dark doings in the aristocracy, unless I miss my guess.'

Somehow Batchelor was not as happy telling Grand's aunt the details of the Duchess of Chilcott's indiscretions as he had been when his audience was Celia Thaxter, but he was saved by the bell, quite literally being rung with some aplomb by Hart, standing at the head of the table, now fully furnished with the Grand family and a strikingly handsome man sitting next to Martha. So, Annie was right about that, at any rate; he certainly was good looking. Aunt Helene had not missed that detail either.

'My land!' she said in Batchelor's ear, with rather more breath than was strictly necessary. 'I do not believe I would kick that one out of my bed should I find him between the sheets.' She paused. 'Excuse my language, Mr Botched, but really; that boy is a looker!'

Hamilton Chauncey-Wolsey would have turned heads anywhere, and Batchelor, though by no means an expert when it came to judging male beauty, could see that he was exceedingly handsome. His hair sprang back in russet curls from a wide and unlined brow. His eyes were a piercing blue and were surrounded by just the right amount of manly crinkles – the eyes of a man who spent his days peering at the far horizon. His nose, both straight on and in profile, was straight off Michelangelo's David and his mouth was well modelled with good-natured, turned-up corners. His chin was if anything a little delicately moulded, but that would just be picky; it suited the rest of his face to a tee. Batchelor comforted himself that the man probably had a cauliflower ear or something otherwise disfiguring; but no, as he bared his pearly teeth in a smile and turned now this way, now that to bestow it around the room, it was clear that his ears were perfect, set neatly against his perfectly barbered hair. *And* he was probably hung like a mule! Taken all in all, Batchelor – and most of the men in the room – hated him on sight.

Matthew Grand, himself no beginner when it came to turning women's heads, spent less time looking at Chauncey-Wolsey and rather more time watching his sister. Martha sat quietly, looking down at her hands, which were clasped lightly in her lap. He had never seen her face so expressionless; usually how she was feeling was writ so large that you could tell at a thousand paces what was going on inside her head. But tonight – the precursor to the rest of her life with the man of her dreams – he could see nothing. Not so in the case of his parents. His father looked like thunder and his mother close to tears. If this wedding actually happened, it would be a small miracle.

At Hart's bell, the soup had appeared, wheeled on a trolley in a huge silver salver. The maids circulated, one with the soup, another with warm sourdough bread. And the courses kept on coming, wave after wave of soup, of fish, more soup, something enormous roasted whole, nuts, ices and cake. Some of the guests, mostly those from the country regions round about, ate heartily and by the end of the meal were nearly unconscious with food. Those from the cities picked delicately at everything that was put in front of them. After all, there were standards in Boston and Washington. Even in Portland. Even after the staff had eaten their fill of leftovers, the hogs in the farm beyond the stables would feed well tonight.

Batchelor, like Grand, was people-watching. Aunt Nell to one side was a picker, so she had plenty of breath left for conversation, which Batchelor let wash over him like the tide. It turned out that she knew more about the British aristocracy and their goings-on than Batchelor had had hot dinners, including this one. What *did* the Prince of Wales see in that gawky Danish girl, the deaf one? Had Lord Palmerston *really* sired a child at eighty-one? And don't get Aunt Nell started on that strumpet Adeline Horsey Brudenell; no wonder her husband, the recklessly brave Lord Cardigan, had fallen fatally from his horse. To his other side, a country neighbour was digging in with a will and didn't say a word except to the staff; that word was usually 'More?' Batchelor got the distinct impression the man was stocking up for a siege of some kind. The man must have read his mind. His one word to Batchelor all night was 'Vicksburg'. Batchelor made a note to ask Grand about it later.

Across the table, beyond the monstrous arrangement of hothouse flowers and dripping candles, Batchelor could just make out Celia Thaxter, making polite conversation to a weasel-faced man who was not taking the blindest bit of notice of her. Batchelor had not known her long, but even he could tell that what she really wanted to do to the ignorant pig was to rip his arm off and beat him to death with the wet end. She could do it too, smiled Batchelor to himself, picturing the scene – he weighed nine stone wringing wet and had a petulant, womanly look about him. He would have been fairly good-looking even so, had he not been in the same room as the groom. Using his enquiry agent skills, Batchelor noticed that the rather over-dressed and sulky woman sitting alongside Grand at the top of the table kept glancing down at the weasel and he – correctly, as he later discovered – decided they were husband and wife. They looked as if they probably deserved each other, too.

As the ruins of the table, petals falling in the heat, nut shells scattered like sea shells on the beach, were cleared away, Hart made everyone jump with another ringing of the bell. This time, he made an announcement as well.

'Ladies and gentlemen . . .'

This sounded odd to Batchelor, but he realized with a start that even in this well-heeled company there were unlikely to be any lords.

'Coffee is served in the drawing room; if the ladies would care to follow me . . .' He gestured towards the door and there was a general scraping of chairs as the women got up to leave. Batchelor was disconcerted but not surprised to feel a hand squeeze his thigh as Aunt Nell stood up to go.

'Later,' she breathed in his ear. It sounded to Batchelor more of a threat than a promise. Across the table, Celia fluttered her fingers to him as she too turned to go.

The port had miraculously appeared in front of Andrew Grand and Josiah was eyeing it with an avid look. The maids, two at a time, were wrestling the enormous flower arrangements off the table and on to the sideboards. The shells and general detritus were being flicked into dustpans by dextrous-wristed footmen, hired for the occasion. With the ladies gone and the table bare, it was finally possible to get a general overview of who was present – and it was certainly a very mixed bunch.

Instinctively, the inner coterie drifted to the top table to fill the ladies' vacated seats. The others, the less great or good from Rye and the islands, took refuge in the beer provided for them and Hart prowled their tables, ready to eject anybody who couldn't hold their liquor.

That didn't go for Uncle Josiah, of course, who, after all, had done little else than hold his liquor for years. 'Are you gonna pour that, Sam?' he croaked to the famous author at his elbow, 'or are you gonna chaw the hind leg off a mule all night?'

Clemens laughed and passed him the port. 'If you knew how much I get per word on my lecture tours, Josiah, you might have a little humility. Cigar, Mattie?'

'Thank you, Sam.' Grand reached over and took the cheroot. 'James?'

Batchelor took one too and all three lit up.

'I understand you're staying at the Appledore, Mr Latham?' Batchelor took the port, much lower in the decanter now, from the journalist.

'I am,' Latham said, blowing his own smoke to Andrew Grand's panelled ceiling. 'Very . . . homely.'

'How's the landlady?' Matthew Grand asked, beaming at Batchelor.

'Similar to her hotel,' Latham said. 'Has delusions of being a writer.'

'I hear she's very good.' Batchelor knew a trap when he fell headlong into one, but he couldn't stand by and not defend the girl. As for his adulation of the great Edward Latham, that had disappeared by the fish course.

'Do you?' Latham swilled the ruby contents around his glass and held it up to the candlelight. He turned to Andrew Grand. 'Charitable of you, Mr Grand, to invite me this evening.'

'Nothing's too good for my Martha,' the old man said. 'As long as what you write is the truth.'

Latham smiled. 'I write for the *New York Times*, sir,' he said. 'Can you doubt it?'

'What about this Depression, Latham?' Hamilton Chauncey-Wolsey asked him from across the table. 'We hear much about it on Wall Street.'

'I'm no economist,' Latham said. 'I'm here to cover this wedding. What the bride wore. What the groom wore. That sort of thing.'

'Horseshit!' All eyes turned to Uncle Josiah, who was trying to light his cigar. Somebody took pity on him. Hart, loyal, perfect, was the first with a match.

'Come, come, Mr Latham,' Chauncey-Wolsey smiled acidly. 'You may write for the *New York Times* now, but before that you were with the London *Times*, weren't you?'

Latham raised an eyebrow. 'You're remarkably well-informed, sir.'

Chauncey-Wolsey laughed. 'Andrew and I didn't get portfolios the size of ours without being well-informed,' he said. 'If there's trouble on your Stock Exchange, chances are it'll be winging its way west before too long. I, for one, would like to be ready.'

'These things are relative,' Latham said, flicking his ash carefully on to the tray. 'We are the workshop of the world, it's true; but how long can that last? My first job in the newspaper business took me to the Crystal Palace, the Great Exhibition. I remember looking at the American stall and seeing two gadgets there I'd never seen before. Two gadgets that weren't on anybody else's stall either – the McCormick reaper and one of Mr Colt's revolvers. The gadgets that no one else in the world had at the time. Two gadgets that have gone on to revolutionize the world, in their own way. You have no need to fear a recession in our economy, gentlemen. You have a vibrant economy of your own.'

Jeremy Zzerbe, sitting weaselly next to Latham, nodded and smiled as though he was personally responsible. 'Here, here,' he muttered into his glass.

'We didn't invent the reaper or the pistol,' Clemens said, giving Zzerbe a rather dubious look. 'You're giving us too much credit, Mr Latham.'

'You didn't invent the railways either,' the journalist nodded, 'we did. But you've got more track and rolling stock than we could fit into Britain.'

There was gentle laughter all round.

'Over-investment,' Andrew Grand said. 'That's the way the wind's blowing. Mark my words; it'll do none of us any good.'

'Least of all "Boss" Tweed,' Latham said, looking carefully at the end of his cigar.

There was a silence.

'Who?' James Batchelor was more than a little lost in this conversation. He felt like a little boy at a prefect's table at school.

Nobody seemed inclined to answer, so Clemens did the honours. 'Not our finest hour,' he said, smoothing his moustache. 'William Tweed was mayor of New York until recently. He was on the take, big time, handing out jobs for the good ol' boys in the Democrat party, charging a fortune for services and drawing up leases on property that didn't exist.'

'Democrats have a lot to answer for,' old Josiah nodded sagely, drawing impressed looks from his fellow guests.

'What happened to him?' Batchelor asked.

'They finally got him last November,' Clemens said, 'guilty on 204 out of 220 counts. Got thirteen years and a fine of $12,500.'

Batchelor whistled through his teeth.

'That was the end of the Tammany Hall ring,' Clemens said. 'Corruption in high places. Leaves a nasty taste in the mouth.'

'Not quite the end.' Latham was refilling his glass before the decanter passed Uncle Josiah's way again. 'You see, we don't *quite* know how big this Tammany ring was. Oh, they caught James Ingersoll – the press called him the "carpenter". Then there was Andrew Garvey, "prince of plasterers", and John Keyser, "the plumber".'

'And?' Batchelor was agog.

'There was another man,' Latham assured him, looking around the company through the haze of cigar smoke and candlelight. 'We don't know his name, but the press called him the "painter".'

'Stuff and nonsense!' Chauncey-Wolsey's cigar had gone out and he puffed it back into flame. 'Journalese, that's all.'

'Oh, no,' Latham said. 'The painter is real enough, I assure you.'

There was another silence.

'Is that why you're *really* here, Mr Latham?' Matthew Grand asked, looking levelly at the man. 'Are you looking for the painter?'

Slowly, Latham smiled. 'I told you,' he said. 'I'm covering a wedding. Talking of which,' he smiled at Chauncey-Wolsey, 'doesn't a groom usually have a best man?'

'He does,' the groom nodded, 'and I do. George Poindexter.' He checked his silver hunter. 'He should have been here hours ago.'

'Oh,' Latham reached for his port, 'I expect he's been detained. Gentlemen, may I propose a toast?' He held up his glass. 'To Mr Hamilton Chauncey-Wolsey. May his life – and that of his bride-to-be – be strewn with roses.'

'Roses,' everyone chorused, and the glasses chinked together.

In the drawing room, the fire was burning and the candles on every sconce threw reflections across the space, lighting a diamond here, a ruby there. The fashions encompassed about three decades, the country ladies dressed in what had once been all the rage, the city ladies dressed in what might be the rage if their dressmakers had their way. The whole room smelled of lavender water and gossip.

As befitted their status as the wedding party in chief, Martha, her mother and Jemima Zzerbe took their seats on the Spanish sofa in front of the fire. Hamilton's sister, Sarah, should have been there too, but she had sent her apologies as she left the dinner table; she had suddenly thought of a new scene for her latest novel and had to write it down when it was fresh. Mrs Grand was not impressed. In a family which boasted Sam Clemens, some scribbling woman was nothing special. If it could be said that the Grand family were lukewarm about Hamilton, they were room temperature about his sister.

Space had been left in front of the sofa so that the rest of the ladies could pay a visit in ones and twos, then move on. While this pavane was in motion, conversation was desultory, but as soon as everyone had paid their respects and passed on their congratulations, the company broke up, as everyone knew it would, into little knots circling the small tables dotted around, supplied with coffee pots and cream jugs and little dishes of lump sugar.

Martha, stuck for the evening with her mother and Jemima, was wishing that the port – and more especially, Hamilton – was not in the other room. She could do with a nip about now and the smell of the coffee was making her queasy. Her mother had poured a cup and was offering it to her, an anxious look in her eye.

'Martha, sweet girl, do drink a cup of coffee. You hardly touched your dinner and you need to keep up your strength.'

Martha's head snapped up and she stared at her mother. 'Why?'

'Why? Because you're getting married tomorrow, silly girl. It will be a long day and . . .' The usual silence ensued as the subject of the night after the wedding day came into view.

'Oh. Well, Mama,' Martha took the cup and held it as far from her nose as she decently could, 'it's just a day, you know. The usual number of hours. Think of it as . . . oh, I don't know. Think of it as being a party, just like any other, but in the daytime. In fact,' she waved her arm around the room, 'a lot less like hard work than this, I would imagine.' She patted her mother's knee, slippery in her new silk dress. 'Don't worry about me. Hamilton will look after me.'

She waited for her mother and Jemima to chime in with agreement.

'He will. He loves me and I love him. We have a dear little house waiting for us when we get back from our honeymoon and everything will be wonderful, just you see. Now, I'm going to go and speak to our guests.'

'Oh, no, Martha!' Jemima could see an etiquette slip coming a mile away and moved to stop this one. 'No. The bride must sit still and wait to be visited.'

'Don't be ridiculous, Mima,' Martha snapped. 'Everyone has trailed past and smiled and shaken my hand. Now I want to actually talk to people. To hear their news. I won't have time for that tomorrow, as has been made quite clear.' She put down her cup on the small table and got up, a hand to her back.

Her mother, missing nothing, grabbed her arm. 'Have you hurt yourself?' she asked. 'I told you you were doing too much. What is a lady's maid for if you . . .'

Martha smiled and looked down at her mother fondly. If there was nothing to worry about, her mother would invent something. But even so, it was a warning. She had completely forgotten that she should show no sign of her impending event. But the corset Annie had wound her into for this evening was killing her, poking into her back and giving her cramps. Perhaps walking around would ease it. 'Just a cramp, Mama,' she said. 'I may have lifted something awkwardly this afternoon. It will pass.'

Liza Grand looked at her, a penetrating look that only mothers can ever really perfect. But the expression on her daughter's face was innocence itself and she had to let it go. 'Well, take care, then. And don't tire yourself.'

Martha bent with difficulty and kissed the top of her mother's head. 'I will. And I won't. I'll leave you to chat with Mima. You have a lot to catch up on, I'm sure.'

As she walked away, she glanced back. Her mother and

Jemima were both staring straight ahead into the flames, no doubt thinking their own thoughts. Martha thought she could probably hazard a guess at what they were.

Turning back to the room, she found herself in the middle of a gaggle of her friends from school. She had been given no limit on the number of people she could invite. Indeed, she had been told to invite as many as she could. This wedding might be arranged in a hurry, but there was no need to look tight-fisted. So she had padded out the list with girls she hadn't seen for years and who, now they were gathered in a grinning bunch, she was hard pressed to identify. That didn't matter too much. They were all talking at once, the married ones holding out their hands as proof that they, too, could catch a man. The single ones kept their hands behind their backs, but made it quite clear by nods and winks that they had their moments.

Martha stood there, leaning on the back of the sofa, looking at their kind, well-meaning, slightly shiny faces. Yes; the room was very hot. And suddenly, very small. And loud. And, for some reason she couldn't quite fathom, tilted rather alarmingly to the left. No . . . the right. No . . . and with a small sigh, Martha Grand, soon to be Mrs Hamilton Chauncey-Wolsey, folded neatly to the ground and everything went black.

SIX

'So, how long have you been with the *New York Times*, Mr Latham?' Samuel Clemens was asking.

'For ever.' Latham was unbuttoning a little as the evening wore on. Andrew Grand's excellent port had been replaced by Andrew Grand's excellent brandy. 'Since last November, in fact. I had my baptism of fire literally. Boston.'

'That was a bad business,' Clemens nodded, turning his chair to face the man.

'It was,' Latham agreed. 'I've seen it all in my time. Cawnpore in the Indian Mutiny. Shiloh. Chancellorsville. But that . . . I don't know why, there's something about fire, isn't there? The smell. The roar of the flames. And the speed of it. Terrifying. Just terrifying.'

'Three days, huh?' Clemens checked.

'All of that,' Latham said. 'I got there on the second. There were fourteen dead by then – that's just the ones we know about – and two churches gone.'

'How did it start? Did anybody find out?'

Latham shrugged. 'Engine room of a downtown building, apparently. Company called Tebbetts, Baldwin and Davis along Summer Street. Never made very clear, though. Some said, of course, that it was the hand of God. Hell of a coincidence that the fire wagons were out of action on account of the horse flu.'

'I guess you Limeys could say it was payback time for the Tea Party,' Clemens nudged his man, grinning.

'Not to mention the snowballs and Bunker Hill,' Latham grinned too. 'I remember explosions – that was the granite blocks of the buildings bursting in the heat.'

'Worse than Chicago, they say,' Clemens said.

'Well, there, of course,' Latham remembered his geography, 'you have the constant wind. God's breath. In Boston, there's nothing like that.'

'God's breath be damned.' Uncle Josiah staggered past briefly. Somehow the brandy had not come his way and he had gone in search of it. 'I don't know about Chicago, but in Boston, let me tell you—'

Suddenly, the door crashed back and Jemima Zzerbe appeared, drama in every line of her body. All the men turned to her and half of them were on their feet in seconds. Only her husband ignored her, taking a steady sip of his brandy and slipping a nonchalant hand into his pocket.

'Mattie . . . er . . . Hamilton! Come quickly! Martha has collapsed!'

Matthew Grand knew that Jemima was rattled by the mere fact that she had used not just a gentleman's given name, but a nickname at that. He was first through the door, Hamilton a close second.

It was easy to see where Martha had collapsed. All of the women in the drawing room were gathered around, looking

down at the floor behind the big Spanish sofa, which had been
pushed back from the fire.

'Give her some air,' Grand said. 'Don't smother the poor
girl. Come along, ladies,' he chivvied them kindly, 'let the dog
see the rabbit.' He had never really known what that meant, but
he heard it constantly on the streets of London and it just came
into his mouth. Despite the fact that he seemed to be talking
gibberish, the women backed away and revealed Martha, still
lying unconscious, tucked into the lee of the sofa.

'Hamilton,' Grand turned to check that the groom was still
there and saw to his relief that Batchelor had come in as well; he
had set Chauncey-Wolsey to guarding the door against all-comers.
'Oh, James. Even better.' Over the years, Grand and Batchelor
had lifted their share of unconscious bodies, albeit mostly that
way through drink. But they had a technique and they fell into it
seamlessly now. With Grand at the head end and Batchelor at the
foot, they had Martha out of the room and across the hall in
moments, leaving the twittering women behind. Hamilton would
be more than adequate to their gossip needs, Grand knew. He had
gathered already that his brother-in-law-to-be was not slow with
a word when it was needed.

At the foot of the stairs, the enquiry agents paused and carefully placed their burden on the lowest step, her head between
her knees. Grand patted her back and immediately grimaced.
'For heaven's sake, Martha,' he muttered. 'Why is a young
thing like you all trussed up like this?' He looked up at Grand.
'No wonder she fainted,' he said. 'Her stays are as tight as a
gnat's unmentionable. Let's get her upstairs and Annie and
Jemima's maid – what's her name? Can you remember?'

'I don't think I ever knew it.' Batchelor had been aware of
a scurrying presence on the middle landing, but beyond that,
nothing. The house seemed full of maids of every persuasion.

'Well – her. Annie and . . . whatever her name is . . . can
get her out of them and into bed. It's ridiculous what these girls
will go through to have a trim waist. I'm surprised at Martha.
She never struck me that way.'

'She was a little girl when you saw her last,' Batchelor
reminded him. 'And now she's a bride.'

Grand looked a little crestfallen. He sometimes wondered

where the years had gone. 'You're right. Give her to me.' He held out his arms. 'I'll carry her up. It's safer on the stairs. Go and call Annie. You only have to call. If I know my Annie, she won't have a moment's rest until Martha and I are both tucked up with a mug of cocoa.'

'Just call? Really?'

'Try it. Trust me, this is not like dealing with Mrs Rackstraw.'

Batchelor helped Grand raise Martha to her feet. Her eyelids were quivering from time to time now and her breathing was less shallow. Grand put one arm under the girl's knees and one in the small of her back and took the strain.

'Are you balanced?' Batchelor asked, stepping back but keeping his arms out.

Grand hefted his burden a little and nodded.

Batchelor took the stairs two at a time and, once on the landing, cleared his throat and called, 'Annie?'

Within less than a second, a door swung open and the old nanny stood there, fully dressed, her hair as neat and tidy as if it had been the middle of the afternoon. 'Yes?'

Batchelor blinked. She must have been standing there with her hand on the doorknob, just waiting. How many years of her life had she spent doing just that? Did she never sleep? 'It's . . . it's Miss Martha, Annie. She fainted.'

With a click of the tongue, the little woman elbowed Batchelor aside and scurried to the top of the stairs, just as Grand appeared in view.

'She's as white as a sheet,' she said. 'I told her those stays would come to no good, but she would have it . . . Come on, Master Mattie. Bring her in here, into her room.' She led them to the door she had just come out of. Catching Batchelor's eye, she said, truculently, 'I always put Miss Martha to bed after a dinner, and always will. She gets herself too excited and it isn't good for her. Especially . . .' She let her words die away.

The bed was turned down and she pulled the sheets right back so that Grand could lie Martha flat. The nanny looked at them with a gimlet eye.

'Well, don't just stand there,' she said. 'I'm not going to undress the poor thing with you standing there. Fetch . . .' She paused. She had been going to say 'her mother' or even

'Miss Mima' but stopped herself in time. 'Fetch that fancy maid of Miss Mima's. She'll either be in her room up on the top landing – third on the left, Master Mattie, as was Florence's in your day – or in Miss Mima's room, just opposite.' She flapped her hands at them. 'Go on. Go.'

Before they were out of the room, she was unbuttoning her darling's dress, crooning to her, weeping hot tears which splashed unheeded on the girl's white face.

On the landing there was, as might have been expected, the embryonic crowd of well-wishers and generally nosy people. Front of the line was Mrs Grand, wringing her hands and weeping. Mr Grand stood by her side, his face expressionless. Of Hamilton Chauncey-Wolsey, there was no sign. Jemima and Jeremy Zzerbe came next, not touching in a way that was more noticeable than a complete clinch would have been; there was virtual frost forming down their sides where they didn't quite meet. The rest were rabble and easy to dislodge. Moving seamlessly into their normal roles, Batchelor went in search of the maid while Grand dispersed the people – to each his own talent and by now they had it off to a fine art.

Batchelor tapped first on the door opposite Martha's. When there was no answer, he pushed it open. A dim lamp burned on the small table beside the bed but the room was empty. The bed was narrow and tightly tucked in; somehow, a complete metaphor for its temporary occupant. He closed the door and made for the stairs up to the next landing. What had Annie said? The something door on the left. It had been Florence's, he knew that, but that was of little use to him. When she had been its incumbent, he had still been struggling with his Shakespearean sonnets at Mr Latymer's school in Covent Garden. Third. That was it; third door on the left. But he immediately had a problem. The landing went both right and left from the head of the stairs and there were doors on both sides. So was it the third door on the left, going to the left, or the third door on the left going to the right? He was still standing there dithering when Grand came up behind him.

'Come along, James,' he said, briskly. 'Third door on the left.' And he went down the right-hand landing and knocked sharply on the relevant door.

Nothing.

'Knock again,' Batchelor said. 'She can't be asleep or anything. From what I have seen of her mistress, I doubt she has permission to ever close her eyes.'

Grand chuckled. Batchelor had Mima pegged right from the get-go and that was a fact. He knocked again.

The door behind him flew open and an irate woman stood there, night-gowned and curl-papered, she was not a pretty sight. 'Look here, you . . .' She stopped when she saw who it was. 'Sorry, Master Mattie.' She bobbed instinctively. 'I thought it was that other fella. Who is it you want?'

'Umm . . . I don't know her name. Miss Mima's maid.'

The snort the woman in the doorway gave spoke far more than words ever could. 'Magda, she calls herself. Alice, Miss Mima calls her. And I won't tell you what the other fella calls her. It makes me blush just to think of it.'

Grand and Batchelor gave her a funny look. She certainly had a bee in her bonnet about this other fella, whoever he was, but for now, there was an unconscious bride to deal with.

Grand called softly at the door, 'Magda, Magda, are you awake?'

No reply, not even the sound of feet on the boards coming to open the door.

'Alice.' He made his voice sharper, more like a command from on high, but there was still nothing.

'If I was you,' said the curl-papered maid whose name, Grand suddenly remembered, was Maisie, 'I would just go in. She don't lock the door. Because of . . .'

'. . . the other fella. I did wonder.' Grand turned the handle and pushed. The door opened easily on hinges that felt newly greased.

Magda had certainly made herself at home in her brief tenure. There was a pile of clothes tumbled on to the bed and in the faint light from the landing he could see a shoe discarded in the middle of the floor. He had seen a lot of maids' bedrooms in his time for one reason or another and this was by far the messiest . . . He looked closer and then turned to Batchelor. 'Keep Maisie out and tell her to go into her room and lock the door,' he hissed.

'Why?' Batchelor looked at his friend's face and his stomach knotted. 'Why?'

'Because someone has stove in Magda's head, James,' he said, quietly. 'We have a murderer in the house.'

It wasn't as easy to keep Maisie out as Grand had hoped. She was already several paces into the room, her curl papers a-quiver and her knuckles to her mouth. Batchelor saw the colour draining from her face and shook her quickly before she keeled over. How many fainting women could one evening take? She came to with a start, her colour came back and she looked at Batchelor with round, uncomprehending eyes.

'Is . . . is that . . . Alice? Magda?' she whispered.

'Yes,' Batchelor said, speaking sharply, not because he under-estimated her shock and distress, but because he had learned over the years that it was the best way to get someone back on to an even keel as quickly as possible. 'She seems to have had an accident. Now, Maisie, I want you to do something for me.'

She looked at him, still not really taking it in.

'Maisie!'

She jumped and blinked. 'Yes, sir?' Years of training were not forgotten just like that, no matter how deep the shock.

'I want you to go down to Miss Martha's room. Annie needs your help. Miss Martha has fainted with the heat downstairs and Annie needs someone to help get her undressed and into bed.'

'Oh, no, sir.' The maid was horrified. 'I'm just the maid for the rough upstairs. I never did no undressing.'

'Maisie.' Grand stood up and towered over the woman. 'You've undressed yourself, haven't you?'

'Oh, sir!' Maisie was outraged.

'Don't be a silly girl. Just go down and help Annie.'

Her feet seemed to be stuck to the floor.

'Don't stop to dress. Just go down and do as I say. And, Maisie . . .'

'Yes, sir?'

'Don't tell anyone what has happened up here. Do you understand me?'

She nodded. 'Yes, sir. Don't tell nobody.'

'Right. Now, off you go. Don't stop to get dressed, Maisie.'

He had seen her suddenly realizing she was only in her nightdress. 'Just get down there.'

She took one look at his face and fled.

'That was a bit harsh,' Batchelor remarked.

'You don't know Maisie, like I know Maisie,' Grand grunted. 'She never could make a decision to save her life. I once found her halfway up and halfway down the stairs, couldn't decide which way to go; turned out she'd been there an hour, one step up then one step down. She needs direction.'

'Will she be much help to Annie, then?' Batchelor just had to ask.

'None at all, but we had to send someone.' Grand turned back to the body, lighting the stub of candle by the bed. 'Look here, at this. I haven't seen anything this savage since . . . ooh, where was that one we looked into, the one near the station?'

Batchelor grimaced at the memory. 'King's Cross,' he said. 'Crestfield Street, if memory serves.'

Grand was impressed but didn't show it. Batchelor had an encyclopaedic recall when it came to anything in the capital. Anything in the country and he was all to blazes, but put him on a sidewalk with the smog in his nostrils and he was close to being a genius.

Batchelor looked closer. 'It is like the Crestfield Street murder,' he agreed. 'Whoever it was caught her from behind, so either she was comfortable with whoever was in the room and turned her back on him . . .'

'. . . or he crept up on her. We're agreed it had to be a man?'

Batchelor pointed, careful not to touch the ravaged head. Reaching round, he put the back of his fingers to her cheek.

'Still warm,' he said. 'What would you say? Half an hour?'

'Can't be much more,' Grand agreed. He straightened, looking down at what was left of the girl's skull, her hair a matted mass of blood, her cap and much of her cranium gone. 'Look,' he said. 'Bone splinters and the blood and brain – up the wall six feet. It had to be a man; no woman would have the strength. Where were you half an hour ago, James? Let's be generous – an hour ago?'

Batchelor straightened too and looked at him. Was his colleague suggesting something? Then it dawned on him. 'Ah, yes, I see.

Yes. Quite. Has to be somebody in the house. If it's an hour ago, even half an hour ago, we were still together, eating.'

'Thirty-eight of us,' Grand said.

'You counted?' Batchelor was amazed.

'No. The number is etched into my brain by my mother and father. In the process of an emotional reunion with them, the subject naturally turned to money – the other woman in Pa's life, I discovered a long time ago. I won't embarrass you by telling you the total cost of the wedding, but the number thirty-eight certainly features.'

'Thirty-eight,' Batchelor nodded. 'But we were all together. How?'

'Were we?' Grand looked at him. 'Think back, James. How often did you take a leak?'

'Er . . . just the once, I think.'

'Uncle Josiah was in and out like a jack-in-the-box. I noticed Sam nipping off for a smoke.'

'Latham forgot his cigars,' Batchelor remembered. 'He went to get them from the cloakroom.'

'Taking how long?'

'Hmm.' Batchelor saw the point exactly. A sudden thought occurred to him. 'We could save some time,' he said. 'We'll have to speak to Maisie.'

'Maisie? Why?' Grand couldn't think what Maisie could have in her brain that could help them.

'The other fella. If we can identify him, we may have our murderer, right there.'

'Ah. I'd forgotten about him. We'll need to get a description out of her if we can. One thing you have to remember about Maisie. She has the average memory retention of a guppy. So . . .' A noise from behind made Grand spin round.

They had been so intent on the body and what it could tell them that they hadn't noticed a soft footfall in the corridor outside. They turned as one to see a pile of pale pink froufrou on the floor just inside the door.

'Oh, for the Lord's sake!' Grand stepped forward, checking his hands for gore as he came into the brighter light of the corridor. 'It's Mima. I should say, perhaps, Mrs Jeremy Zzerbe. I might have known she couldn't keep her nose out.'

Batchelor looked down at the pink heap on the floor. 'I suppose . . . well, it *is* her maid. She was probably worried.' Grand snorted. 'Worried? Mima worried about anyone else? If that's so, it will be for the first time in her life. Look, James, we can't do anything in here, not in this light. We'll seal the door and wait till morning. And we'll have to send for the police.'

Batchelor was searching among the frills for Jemima Zzerbe's armpits. Dragging her on to the landing was not the most elegant way of moving her, but it was important to disturb as little as possible in the room, and lifting her on to the bed was clearly out of the question. Locating a suitable body part, he lugged her out of the room. Grand followed and stepped over the prostrate woman to forage in his wallet.

'Damn it,' he muttered, pulling out a strip of stamps and tearing three off. 'I've only got three-ha'penny ones. Never mind, it's cheap at half the price.'

Despite the circumstances, Batchelor had to smile. 'Matthew,' he said, lugging Mima Zzerbe out of his partner's way, 'we'll make an Englishman of you yet.'

Grand looked down at him, confused. 'Why?'

'Not only can you trot out a meaningless platitude on any occasion, but you also moan about the cost of postage. And why now, I have to ask?'

'I'm sealing the door.' He licked the stamps, one by one, sticking them across the door where it met the jamb. 'This means that we'll know if anyone has been here, tampering with the evidence.'

'But . . .' Batchelor had spotted a flaw. 'Can't someone just replace the stamps?'

'Who is likely to have a three-ha'penny British postage stamp in their wallet, let alone three? For example,' Grand gave the third stamp a hard press with his thumb to keep it in place, 'have you?'

Batchelor admitted he had not.

'Latham doesn't strike me as the kind of cuss who'd ever post anything for less than a penny. Anyway, he's been in New York for too long.' Grand looked down at Jemima, just beginning to stir. 'We'll have to do something with her,' he said. 'Go down and get that useless husband of hers. It's time he did something other than drink and sulk. I'll stay here with her until you come back. She's just as likely to burst back into the room and faint again.'

Batchelor made for the stairs and, as he turned the corner, hanging on to the banister against the steep flight down, he looked back, to see Grand looking down at Jemima with an unfathomable expression on his face. It was the kind of look, half hatred, half love, with an overlay of contempt, that no man wants his friends to see. Dipping his head to avoid the low beam, Batchelor went off in search of Jeremy Zzerbe.

Josiah was alone. There was some kind of hubbub upstairs, probably Martha showing off her honeymoon falderals to the ladies. Odd that the men had gone too, but maybe, Josiah reasoned, that was how it was done these days. Reason and Uncle Josiah were strange bedfellows and he had no interest in ladies' falderals, not since the winter of '53, forever etched in his memory. No, Josiah would sample just a *little* more of Andrew's special reserve.

And that's how he saw him first – through a glass, darkly. The facets and the candles meant there were a dozen of him, perhaps more. Josiah sipped and lowered the glass and the dozen strangers became one. A large man, with a full beard and uncombed hair, had wandered into the dining room. There was an indefinable smell about him that Josiah couldn't place. The old man might be losing the rest of his faculties, but his nostrils were still with him.

The man crossed the room, taking in the scattered plates, the ribbons and fancies. 'Looks like I got here too late.'

Josiah tried to focus. 'I didn't know you were invited, sir. Who the hell are you?'

The man crossed to Josiah's chair and thumped his heavy canvas bag down on the carpet. He slid back a chair of his own in front of the old man and looked him straight in the eye. 'It's me, Uncle,' he said. 'Ira.'

A thousand emotions flitted across the old man's face. Ira didn't recognize them all. But then, after so many years, he hadn't expected to see Josiah in this house at all. Hell, after so many years, he didn't expect to see Josiah alive. The old man's nose was cherry red, the veins running along it like something in a butcher's shop. His eyes, pale and glistening with unshed tears, tried to take in the man before him.

'Ira?' he managed at last. 'Phil's boy? Ira?'

'The very same, Uncle,' Ira nodded, gripping the man's bony hand in both of his.

'The last time I saw you,' Josiah said, leaning back and looking his nephew up and down, 'you and your pa were like to kill each other.'

'We were.' Ira nodded.

Josiah frowned, suddenly gripping his nephew's hand. 'You know he's gone, Ira – your pa?'

'I know,' Ira sighed. 'Wish I'd had a chance to put things right, but it wasn't to be.'

Suddenly, it all came flooding back to Josiah – the indefinable smell that seemed stitched into his nephew's clothing. 'You're a whaler,' he said.

'I've hurled a lance or two,' Ira nodded, 'but that's a young man's game, Uncle. I reckon the US whaling fleet'll just have to get along without me.'

Josiah laughed. 'Where are my manners?' he asked, fumbling for a glass. 'Hair of the dog, Ira? We've got some catching up to do.'

'Hair of the dog it is, Uncle,' Ira beamed. 'But . . .' he reached down into his sea-bag, 'my dog, if you don't mind.' Josiah took one look at the rum bottle that Ira was holding and didn't mind at all. 'But what's going on here?' the ex-whaler asked. 'I feel like I've missed the party. I rang the bell, but nobody answered. I heard times were hard these days. Uncle Andrew can't afford the staff like he used to, huh?'

'Your timing's damn near perfect, my boy,' Josiah said, his old eyes lighting up as he watched Ira pour for them both. 'Little . . . Thing's getting married tomorrow. Martha.'

'Martha?' Ira's eyes widened. 'Married? My God!' He laughed. 'When I saw her last, she was all pigtails and goofy teeth.'

'Well, the teeth are still a trial, though her fella doesn't seem to mind. Pigtails have gone, though, if I remember right.'

Uncle Josiah looked into an invisible distance and nodded to himself.

'Where are they all?'

'I don't rightly know.' Josiah looked about him, still a little bewildered by the evening's events. There was a scream from the landing and Ira was at the foot of the stairs, looking up. The staircase had been empty a moment ago, but now it was full of people, all jabbering excitedly, with anxious faces. In the middle was Aunt Liza, looking pale and ill, held up on one side by Uncle Andrew and on the other by some flunkey. They were bringing her downstairs. The party stopped when they saw him.

'Aunt Liza,' the ex-whaler said. 'What's happening?'

And Aunt Liza screamed again.

SEVEN

Martha's room was an oasis of calm in the chaos that was developing all around. The milling crowd of people in all stages of drunkenness from very to only slightly tipsy – the most a well-brought-up lady would ever admit to – had either become quieter or had gone away. Annie didn't care which; she was just grateful for the relative peace that had descended on the house. Her little girl, her Martha, lay on the bed, so pale and still. She had unbuttoned the girl's dress as best she could, turning her halfway and undoing the slippery little nubs of pearl from her shoulder-blades to her waist, but when they disappeared into the gathers of her skirt, she needed more hands than she had at her disposal. She remembered, so few hours ago, lacing her into her stays, then buttoning her into the dress, telling her, over and over again, that she couldn't go a whole evening trussed up like that. The baby was growing, she would feel the quickening soon; this was no time to wear a corset. But, Martha had said, it was just for tonight. After the wedding, once they were on their honeymoon and no one would know how long they had been married, she could wear the loose dresses Annie had been sewing in secret for the past weeks. She hadn't told Hamilton yet, so she had to wear stays. Just this last time . . .

Annie wept some more, just thinking about her girl, her sparkling eyes every time she spoke of that animal, that Hamilton; handsome is as handsome does, and he had not behaved so handsomely.

And meanwhile, where was that Magda, Alice, whatever she called herself? No better than she should be, or so Annie had heard. Men in her room. And in the afternoon as well. Broad daylight! Annie had not lived as sheltered a life as the family believed; she had had her moments, oh, yes, indeed. But never, *never* in the light. Always at dead of night. Hearing the creeping footsteps along the landing. Blowing out the candle. Waiting in the dark . . .

She shook herself. None of that nonsense any more, no indeed. But where . . .

The door creaked open and Annie jumped up off the bed, turning, ready to scold, but the words died unspoken. Maisie stood there, in her nightgown, her hair in curl papers. That alone would have been reason for surprise. But it was her face that stopped Annie in her tracks. She was as white as a sheet and her lips were trembling. As if to stop them, her fingers strayed to her mouth like fluttering moths to a flame and then her hand would drop, before lifting again to pat her curls and touch her mouth. She looked as though she had seen a ghost.

'Maisie,' Annie whispered. Even in shock, she wouldn't forget her baby lying insensible on the bed. 'Whatever's the matter? Where's Magda?'

Maisie buckled at the knees and held on to the corner of the clothes press just inside the door. 'She's . . .' Her voice came out too loud and she started again, pitching it to a whisper, like Annie. 'She's dead, Annie,' she said. 'She's dead. It's horrible. Her head . . .' Her fluttering fingers went round to the back of her own skull, as though checking it was not crushed like Magda's.

Annie's first reaction was to disbelieve every word. Her second was to believe it, because Maisie simply didn't have the brainpower to make something like that up. And she knew that, had it been possible, Master Mattie would have sent Magda down to help his sister as quickly as he could. And if he had sent Maisie, it really had to be because there was no other option.

Annie grabbed the woman by her shoulders and shook her gently, setting the curl papers bouncing on her forehead. 'Come on,' she said, not unkindly. 'Come on, Maisie. We'll talk about it later. You can have a good cry, but for now we must get Miss Martha out of these stays. She's been in a faint for far too long. Come on. Help me, there's a good girl.'

Maisie squared her shoulders and, with an enormous sniff, stepped into the breach. She held Martha Grand over on her side while Annie undid the dress and then the stays. Then, she helped her slip them down her legs and over her feet and the girl was free. She lay there, naked as a jaybird on the bed and took a deep breath, wriggling further into the mattress and falling into a natural sleep at last. The colour came back to her cheeks and she put a hand on her stomach. Her lips parted and her eyelids fluttered.

'Hamilton,' she murmured.

Annie turned sharply and faced Maisie square on.

'I know you're none too bright,' she said, mincing no words. 'But I know you know how many beans make five and if you breathe a word of this, so help me, I'll flay your stupid skin off your back myself. There now!'

Maisie looked down at the angry little woman in front of her and smiled. 'No need to get yourself in a spin,' she said. 'So, she's expecting. What of it? I know you think that the Grand family's shit don't stink, but all of us down in the kitchen know different. Why, I could—'

'If you say a word of this,' the nanny said, between clenched teeth, 'I'll kill you. I swear it. Now, back to your bed and we'll put this night behind us.'

Maisie deflated and made for the door. Then, with temporary bravery, she turned and faced the woman down. 'Hah!' she said. 'I reckon you've got some nerve, threatening me with Magda dead and cold upstairs. When they find that fella as was visiting her all afternoon, I reckon they got a murderer on their hands. And what if it was your precious Master Mattie, eh? Or

Mr Hamilton, who obviously knows what to do with it? Eh?
What then?' And she slammed the door behind her.

Martha flinched in her sleep and gave a little cry. Annie
turned to the bed and covered the girl up, crooning a lullaby.
What was to become of them? Any of them in this world turned
upside down?

James Batchelor got down to the next landing and found it
empty. However, the noise from the hall below sounded like
the seventh circle of Hell, so he went on down. Where there
was noise, there were people. And, hopefully, one of them would
be Jeremy Zzerbe. He had to squeeze past a mob at the bottom
of the stairs to get into the hall at all. In the middle of the
throng there seemed to be a rather disreputable-looking man,
bending down and shouting. The women were all clustering
around someone who seemed to be on the floor. Batchelor rolled
his eyes. Did these women do nothing but faint? He scanned
the crowd, hoping that he had made the right identification over
dinner of Mr Zzerbe. He remembered him as weaselly; sadly,
as he looked around, that designation fitted more than a few
people.

'Are you looking for someone specific, sir?'

Hart's voice, coming suddenly out of nowhere, made him
jump. He turned to see the butler standing to one side, seemingly impervious to the jostling of the crowd. 'Yes,' Batchelor
said, 'but first, can you tell me what's going on down here?'

'Yes, sir, of course.' Hart had the kind of voice which novelists
described as 'colourless', but this was in fact unfair. Everything
that anyone heard spoken by him above stairs was actually carefully couched in level tones designed to give away nothing. When
letting down his hair in the servants' quarters, he had access to a
vocabulary that could turn milk. Blandly, he said, 'Mrs Grand
has fainted, sir. I believe it was from shock at seeing her husband's
long-lost nephew, Ira, standing in the hall. I understand he has
been absent these fourteen years, on a whaler, sir.'

'Er . . . thank you.' James Batchelor, in all his strivings to
write the Great English Novel, would never use a storyline so
clichéd. 'I see. And meanwhile, do you know where Mr Jeremy
Zzerbe is?'

'Mr Zzerbe. I believe the last time I saw Mr Zzerbe, he was in the library, sir. Addressing the brandy, if I remember rightly.'

Batchelor had remembered that Zzerbe rather liked the liquor so he wasn't surprised. Now, all he had to do was remember where the library was.

Reading his mind, Hart pointed to a door in the corner of the hall, fortunately not one which involved making his way through the milling crowd.

'Thank you, Hart,' Batchelor said, edging round the rather large woman standing in his way and showing no signs of moving.

'You are very welcome, sir,' Hart said, standing aside to let him pass. When he was out of earshot, he muttered, 'Good luck.'

Jeremy Zzerbe had addressed the brandy until only the fumes remained. Uncle Josiah had not known that the bottle was in the library, or there might have been an unseemly scuffle, but as it was, Zzerbe had had the bottle to himself. He was sitting in a chair in the window bay, head back, snoring like a pig. His tie was loose and his shoes kicked off; he had reached that stage of drunkenness when he scarcely knew nor cared where he was any more. Batchelor was now in a quandary. He should at least tell him that his wife was in a fainting condition on the servants' landing. But it seemed hardly worth the effort, when he would not be able to be of any help at all. He stood, looking down at the man, probably no older than himself. He saw the thread veins already appearing on the cheeks under the tan. The hair thinning, though the carefully combed-over strands hid it in most circumstances. The open mouth let him see the coated tongue, the missing tooth. In short, here lay Uncle Josiah, a lifetime ago. He kicked the man's foot, not hard, but enough to wake him should he be wakeable.

One crusted eye opened and Zzerbe looked up at him, without too much enthusiasm. 'Who're you?' he slurred. 'Whaddya want?'

'I'm James Batchelor,' Batchelor said, with exaggerated enunciation. 'I need you to come and help me with your wife.' As he spoke, he knew he could have worded it better.

The drunk barked a laugh. 'The goddamned Limey. And good luck with my wife,' he said, closing his eye again. 'I haven't called in help, I grant you, but I've got nowhere with her this three years.' He chuckled his way back to sleep, muttering incoherent words which Batchelor was glad he couldn't make out.

'Your wife has fainted,' he said, leaning down as far as he dared without getting engulfed in alcohol fumes.

The eye opened again. 'Fainted? She's on the faint already? She usually has a few days of headaches first.' Zzerbe focused briefly on Batchelor before the effort was too much. 'Y'must be a faster worker than I am, Mr Limey.'

Batchelor shook him by the shoulder, but it was no good. Jeremy Zzerbe would not be coming up two flights of stairs to help with his wife. Not this side of hell freezing over, at any rate.

'Can I be of assistance, sir?'

Hart's voice in Batchelor's ear made him jump again. The man's shoes must be soled in flannel.

Batchelor made a snap decision. There were so many unconscious women in this house, one at least had to be dealt with. 'I think you can, Hart,' he said. 'Could you find Miss Thaxter for me and then come up with her to the top floor? We have a bit of an emergency up there.'

Hart looked at him, unperturbed. 'May I ask . . .?'

But Batchelor had gone.

Up on the top landing, Matthew Grand was getting a little testy. Time always lags when in the company of a comatose woman, he knew that, but he was wary of Mima Zzerbe, ever since that time when he was sixteen in the shrubbery. He still couldn't remember it without sweating. He was sure he had sent James in search of her husband hours ago. She was beginning to stir every once in a while, only to fall back again swooning whenever she saw the door, sealed with his three-ha'penny stamps.

Finally, Batchelor's feet were on the stairs and Grand wasn't alone any more.

'Where in hell's name have you been?' he snapped. 'And where's her husband?'

'Out cold in the library,' Batchelor explained. 'If things go on like this, we'll be the only ones in the entire house still conscious. I have Hart and Celia on the way.'

Grand tried not to let Batchelor know when he was impressed, but he was impressed now. Of the whole household, he had instinctively chosen the only two people who would be the slightest good in any kind of crisis. But before he could tell him so, the two were on the landing, going into action like a well-oiled machine.

'If you could take Mrs Zzerbe's head, madam,' Hart said, smoothly, 'I will take her feet.' The perfect butler was all about decorum. Even in a crisis, there were parts of a lady's body that a mere servant never thought about, let alone handled.

'Upsidaisy,' Celia said, brightly. She beamed at Grand. 'Mattie. We haven't had a chance for a chat, but we must before tomorrow evening.'

He nodded, with a tight smile.

She smiled at Batchelor as well, as she hefted the weight to be more comfortable. 'I knew that first-aid I did in the war would come in handy,' she said. She looked at the butler. 'Shall I go down first, Hart?'

'If you would, madam,' he said, smoothly. 'I am not really supposed to lift anything heavy, although Mrs Zzerbe cannot be said to be heavy, of course. So please, if I need to put her down . . .'

'Oh, heavens, Hart, I had forgotten.' She looked at Batchelor. 'James. Would you? Hart has an old war wound and mustn't lift . . .'

Batchelor took the woman's head end from Celia, one armpit at a time and Celia manoeuvred her way to the feet. The butler stepped back.

'Thank you so much, sir,' he said. 'I would do it, but—'

'No, no,' Batchelor said, disappearing around the corner with his burden. 'A war wound is a war wound, when all is said and done. If you could come down after us, though, to open doors and so on.'

'Indeed, sir,' Hart intoned. 'I will be right behind you.' He watched them disappear. Then he turned to Grand. 'Is there anything wrong, sir?' he asked. 'Because, I wondered why Mrs Zzerbe was in a fainting condition up here of all places.'

'There has been an accident, Hart,' Grand said. 'Mrs Zzerbe's maid is . . . unwell.'

'Unwell, sir?' Hart's eyebrow disappeared under his hair.

'Well, dead, actually.' Suddenly, Grand no longer had the energy to dissemble. 'Bludgeoned, not to put too fine a point on it. But I would prefer you not to mention it to anyone. Especially in the servants' hall. Gossip, you know . . . and we don't want to spoil Miss Martha's wedding.'

Hart gave the small bow he used when asked to bring the tea things in. 'Understood, sir. I won't say a word to anyone. Do . . . do you and Mr Batchelor have any clues as yet, sir?'

'Not a thing,' Grand sighed. He held out a hand towards the stairs. He had seen enough of the landing to last him for a while and, as long as no one else fainted, he would rather be downstairs. 'Shall we?'

Downstairs, the crowd had largely dispersed. From outside came the voices of coachmen coaxing their teams out into the drive, setting out on their journeys home. Latham was waiting just inside the doorway for Celia Thaxter. He knew in principle how to row, he just didn't intend to do it and especially in the dark. He had to wait for his oarswoman to take him back to the hotel. Celia Thaxter had been rowing with her father since she could hold an oar in both hands and she had the biceps to prove it. Jeremy Zzerbe was visible through the library door, still slumped in his chair. Ira was around somewhere by the smell, but it was becoming more elusive now he was in the environs of so much orange blossom, so many lilies. He was sitting with Uncle Josiah on hard hall chairs, reserved for unwanted guests. They were both smoking cigars and passing a dark bottle from hand to hand.

Latham saw Grand and came over. 'Have you seen Miss Thaxter?' he asked, a little testily. 'We should have set off to the island long before this.' He had the landlubber's whine in his voice. 'How will we find our way in the dark?'

Grand forbore to mention the enormous lighthouse. It seemed such an obvious thing that he was sure an investigative journalist of Latham's standing must have noticed it already. 'Miss Thaxter is tending to Mrs Zzerbe,' he said. 'She fainted.'

'Another?' Latham had little patience left. 'Do the women in this county do nothing but pass out? First Miss Grand, then Mrs Grand . . .'

'My mother fainted?' Grand was unaware.

Latham waved a careless hand. 'Yes. When that whaler walked in. What's his name? Irene? No, that can't be right.'

'Ira?' Grand's eyes were like marbles. 'Ira's here?'

'Can't you smell him? What with the blubber and the rum, it's quite unmistakeable. He's over there, with your uncle.'

'His uncle, too. Well, well, well. Ira's home. There's a thing.' Grand shook himself. 'But . . . my mother?'

'She was taken up to her room. But she had come round all right. Nothing to worry about.'

'Perhaps nothing to worry *you.*' Grand was already on his way to the stairs. 'But then, she's not your mother.' And he took the steps two at a time, the impending mortality which accompanies any sign of frailty in a parent sitting on his shoulder, digging in its cruel claws.

Latham watched him go and shrugged. Then a thought came to him. A whaler? He could probably row . . . He moved across the hall on silent, journalist's feet.

'Ira?' he asked in oily tones. 'Can I have a word?'

Grand tapped first on the door of Jemima Zzerbe. Batchelor opened it and oozed out on to the landing, closing it quietly behind him.

'She's better,' he said, quietly. 'She wouldn't let Celia so much as loosen a button. Screamed blue murder every time she tried. She may do better with me out of the room, but Celia was a little unwilling to be left alone with her. Apparently, Mrs Zzerbe has been known to bite.'

'Not since she was about six,' Grand said. 'But she has a nasty temper on her, it's true. Look, pop across to Martha's room and see if Maisie is free to help Celia.' He ran a hand through his hair. 'This is like a game of tic-tac-toe. I'm going in to my mother. She fainted.'

Batchelor opened his mouth, framing a question.

'Don't ask. Long story. Hopefully my father will be with her, or at least not far away. I'll get him to send for the police.'

In all the excitement, Batchelor had almost forgotten the bludgeoned body on the floor above. 'Are there police around here?' he asked.

'Good Lord above, James.' Grand was getting tired and near the end of his leash. 'This isn't the back of beyond, you know. We have all the conveniences here. And a police station is one of them.' He considered. 'Not a police station as we would understand it, but we do have a constable. Doubles as a blacksmith. So don't worry. He will be here in a jiffy and can at least guard the door properly. Off you go, get Maisie and then go downstairs for a drink and a rest. You look done in. Hart was off to arrange a cold collation when I saw him last, after he'd seen to the fires, checked all the windows and doors, drawn the curtains; I understand his motto is that if a thing's worth doing, it's worth doing yourself.' He patted his partner on the back. 'Off you go.'

Liza Grand lay in her big feather bed, capped and beribboned as though nothing untoward was going on at all. Her hands plucked at the coverlet and that was the only sign that she was not simply sleeping. Andrew Grand sat on the foot of the bed, leaning on the post and looking at his wife. If his son had been asked before that moment whether his parents loved each other, he would have been stuck for an answer, but the look on his father's face cleared up that conundrum. The look of naked adoration, not unmixed with fear and sorrow was gone in a second when he heard the click of the door, but it made Grand's heart leap in his chest.

He crept up to the bed and whispered, 'Is she going to be all right?'

His father nodded. 'She's sleeping,' he whispered back. 'She's had one shock after another tonight and what with all the worry over the food, the flowers, the guests . . . it's just been too much. She'll be up and about for tomorrow. I can't imagine that there will be any more alarms tonight.'

Grand looked at his father and pulled a rueful face.

'What?' The word came out too loud and his wife flinched in her sleep. 'What?' he repeated, more quietly.

'We must talk about this outside,' Grand said. 'We don't know how much she can hear.'

Andrew Grand got up slowly from his place of vigil and, walking to the head of the bed, kissed his wife's forehead tenderly. Then he led the way out of the room. If this boy of his had started a mare's nest just because he was involved in some consarned police nonsense these days, there would be another crisis in the house, the bride's brother with a black eye.

On the landing, Grand told his father about the gruesome find. He waited for the shock and horror, but there was little to see.

'So, Pa,' Grand always hated the way he reverted to the schoolroom when he was at home with his parents, 'we'll have to call the police. Is the constable here still old John Johnson?'

'Dead,' his father said, shutting his mouth with a snap.

'Right. Well, he was getting on, I suppose.'

'Not old age. Bullet. Last Fall. Hunters mistook him for a deer.'

Grand did a quick calculation. 'That's six months ago,' he said. 'Who is the constable now?'

A shrug. 'Nobody. We haven't had the elections yet this year.'

Grand tried to imagine a policeman in England not replaced for half a year and it just didn't make any sense. But this was *New* England and they did things differently here. Suppressing a sigh, he said, 'So, where is nearest then, do you think?'

Andrew Grand was trying to keep his temper. His wife was ill, he had to admit that. His daughter seemed to be the same. There were thirty-eight guests for the wedding tomorrow, plus the inevitable sightseers from the town. There was no best man yet. The bridesmaid, it turned out, had also fainted. What was wrong with these women? Their mothers had been pioneers, seeing off a couple of dozen coyotes and a rattler or two before lying down in the mud and giving birth to triplets – or so the story went. And now they passed out like ninepins. Just because some foreigner had been hit over the head. He couldn't see for the life of him what all the fuss was about. 'Boston,' he snapped.

'Boston? That's out of state. There must be somewhere nearer, surely?'

'Can't think where that would be. Exeter's got one officer, I think. There's a cop of sorts in Portsmouth, but he's contracted to the harbour. You do what you like, Matthew. I'm going back to your mother. A dead maid means nothing to me right now. Why don't you just get the Zzerbes to bundle her up, take her home and deal with it there? Best way. Now, if you'll excuse me . . .' and he swept back into his wife's bedroom, only just remembering not to slam the door.

Needless to say, the imperturbable Hart had the answer. While Grand wrote out the wire, the butler roused the boot boy and told him to get to the rail terminus as quick as he could, to send it to the police in Boston. The boy's eyes were wide with wonder and they got wider when nice Master Mattie gave him a dollar for himself. It was the most money he had ever had at one time and that fact alone was so exciting he hardly listened as the man at the telegraph station, grumpy with sleep, read out the words as he tapped them into his machine. Something about somebody being dead. What did he care, with a dollar in his pocket?

EIGHT

The drunks and good-time girls were already lined up at the station house by the time the telegram arrived. Sergeant O'Farrell had been one of Boston's finest, ever since he stepped off the cattle boat from Connemara. He had been ready to shoot someone since he started his shift and it wasn't midnight yet.

'Telegram for the chief,' the boy said, holding out the paper.

'Chief's not in,' O'Farrell muttered, not looking up.

'I just deliver 'em, Sergeant,' the boy said. 'I can't take 'em back.'

Now O'Farrell looked up. 'Don't smart-mouth me, you little son of a bitch. I'll take my belt to you.'

The boy didn't doubt it. There was something in the ox-like shoulders and the Irish temperament that he'd rather not tangle with.

'Yessir,' he intoned. 'Sorry, sir.'

O'Farrell snatched the paper. 'Now, get your black ass out of here.'

And the boy was gone.

They didn't get that many telegrams at the station house. Most people reporting a crime came in person. Most people complaining – and that *was* most people – made a beeline for Sergeant O'Farrell's desk and bent his ear about the cost of policing in Boston's fair city and how it wasn't safe to walk the streets at night.

'What we got, Sarge?' the other desk man wanted to know.

'Some lady's maid's got herself killed in a country house.'

'Chief ought to be told,' the constable said.

'Yeah, and I ought to be mayor of Boston by now, but I ain't. And I ain't gonna bother the chief over a Goddamn lady's maid, Berlowski. Anyhow, it's out of state.'

'It is?' Tadeusz Berlowski may have been from Poland originally, but that was a long time ago. He was all-American now and the mysterious workings of the federal system fascinated him.

'Rye.' O'Farrell pointed to the wire. 'That's Maine, Berlowski; the far side of the moon.' He lobbed the paper neatly into the litter basket, looked up at the face in front of him and sighed. 'Lulu,' he said, peering past the paint on the face in question. 'Have you been pestering honest gentlemen going about their business again? I only ask, because this is the third time this week.'

Liza Grand had dreamed about her daughter's wedding day since Martha had first been put in her arms, red-faced, arms flailing, ready to take on the world. It hadn't been an easy road; eligible men had come and gone, far less eligible men had come and stayed for a frighteningly long time before the girl had seen sense. But now, here she was, on the morning of that long-awaited day. She knew she should be happy. Her Mattie was home for the wedding. Hamilton Chauncey-Wolsey was handsome. Martha was blooming, if a little testy. So, why wasn't Liza feeling like a million dollars? This stone in the pit of her stomach wasn't getting any lighter, and what with Ira, smelling like the Lord knew what, and Josiah . . . She thought for a moment and realized there was no way to categorize Josiah these days, except as an old soak. Helene was doing her thing with the young men; she had been all over that nice Englishman at dinner – Liza had hardly known where to look. And Martha fainting. Why would she do that? So mortifying. And Mima too. And what about that husband of hers? Eyes all over the room except on his wife . . .

Liza turned on her side and pulled the covers over her head. She hadn't done that since she was about twelve, but there seemed no other rational option. There was a comfort in the dark.

Martha Grand lay in her bed, curled up like the baby inside her. Annie had told her she would feel it move soon; the quickening, Annie had called it. She lay, concentrating all her love and attention on the tiny thing which, as things stood at that moment, only she and Annie knew existed. Had she known how many in the servants' hall knew by now, she would have pulled the covers over her head like her mother was doing on the other side of the wall, but ignorance being bliss, she stroked her stomach, crooning low in her throat to the tiny scrap of life. She loved Hamilton, she really did. He was so handsome, after all. But if it wasn't for this scrap, she wouldn't be marrying him this morning. She trusted him about as far as she could throw a grand piano – no man that handsome was trustworthy. She had heard Annie whisper it to one of the maids when she had first brought him home to meet her parents. She had let that go – she believed it herself, after all. But now, with what was to come in just a few short months, she was going to have to trust him, handsome or no. She smiled to herself because, after all, if you had to have a husband at all, why not make it a handsome one?

She turned on her back and stretched her arms above her head, pointing her toes and lengthening her legs. Startled at the movement, the baby turned a back flip, as light as a butterfly's wing. But Martha, jumping out of bed and reaching for the bell to summon Annie, didn't even notice.

Jemima Zzerbe woke unwillingly, as she woke every morning. Jeremy was not in the bed beside her – it would have given her the screaming fits had he been – but at least she knew this morning the other place he was not. She was not a vindictive woman, not really, not in her heart of hearts. But the little warm glow that comes with being the winner, the last woman standing, gave her a purpose most days lacked. And, after all, her best friend was getting married today. Time to pin on the smile and be the best maid of honour there ever had been. For a moment, the smile was genuine; at least with that sad sack of a sister-in-law-to-be standing beside her, holding the bouquet, she knew she would be the prettiest woman in the bride's entourage, by a country mile.

Waldo Hart walked along the line, inspecting his troops who would battle with this Day of Days. One word out of place, one eyelash out of line and there would be no bonuses for them. And Hart watched like a hawk; a butler could grow rich on withheld bonuses but Hart, though cruel, was fair. If they did right by him, he would do right by them; all it could cost them was a meagre ten per cent. And who could complain at that? No one moved a muscle. Hart's retribution was swift and no one ever saw it coming. Only the boot boy flinched a little when he was next to come under the butler's eagle glare, but it all passed off well and, with a clap of his hands, Hart released his minions to do what they had to do. He stalked off, stiff and proud as a heron on a fat-fished pond, watching, missing nothing – the perfect butler. He tweaked a curtain into place, picked up a piece of errant paper and straightened the fire irons. Nodding to the perfected room, he went on his way.

Hamilton Chauncey-Wolsey had not slept well. He was in a hotel in Exeter, the little town only a little less sleepy than Rye, it being beyond the pale for him to spend the night before his wedding under the same roof as his bride. As most of his stays with the Grands had involved being under the same sheet as his bride, he could see their point. My God – and he twisted under the scratchy sheets of the hotel bed – Martha was a devil in bed. He didn't bother himself with wondering where she had learned that stuff. After all, he was scarcely a beginner himself. But she really knew what she was doing . . . He mulled over whether it was bad taste for a groom to try and inveigle the chambermaid into joining him in bed for a while on the morning of his wedding. His dilemma was solved when a knock on the door brought his breakfast, carried by possibly the biggest, meanest looking bus boy this side of the Alleghenies.

Jeremy Zzerbe, Uncle Josiah and Edward Latham all woke simultaneously, brought to sudden consciousness by the thud of Ira falling off the sofa in front of the library fire. It was not the usual habit of Andrew and Liza Grand to allow guests to fall asleep hither and yon in the house, especially when at least two of them had perfectly good bedrooms upstairs, but the night before had not been usual and Hart, peering into the gloom of the library before locking the doors and windows for the night, had made a judgement call. There were at least seven hundred pounds of drunk in the room and he had sent most of his staff to bed. Allowing for the fact that he himself was allowed no heavy lifting, he decided to blow out the lamps and leave them to it. Sufficient unto the day is the evil thereof and Hart had had, for one day, sufficient.

Ira had protested that he was in no fit state to row Latham across to the island and the journalist positively refused to trawl this peculiar house in search of Celia Thaxter. So, here he was, still under Andrew Grand's roof.

Silently, the men made their way out of the library, Zzerbe and Josiah Grand to their rooms, Latham and Ira Grand in search of coffee. Lots of coffee. Latham was also looking for a cloakroom to wash up a little. Ira had got out of that habit years before, so coffee was his first and only call. Sam Clemens was already out in the orchard, pacing about as he usually did when ideas were whirling in his head, the smoke from his cigar drifting through the trees.

Slowly, as inexorably as a glacier, the plans for the wedding ground their way through the morning. Annie dressed Martha and then went to dress Jemima, now that she was a maid short. Liza Grand got up finally and dressed herself. She had been brought up plain and simple and, wealthy though Andrew had become over the years, she still liked to do up her own buttons and tie on her own bonnet. The men clambered into their Sunday best, brushed their hair, oiled their moustaches where present and began to assemble in the hall.

The staff began to gather outside, ready to cheer the wedding party off on the short journey. Liza, Jemima and the silent Sarah Chauncey-Wolsey would go in one carriage. She didn't speak; hadn't spoken since she had arrived. Had she been asked for a reason for her silence, she would have parted her lips just enough to explain that she was a writer – did everybody realize that? – and the Muse must not be disturbed. She sat, eyes closed, in the carriage, alone with that Muse. Liza Grand wanted to slap her, but didn't want to cause yet more of a scene, so settled for clenching her fists in her lap. Martha and her father would follow along behind. There hadn't been a wedding in Rye for years and the single street which led to the little clapboard church would be lined with the townsfolk. Some of the more honoured of them would be in the church, having been also at the dinner the night before. All in all, it was like a holiday. Some people had even tied ribbons to the bridles of their horses and others had hung streamers from their windows. It was like Thanksgiving and the Fourth of July all rolled into one.

As James Batchelor strolled along towards the church with the other walking gentlemen, he found it hard to keep a smile off his face. Yes, there was a dead maid in one of the attic rooms. Yes, he was far from home. But there was something about being out on a spring morning, with a waving crowd on either hand and the smell of the salt spray, that made you feel good to be alive. He put his natural pessimism to one side. Nothing could go wrong; had not enough gone wrong already? One dead maid, three fainting women and – according to the urgent message which had arrived by sweating messenger not half an hour before – no best man. Matthew Grand had stepped into the breach and would be joining the party from the other side, as it were, at the church. Yes. Batchelor inhaled the brisk spring air, tinged with early blossom and the tang of the sea; it was as good a morning as any to go to a wedding.

An arm slipped through his and he turned to see that he had been joined by Celia Thaxter.

'Good morning, Mr Batchelor,' she said, squeezing his arm in her rather vice-like grip.

'Good morning, Miss Thaxter,' he said, formally. 'Um . . . have you come over from the island this morning?'

'No,' she said. 'I stayed the night. What with Mrs Zzerbe and all the other kerfuffle, I missed the tide and then Mr Latham seemed to disappear. I stayed in the last guest room, I would imagine. It was a good thing I had already decided to wear my best jacket to come over for the dinner, or I would have been unable to attend the wedding.'

Batchelor raised his hat. 'You look delightful,' he said, politely.

'Do you think so? How kind you are!' She tapped her head. 'This is one of Mrs Zzerbe's hats. Can you believe she brought nine hats? For a stay of less than a week! That maid of hers must have the patience of Job. A shame that she was taken ill, but I would put it down to exhaustion, having spent a while in her mistress's company. How is she, by the way? Do you know?'

Batchelor thought fast. 'I believe she is much as she was yesterday,' was all he could come up with.

'Oh dear. Poor thing.' She squeezed his arm again. 'I *am* looking forward to the wedding though, aren't you? Hamilton Chauncey-Wolsey is so *handsome*.'

Batchelor smiled a wintry smile.

'Tell me, as one of the family party, or more or less, you will have met Mark Twain of course. What is he like? I've seen him before, of course, when he visits the family, but never really to talk to. I didn't like to push myself forward last night.'

Batchelor was on firmer ground here and chattered happily to the woman as they approached the church. It only had a single bell and the minister didn't think it sounded festive enough for a wedding, so he had mustered the choir outside and they were letting rip with some of the rather more catchy hymns from Mr Wesley's repertoire. Once inside, the harmonium would take up the slack. The minister, a tall, cadaverous individual with a shining white surplice over his rather dusty cassock was patrolling the ranks of the choirboys, flicking a bony finger on to the heads of those found singing alternative words. The porch was decked with white flowers, brought in by the cartload from Boston's hothouses at what Andrew Grand considered ruinous expense.

The growing crowd were ushered into the church and took their sides. Because the groom's side was a little thin on the ground, the good-natured townsfolk allowed inside chose to sit there. The whole church, like the porch, was a mass of white blossom and here and there some sneezes could be heard, rather delicate from the ladies, stentorian bellows from the men. But, as the minutes passed waiting for the groom to arrive, everyone settled down and the conversation became just a susurration, like bees on clover.

With a rustle and a stir of attention, the groom and his best man arrived and took their places at the front. Everyone's ears strained for the sound of carriage wheels at the door and heard first one, then another. Liza Grand slipped up the aisle and took her place in the front pew, leaving room on her left-hand side for her husband. Then, the harmonium gave a wheeze and a judder and the opening bars of the *Wedding March* and everyone stood, in a rustle of lace and starch and Sunday best.

James Batchelor let out a breath he hadn't realized he was holding. The groom was here. The bride was here. This wedding was going to happen, after all.

The sun was still shining and the crowd was still outside when Mr and Mrs Chauncey-Wolsey came out of the little church in Rye into a hurricane of rice. With cheers ringing in their ears, they climbed into the little two-seat gig to be driven back to the house for champagne and oysters. Mrs Grand had tried to persuade her husband that another sit-down dinner was the done thing these days in polite circles, but he had put his foot down on that request. His foot had gone down a lot over the weeks of planning the wedding, but this time, he really meant it and the staff, as a body, had given him three hearty cheers in the privacy of below stairs. The glasses might need a bit of washing and polishing, but who could object to oysters – a few big platters and a burlap sack to collect the shells and it was all fine as fivepence, as Grand would doubtless have said in his embryonic persona as Cockney sparrow.

The gig went the pretty way, but even so the happy couple

were the first to the house. Hart positioned them neatly just inside the door, to welcome their guests as they arrived. While they waited, arm in arm, wreathed in smiles, the new Mrs Chauncey-Wolsey went up on tiptoe and whispered something in the groom's ear. Two maids standing further back in the hall nudged each other and mouthed 'Awww' to each other. It was lovely to see Miss Martha so happy. And wasn't he *handsome*! They missed how pale he had gone, but the light wasn't that good in the hall, especially as the happy pair were outlined against the sun.

Soon, the hall was full of people, all kissing, shaking hands and generally doing what was expected of a wedding party. The bride and groom went up to dress and the gossip started in earnest, but it was all good-natured and how could it be otherwise? The sun was shining, the birds were singing, the bride and the groom had both turned up, and didn't they make a lovely couple? The champagne was chilled, the oysters fresh from the bay; all in all, a success. Mr and Mrs Grand toasted each other without speaking, each wishing for the same thing; a quieter life, now Martha was off their hands.

Mr and Mrs Chauncey-Wolsey went up the stairs and along the landing to what had once been Miss Martha Grand's bedroom. They waved to the odd lingering guest who was up on that floor out of simple nosiness, went inside and closed the door.

'You're *what*?'

'Hamilton,' she said, calmly, unfastening her veil and laying it down carefully on the bed. 'I'm not sure of the right part of speech, but that sounds very ungrammatical to me.'

He stood with his back to the door; his handsome face pinched and white. His eyes seemed to be more protuberant than she remembered, somehow. She turned her back to him while she waited for his reply, gesturing for him to undo her buttons at the back. He did so almost without thinking and she stepped out of the dress and gathered up the silken cloud and lay it alongside the veil on the bed.

'You didn't tell me.' It wasn't much, but it was all he could manage.

She turned to face him. 'And if I had?'

He blinked.

'Would you have still married me?'

'Of course . . .'

She looked at him carefully. 'I believe you might at that,' she conceded. 'But I would never have known why. At least like this, I know it might be because you love me, not because I am having your child.' She turned her back on him again. 'Unlace my stays, will you, please, Hamilton?'

He started to untie the tightly wound strings and then stopped. 'I don't want a child,' he said, bleakly. 'Not yet. I wanted . . . I wanted to just be the two of us.'

Without turning round, she answered him shortly. 'It's not a case of wanting, Hamilton,' she said. 'It's a case of what is going to be. And what is going to be is that you are going to be a father before the summer is out. So you will have to live with that. Or leave me. It's up to you.'

He felt he had a wolf by the ears. His little Martha; a demon in the sheets, it was true, but in all other respects as demure a wife as any man could want. Without thinking, he carried on unlacing her stays. 'I . . . I have to think, Martha. What will people say, for one thing? I have a position to consider.'

'A position to consider.' She spoke quietly. 'Then perhaps you ought to have married Jemima. She likes to consider her position as well. She wouldn't have worried you with children, because I don't believe she actually indulges in what makes children appear. And you, Hamilton,' she said, turning as the last lace fell away, letting the stays slip to the floor, 'you do like your indulgence, don't you?'

Freed from the constriction of the corset, the mound of her belly swelled beneath her breasts, smooth and rounded. She took his hand and lightly pressed it to the skin, feeling the dry warmth of his palm. He didn't speak; he couldn't. Right on cue, the scrap that was the first of the new Chauncey-Wolsey dynasty flipped over with the sheer joy of being unconfined.

Martha looked into his face, which was alight with wonder.

'Who cares what people say?' he said, taking her in his arms. 'Who cares?'

*   *   *

Hart appeared as if from nowhere and rang his bell at the foot of the stairs.

'Ladies and gentlemen,' he intoned. 'May I present, the happy couple, Mrs and Mrs Hamilton Chauncey-Wolsey.'

A storm of clapping burst out from the assembled guests. This was a clever move on Hart's part, because when the glasses and oyster plates had been discarded in the applause, his staff moved among the guests like ghosts and removed them. A much politer way of getting rid of people, the butler had found, than actually putting on their coats for them and showing them the door.

Martha and Hamilton came down the stairs, arm in arm, beaming like two Cheshire cats. He was dressed for travelling in a pale grey serge, immaculately tailored and matching his low-crowned top hat to perfection. She was wearing a pale green travelling cape, generously cut, but not so generously that it could hide the dress beneath it, with a cunning pleat let into the front to accommodate a clearly swollen belly. The clapping continued – no one there was rude enough to stop, except Sam Clemens, who was wrestling with a recalcitrant cigar – but the gossip later that day among the ladies would not be as good natured as it had been before. Hamilton Chauncey-Wolsey was handsome, yes, but . . . was there any need to go *quite* that far?

Nodding and smiling to everyone, they got into the gig at the front of the house, the chestnut shifting in the traces. The bride, smiling, turned her back and threw her bouquet into the crowd of waiting single ladies. It was caught – a poisoned chalice – by Hamilton's unsmiling sister Sarah, who, too cerebral for such trifles, passed it briskly to the woman to her left, a delighted Helene. She brandished it at Batchelor, who went white.

'It's never too late,' he heard her say.

The back of the gig had so many streamers, old boots and other impedimenta attached to it that it was a wonder the sorrel could move. The rice in the air was thick enough to trot a mouse, as Grand would doubtless have said, had he had the time. But Batchelor, looking around, could see no sign of him; surely he wouldn't miss his sister's going away, especially as it was such a very spectacular event. It wasn't every day a man learns he is to be an uncle whilst attending his only sibling's wedding.

As the gig reached the corner of the house, Matthew Grand stepped out from behind an oleander and grabbed the horse's bridle. The coachman pulled up and Grand hopped up on to the buckboard and spoke urgently to the groom. After a short conversation, the driver pulled hard on the right-hand rein and the gig turned sharply and went round the back of the house, to end up in the stable yard. Only Batchelor was there to see – everyone else had fled inside, on a fruitless search for their glasses of warming champagne.

NINE

In that indefinable way that news has of leaking out into the world, everyone knew. And everyone had their theories. Waldo Hart had called all the servants together in Mrs Stallybrass's huge kitchen, gleaming with copper and scrubbed wood. There were still guests in the house and who knew, now, when they would go? There would be fires to lay, clothes to be laid out, the usual exhausting physical round they were all used to.

Hart waited until they had all gathered. He waited until they were all silent. He waited until they had stopped fidgeting. Then he folded his arms, fixing his gaze on the littlest and youngest of the downstairs maids, until she blushed to the roots of her hair and dipped her head.

'There is to be an enquiry,' he said, his Silesian accent more to the fore than usual this morning. 'Mr Matthew Grand and his partner in business, Mr James Batchelor, will be asking you questions.'

'Why them?' a voice called. Hart didn't have to glance across the room. He knew who it would be. Jackieboy Thornton was Andrew Grand's groom and only he had had the brass neck to stand up to Waldo Hart.

Hart looked at him under his scowl. If it were not for his old trouble, he would have taken a horsewhip to Jackieboy Thornton months ago. 'They are private detectives,' Hart said. 'Snoopers. They have no powers of arrest and you are not obliged to tell them anything. Is that clear?'

There was the odd murmur. No one in the room had been this near to a murder before. It didn't seem quite real.

'Remember,' Hart was prowling the room now, pausing to look each one of them in the face. 'This Magda girl was not one of us. We owe her nothing. Lottie,' he towered over the little maid. She bobbed, hardly daring to breathe. Truth be told, little Lottie was afraid of her own shadow. 'When Mr Grand – or Mr Batchelor – asks you anything, what will you say?'

Little Lottie wanted the ground to swallow her up, the flagstones to close over her head, keeping her hidden and safe. Instead, she felt everybody's eyes boring into her like red-hot pokers. 'I don't know, sir,' she whispered, eyes wide, heart thumping.

Something like a smile flitted over Waldo Hart's lips. 'Exactly,' he said. 'We don't want outsiders snooping, do we?'

He lashed them all once more with his stare, then clapped his hands. 'Come along, my children, this house won't run itself.' And they scattered with a rattle of starch and a clatter of heels.

'Rachel.' Hart closed to the cook. 'A word.'

Mrs Stallybrass was a large woman, the inevitable result of sampling too many of her own delicious puddings, but her eyes were kindly and, old grouch that he was, she carried something of a torch for Waldo Hart. She followed him into the pantry and closed the door.

'What have you heard?' he asked her.

'Gossip, Mr Hart,' she shrugged. 'You know, the usual. Miss Martha's news has rather taken over with some of the younger ones. But as for the . . .' she stuck a little on the word, '. . . murder, you know, the usual.'

Hart was left wondering what the usual gossip was when murder had been done. 'Who's your money on, then?' he asked.

'I don't know what you mean.' She decided to be the arch-professional. If it didn't happen in Rachel Stallybrass's kitchen, it didn't happen.

'Come on, Rachel. Who killed that wretched girl?'

Mrs Stallybrass's eyes widened. 'Mr Hart, I have no idea. I don't even know how she died.'

He closed to her. 'But what have you *heard*?'

She looked at him, weighing up her options for a moment, as though deciding on sugar or flour. 'Knife,' she whispered. 'Through the throat, I heard.'

Hart's eyelids flickered, then he crossed to the rack on the far wall. 'One of these, perhaps?' he asked quietly.

'No!' Mrs Stallybrass didn't like the way this conversation was going. 'Not one of my knives. Never.'

'Whose, then?' Hart wanted to know.

Mrs Stallybrass checked that they were quite alone and joined him by the knife rack. 'That Mr Ira,' she said. 'They say he's a whaler.'

'They do.' Hart nodded.

'He'll have a knife,' she said. 'I'm from Nantucket, back in the day. They all carry 'em, whalers. Great Bowie knives. Sharp as razors. And that's another thing.'

'What is?'

'Do you know this Ira?' she asked.

'Never seen him before,' Hart said. 'In fact, I didn't know he even existed.'

'Darn tootin'.' Mrs Stallybrass was getting into her stride now. 'Don't you think it's strange, Mr Hart, that this black sheep of the family, or whatever he is, should turn up, unannounced and uninvited, on the *very day* that a poor girl is murdered? If that's coincidence, I'm a Smuttynose Lobster.'

'Hmm.' Hart was chewing the idea over. 'Mr Ira, eh? Let's keep this between ourselves, Rachel. No sense in frightening the staff.'

'What about the Limey?' she asked.

'Which one?' Hart asked.

'Batchelor.'

'What about him?'

'My granpappy used to say that folks from England are just

itching to get back at us after what we done to them in the Revolution.'

Hart frowned. 'Well, perhaps,' he said, 'but I don't see how killing a maidservant is much in the way of revenge.'

'I still don't like him,' Mrs Stallybrass said. 'Shifty eyes. Like a pine marten. Or a skunk. Weaselly.' Rachel Stallybrass could have listed the less reputable members of the animal kingdom all day, given half a chance.

'I'll tell you what, Rachel,' Hart said. 'You keep your eyes and ears open. Between you and me, I wouldn't trust *any* of those folks upstairs.'

'Darn tootin',' Mrs Stallybrass agreed.

Andrew Grand had called the menfolk together in the library as soon after the midday meal as was practical. He knew if he left it too long, most of them would be in a post-prandial doze and he wanted them as lively as they could ever manage. He stood with his back to the fireplace, the logs spitting behind him now and again. His arms were locked behind his back.

'I won't mince words,' he said. 'We have a tricky situation on our hands.'

'Nothing the police can't sort out,' Sam Clemens said, his face wreathed in smoke as he lit a cheroot.

'Police be damned,' Andrew snarled. 'If they come at all, they'll be too late. Miscreant'll be long gone.'

'You think it's an outsider, Uncle Andrew?' Ira asked. For the wedding, he had worn a hand-me-down of Andrew's, but now he had reverted to his pea jacket.

'Stands to reason,' Andrew said. 'Couldn't be anybody in the house.'

'What does Mattie think?' Clemens looked around the room. 'Come to think of it, where *is* Mattie?'

'Matthew won't be joining us,' Andrew said. 'Neither will the ladies. Family only this afternoon. The inner circle. Us.'

'So . . .' Clemens thought he ought to say it, 'shouldn't the blushing groom be here? Family and all?'

'We'll let him earn his keep first,' Andrew said. 'Josiah!' His voice had grown louder. 'Are you listening to me?'

'Every word, old boy,' Josiah said, but he was already having difficulty with the decanter-stopper. 'Every word.'

'I have not asked Matthew along because he has taken it upon himself to behave like a policeman, asking questions.'

'Asking questions of whom?' Clemens asked.

'All of us,' Andrew said.

'Well,' Josiah, tricky task accomplished, sank back in his chair, 'I've got nothing to hide.'

'Oh, Uncle,' Ira shook his head ruefully. 'We've all got *something* to hide.'

'You can imagine,' Andrew went on, frowning, 'I'm not exactly cock-a-hoop about my own son snooping on his family, but there it is. Liza thinks it's for the best.'

'Has to be a stranger,' Clemens was chewing over the idea and his cheroot-end.

'What's the motive?' Ira asked.

'Robbery gone wrong.'

'Perhaps,' Ira said, 'but the girl was murdered in her own room in a house full of people.'

'So?' Andrew snapped. 'I don't follow.'

'It's a brave burglar who enters a house packed to the gills with folks,' Ira said.

'If it's entering he did, it's not technically burglary.' Clemens felt he ought to point it out. Rumours, he knew, spread like wildfire.

'Whatever,' Ira shrugged. 'That's the first point. The second is he ends up in the maid's room. And there's only one thing worth taking in there.'

'What's that?' Andrew asked.

'Her virginity,' Ira smiled. 'Assuming she was still the proud owner of it, of course.'

'Ira's right,' Clemens said. 'Look at your volumes here, Andrew. That's an early Boswell's *Johnson*. You've got the complete set of Gibbon and that Hawthorne would keep me in cigars for a lifetime. A discerning burglar would have come here.'

'And a non-discerning burglar would have been looking for the family silver,' Ira nodded.

'So, what are you saying?' Andrew asked.

'It may be that Sam's right,' Ira said. 'Our killer is an outsider, a stranger to the house. But he wasn't, I'm thinking, a stranger to the maid.'

Andrew looked at Josiah. 'I don't suppose you'd care to contribute to this conversation, brother?'

Josiah slammed down his glass. 'Do you know what?' he shouted, eyes swivelling, 'I'm tired of being treated like a liquored-up old bastard. It might interest you all to know that I know things. When folks are jabberin' and think I'm asleep, I'm not. Take old . . .'

But Josiah never finished his sentence. The door swung wide and Hamilton Chauncey-Wolsey stood there, a letter in his hand. He took in the gathering of the Grand clan and sensed that something was afoot. But his need was greater. 'Andrew,' he said. 'Pa?'

'I'd rather you didn't,' Andrew muttered.

'Andrew,' Chauncey-Wolsey, despite a trying day or two, was too well-brought-up to be fazed by that. 'I'm sorry to burst in like this, but we need to talk, you and I.'

'They're not coming, Matthew.' Batchelor was shaking his head. 'You know they're not.'

Grand nodded. He did know it. Boston's finest weren't moving out of Boston. He never thought he'd see a day when he quite longed for Scotland Yard; yet, here it was. 'And we have a dead body,' he said.

'And a house full of suspects.'

Grand looked at his colleague. 'Should we go to work, then?'

'I think we should,' Batchelor said and flipped a dime out of his waistcoat pocket. 'Call it,' he said.

'What for?'

'Staff or family.'

'Uh-huh.' Grand shook his head. 'No offence, James, my boy, but you'll get nowhere with the Grands. They'll close ranks tighter than Stonewall Jackson, believe me – and he was on the other side. Anyway, you're good with servants.'

'Thanks,' Batchelor grunted, trying to find the compliment deeply hidden in that. 'What are we going to do about the others? The guests at the dinner?'

'I'll get a list from Pa,' Grand said. 'And we'll get to them when we can.'

'And if one of them's done a runner?'

Grand shrugged. 'Then it's a fair bet we'll have our man – in absentia, so to speak.'

It made sense to begin with Hart and Batchelor tracked him down to his parlour, a spartan little room out towards the stables. As far as the butler was ever off-duty, he was now – the bottom button of his waistcoat was undone.

'Enquiry agent,' he read aloud from Batchelor's card.

'I should point out,' Batchelor said, 'I have absolutely no jurisdiction here and you have no obligation to answer my questions.'

Hart looked at him solemnly. 'Sir, one of the staff has been savagely murdered. I fear the word has got out and is the sole topic of conversation below stairs.'

Batchelor nodded. It would have been exactly the same back home. 'Your point?' he asked.

'My point is that no one bludgeons a maid in my care and walks away. As I see it, and as things stand, you are the professional. I will do all I can to help.'

'Good.' Batchelor flicked the notebook from his pocket. 'Let's start with you. Full name.'

'Waldo Hart.'

'Where are you from, Hart?' Batchelor asked.

'New York, sir. Hell's Kitchen.'

'Hell's . . .' Batchelor had heard of that place. And what he had heard, he didn't like.

Hart held up his hand. 'I know,' he chuckled. 'And, yes, Mr Batchelor, it *is* aptly named. My parents drifted there from Silesia before the Zollverein.'

'I *thought* I detected an accent,' Batchelor said. 'You're German.'

'No, sir.' Hart bridled a little. 'I'm Silesian.'

'You don't approve of the new Reich, Hart?' Batchelor smiled.

'I do not,' the butler told him. 'No good will come of that if you ask me . . . But I assume we're not here to discuss European politics, sir.'

'No, indeed.' Batchelor cleared his throat. 'So, you got out
of the Kitchen . . .'

'And became a gentleman's gentleman, sir, yes.'

'And the war?'

'Sir?'

'I was led to believe you were wounded and so cannot
lift . . .'

'I am embarrassed about it, sir, but yes. In sixty-one, my
gentleman at the time was a major in the Fourth Pennsylvania.
As his batman, I naturally had to enlist. Chickamauga. I came
away with . . .' he waved a hand vaguely over his body
'. . . this. My gentleman, he didn't come away at all.'

'And how long have you been with the Grands?'

'I did a brief stint at the Washington house in sixty-nine,
sir. Since then, I have been running Rye.'

'Good to work for, is he, Andrew Grand?'

Hart's face hardened and he looked into Batchelor's eyes.
'You can ask me anything you like, sir,' he said, 'but I will not,
in any eventuality, be disrespectful to my employer.'

'No, no, of course not.' Batchelor shuffled a little. Loyalty
was an admirable trait in a butler; not so much when there was
a murderer loose. 'Now, your people . . .'

If James Batchelor had hoped for juicy gossip from Waldo Hart,
he was to be disappointed. The man was as honourable and
tight-lipped about his staff as he was about his employers. The
detective had secreted himself away in an old storeroom under
the eaves. It was draughty up here and if the fireplace had ever
exuded heat, it was past that now. The soot of centuries had
left its traces among the spiders' webs and the bare boards of
the floor creaked with every movement. Batchelor shook his
head. Downstairs, he knew, Matthew Grand was sitting in the
library or the drawing room or *anywhere* where there was a
crackling fire and a stiff brandy. *He* was among his nearest and
dearest, although deep down Batchelor knew that was only a
figure of speech, while he, Batchelor . . . He flicked through
his notes again. He had enough material here to write a book
on the house's domestic arrangements, if only Isabella Beeton
hadn't beaten him to it. He knew exactly what time the

downstairs maids lit the fires; who polished the silver (Hart did); how Mrs Stallybrass prepared the roast fowl in the kitchen where she was queen. He knew which horse Mr Grand took out for a morning's canter and precisely how Jackieboy, the groom, harnessed the rig. What he did *not* know was anything about Hart's *people* at all.

There was a knock on the door. 'Come in, Mrs Stallybrass,' Batchelor said. He understood how these things worked. In domestic households on either side of the Atlantic, the butler was god, only to be spoken to in hushed, respectful tones and never to be spoken *about* at all. Then came the under-butler, except that the Grands didn't have one and then, in that most rigid of hierarchies, the cook.

Though James Batchelor had never seen Mrs Stallybrass, she had seen him and formed her own opinion. He had to admire her culinary skills, at the very least. Even so, the *two* women who stood there didn't quite have the gravitas he had expected.

'Begging your pardon, sir,' the older of the two bobbed a curtsey. 'Mr Hart says you are looking into the decease.'

'The decease?' Batchelor frowned. 'Oh, yes, that's right. The decease. I take it neither of you is Mrs Stallybrass.'

They both chuckled. 'No, sir,' the older woman said. 'I am Karen Christensen and this is my sister-in-the-law, Anethe.'

Batchelor checked his notes. Those names weren't there at all. 'Er . . . I don't have you on my list,' he said.

'No, sir.' Karen walked forward. 'That is why we asked Mrs Stallybrass if we could see you now. We are not on the establishment of Mr Grand. We help out sometimes, like for the wedding, ya?'

Anethe nudged Karen and muttered something incomprehensible.

'Oh, ya,' Karen nodded and muttered something incomprehensible right back. 'We are from Smuttynose. You know it? The island?'

Batchelor felt the ludicrous, childish hysteria rising in his throat again, but stifled it. Things were different now. A woman lay dead.

'We have to get back before the storm.'

Batchelor looked out of the tiny window. Through the

cobwebs he could see the grey sea, shifting in its mightiness. But the sky was clear and there seemed no wind. 'Storm?' he repeated.

'Oh, ya. We are from Amøyhamn on the island of Skardet. Do you know it?'

Batchelor shook his head, trying to look like someone who *might* know obscure places in Norway.

'It is very small,' Karen said, forgiving him. 'But we know the sea. Like Smuttynose, Skardet faces the Atlantic, but from the other side, you know. We know the weather of this ocean. Our menfolk will be worrying.'

'Yes, of course. I see. Tell me,' he looked at the pair. 'Do you row yourselves?'

'Oh, no,' Karen said. 'We have a handy, odd-job man, Mr Wagner. He will take us.'

'Well, then,' Batchelor suddenly remembered his manners and offered the ladies seats. 'I won't keep you. Just a few questions.'

Matthew Grand had no illusions that he was going to be allowed to question the ladies of the family, any more than he expected to get anything out of the men. His father's foot had gone down and that was that. His mother was back in her room, all lavender and old lace, with Martha sitting in attendance, sewing something small and frilly. Andrew and Liza Grand had taken impending grandparenthood surprisingly well, all things considered. It was hard to worry about that when there were about to be police in the house and a young woman was lying dead upstairs. Liza looked across at her daughter, her head bent to her embroidery, the sun gilding her hair and she smiled. This might turn out all right after all. Annie was also in attendance. They had tried to get her to go back to her semi-retirement in her room along the east corridor, but they had not prevailed. Her darlings needed her and that was that. She did feel strongly that she needed to speak to Master Mattie, though. Not that she knew that Magda, although she had heard things, even in the short time she had been in the house. She liked her men all right. Nothing wrong with that, right time, right place. And right class, she almost added, smiling to herself as old women will.

Martha looked up. 'Sorry, Annie? Did you say something?' The old woman was startled. She knew she talked to herself sometimes, but didn't usually do it in company. She smiled and wagged her head vaguely. That usually did the trick.

Liza Grand sat herself up straighter in the bed. 'I really should get up, Martha,' she complained. 'I am not ill.'

Martha went to her side and sat next to her on the bed. 'The doctor said just one day in bed,' she said. 'Just so you get your rest.'

If truth were told, nobody had much faith in the doctor, Old Brocius, having failed to heal himself, had gone off to the great hospital ward in the sky last year and his replacement was fresh out of medical school.

'Where's Mattie?' Liza had decided to make the most of being an invalid, if invalid she must be. 'Ring the bell and get someone to find him, Martha, there's a dear.'

'I think Mattie is busy, Mama,' Martha said. 'Investigating . . . you know.'

Annie clicked her teeth and struggled to her feet. 'I'll go and find him,' she said. It would give her a chance to speak to him, perhaps, without the others knowing. But her rheumatics were something cruel today – and they usually got better in the spring.

But Martha had already rung the bell. So quickly that it made them all jump, the door opened a little and a head peered in, with a cap at a rakish angle.

'Maisie?' Martha said. 'We don't need the fire making up at the moment.'

Maisie glanced over and could see this was the case, but that wasn't why she was here. She had an arrangement with the upstairs maid that if either of them saw a bell ring, they would answer it. It saved a lot of running about and every step you didn't take was a mercy in a busy house like this. 'Just answering the bell, m'm,' she explained.

'Oh. Oh, well, if you don't mind . . . could you go and find Master Mattie for me,' Liza said. 'I haven't seen him all day and I would love for him to visit.'

'I know where Master Mattie is,' Maisie said. This in itself was a small miracle; Maisie often didn't know where she was herself. 'He's waiting in the library for Mr and Mrs Zzerbe to speak to him.' She looked around the room and decided she was among friends. 'He's still all liquored up and she's locked in her room cryin', so I guess he'll be waiting a good ole while. Shall I fetch him?'

Liza nodded. She didn't like it when the staff gossiped, but who could wonder at it, with everything going to hell in a hand-basket.

When the maid had gone out, Annie gave vent to another of her snorts. 'Liquored up. He's been nothing but liquored up since he stepped into the house,' she said.

'Annie!' Martha was outraged. 'That's my best friend's husband you're speaking of. How dare you?'

'Only the truth,' Annie said, sullenly. 'Never liked the man. Shifty eyes.'

The door opened after a quick knock and the three women looked expectantly at it. It wasn't their beloved Mattie, though. It was Helene, suited and booted and ready for the road. She stood, her parasol digging into the carpet, and waited for one of them to speak. She had been in a haze of outrage since the wedding. She had been put in a pew three back from the front, had been forgotten on the way back, had had to hitch a ride with a grocer of some kind and now was excluded from this family gathering. Not only that, but not *one* of the luscious young men had visited her in her room, though she had left the door ajar and an enticing low light burning all night. It was time she went.

'Liza. Martha. It's time I went home.' She didn't honour Annie with a greeting. She waited for their protestations. It wouldn't take her long to slip off her outside coat and settle down for a gossip. She hadn't even ordered a gig so she needn't even cancel that.

Liza made a lightning decision. 'Helene, my dear,' she said. 'I am so sorry we haven't had a chance to chat. But . . . well, you know that things aren't quite as I would wish them to be at the moment, so . . . can you let us know when you get home? Do you have a telegraph office you can use to send us a message? Just to say you are well and safe.'

Helene was mortified. Even the feather in her jaunty hat, more suited to a woman half her age, drooped. 'But . . . but, should I not *stay*?' she wailed.

'I thought you were going?' Liza asked, innocently.

'But . . . with the . . .' she pointed above her head and mouthed, 'murder.'

'I think that what Mattie has done,' Liza said, 'with the help of Hart and Mr Batchelor, is to take a list of everyone who was in the house. If he or the police need to speak to you, they can easily visit you at home.'

'Police?' Helene's voice rose up the scale. 'Police? At my home? Whatever will the neighbours think?'

Liza already knew what the neighbours thought. No one needed that many delivery boys coming to the house on a daily basis. But Helene was her sister, and harmless enough, really. So she gestured her over to the bed and gave her a kiss. 'Off you go, then, my dear. Martha,' she turned to her daughter, 'can you see if you can arrange Aunt Helene a gig? And if you see Mattie on the way, tell him I am a little fatigued. I will see him later, if he wants me. Thank you, my dear.'

As the door closed behind the two, Liza Grand fell back against the pillows. This house was no stranger to scandal; over the years, it had seen more than its share. But that it should come now – now that she was old and tired – was just more than she could bear. The fewer people here to see it, the better. Annie got up and went over to the bed. Silently, she handed her a handkerchief and stood there, looking down. Two women, the keepers of the Grand secrets, silently communing in this sun-striped room. They would survive.

Martha, turned out of the quiet paradise of her mother's room, with her aunt Helene bristling by her side, had no idea how to go about ordering a gig. She had always had someone else to do that kind of thing, and it suddenly hit her with the power of a sledgehammer that she was the lady of her own house now, albeit one she had not yet even seen. She squared her shoulders.

'Aunt Nell,' she said, decisively. 'Let's sort out this gig.'

Helene shrugged her shoulders. 'As you wish, Martha,' she said. She had not expected to actually be going home; she had expected to be begged to stay. She allowed a little tremor to enter her voice. 'I could do with a lie-down, first, if I tell you the truth.'

Martha grabbed the straw like a drowning person. 'Then so you shall, Aunt Nell,' she said. 'So you shall.'

Watching the woman go down the landing, she waited until she was safely in her room and then flew down the stairs. Hamilton couldn't be far away and it had been absolutely *minutes* since she had kissed his dear lips last.

TEN

At first, when Maisie popped a tentative head around the library door, she wasn't sure whether Matthew Grand was even there. There was still a faint smell of Ira, it was true. The chambermaids had already despaired of ever getting the stink of whale blubber out of his mattress and he did leave a lingering waft behind him wherever he went, though he seemed oblivious to it. There was also a slight Josiah-like whiff; nothing like as unpleasant as Ira's, it was true, but composed of equal parts of brandy, bay rum, cigars and slightly singed vest – a natural corollary, in Josiah's case, to cigars. She smelled another lingering scent too, and looked around, anxiously. But there – no need to worry. Master Mattie was sitting in the deep chair by the window, looking out into the deep, brooding woods that, on windy nights and on still ones, by moonlight or starlight, gave Maisie the shivers.

She cleared her throat. 'Master Mattie?' she said, quietly enough to make him jump.

He looked round the chair and smiled. 'Maisie,' he said. 'Have you spoken to Mr Batchelor yet?'

'No? Yes?' She wasn't sure what was the right answer and liked to please.

'Never mind, I'm sure he'll catch up with you soon. It was just about . . . well, you told us about a man . . .'

'Yes. That other fella.'

'Who is it, Maisie?'

She shook her head. 'Mr Hart doesn't want us talking. He doesn't want us gossiping.'

'It isn't gossip, Maisie, if it's a truthful answer to a question.'

She set her lips in a hard line.

'If I say some names, Maisie, will you nod or something, when I get to the right one?'

She looked puzzled. This hadn't been covered. Mr Hart hadn't said nothing about nodding.

Grand decided to change tack. 'Why did you come and find me, Maisie? Nothing wrong, I hope?'

'No, Master Mattie. Missus wants to see you, in her room, if you don't mind stepping up.'

He jumped up. 'She's well, though?'

'Resting,' Maisie said, smiling. When she had a son, and she hoped she would some day, though time was getting short, she hoped he loved her like Master Mattie loved the missus.

Grand made for the door, holding it open politely for Maisie as he went. 'And you don't think you can tell me, then, Maisie?'

'Uh huh.' Maisie shook her head.

'Another time, perhaps,' he said and made for the stairs. A shadow on the landing made him pause, looking up. Jemima Zzerbe stood there, swaying slightly and looking pale as death. Behind her stood her husband, green where she was white and also swaying just a touch. Grand didn't know whether to hold out his arms to catch them, or step aside and let them measure their lengths on the hall floor.

Before he had to make his difficult decision, Jemima Zzerbe took a step downwards, smiling at Grand waiting at the foot of the stairs. 'Mr Grand,' she trilled, her society voice and demeanour both back in place. 'Jeremy and I were just coming to see you. Is it no longer convenient?'

Grand did not miss the subtext in her question, but ignored it. 'No, it is perfectly convenient. But please, Mrs Zzerbe, don't let's stand on ceremony. It's not as if we're strangers. Matthew, please. And if I may call you Jemima? And Jeremy?'

Jemima spoke for her husband. 'I think, in the circumstances, Mr Grand, we would prefer to keep this formal.' She was at the foot of the stairs now, offering a languid, gloved hand to Grand. Her husband came alongside her and nodded tersely at him.

'As you wish.' He looked around for Maisie, but she had gone, back to her fires and her scrubbing. 'I was in the library. Shall we?'

He stood aside and Jemima swept past him, a susurration of lavender silk and lace. Unless he looked deep into her eyes, Grand could not tell that she was in extreme distress. But he had more or less been brought up with this woman; he had seen her in every mood and he knew that she was on a knife-edge. If she knew anything about the death of her maid, he was certain that he could winkle it out of her. Her husband was less easy to read. His eyes looked half asleep, red-rimmed and sore. But his body was as taut as his wife's and his mouth was like a rat-trap. If he knew anything, he would probably go to his grave without sharing it. He looked that kind of banker.

In the library, Jemima sat on the very edge of the very middle of the sofa facing the fireplace, leaving her husband and Grand to take the chairs on either side. She spread her skirts across the remaining seat; if she had put barbed wire around her, she could have been no more impregnable. She turned her bland face to Grand. She had a touch of powder on her cheeks and just the hint of colour on her lips. Her hair was perfect, swinging back from her temples in two glossy wings. Her day dress was immaculate, her lace crisp with starch. Grand wondered to himself why, when she clearly could dress herself, she had bothered with a maid, a woman for whom she clearly had felt no affection, not even bothering to use the woman's given name. Jemima, without realizing she was doing so, answered his question.

'Do you know, Mr Grand, I had no idea that your mama kept such a well-run house. Why, her chambermaid dressed me today and look at what a good job she made of it; one would imagine she had been trained in Paris. She has a way with hair. I will be speaking to your mama to see if I may engage Alice to be my maid when I go home.'

'Alice?' What, thought Grand, another one?

Jemima laughed her scale and smiled at him. 'I don't know what her name is, of course,' she said. 'Mr Zzerbe and I don't believe in using given names for servants. It gives them ideas above their station and makes them overly familiar. Does it not, Mr Zzerbe?'

Zzerbe lay back in the chair, his eyes closed. 'Can we not drop all this Mister business, Jemima?' he asked, wearily. 'You've known Matthew here since you were in diapers – and don't tell me you never wore them; you are human, or so I was led to believe before we married. It's stupid to call him Mr Grand and stupider still to call me Mr Zzerbe.' He turned to Grand. 'Ignore my wife, Matthew. Just ask me anything you want to know.'

Grand took another look at Jemima and decided that her husband was right. He was not going to get anything helpful out of her if they sat there all day.

'How long had Magda Galatski worked in your household?' he asked.

'Rather less than a year,' Zzerbe replied. 'She came highly recommended from a very good family in Wisconsin. As a rule, of course, my wife prefers a local girl, but Alice – the real Alice, that is – had died suddenly and we needed a replacement quickly. She seemed . . .' he paused to think, 'efficient and very pleasant.'

Jemima snorted, an unexpectedly unladylike sound.

Zzerbe continued, as smoothly as though she had remained silent. 'I believe there were rumours in the servants' hall that Magda was a little . . . loose . . . but she was a very attractive woman. It was hardly unlikely that our cook, for instance, who has a face like a gopher and a backside like a drayhorse, shouldn't be at least a little jealous. Personally, I didn't see her behaving anything other than totally appropriately.'

Grand prided himself on being able to read a man beyond what his words conveyed. He was watching Zzerbe with an eagle eye as he spoke and thought he detected an inner amusement, which had to be directed at his wife. 'So, you never saw her with men, Mr Zzerbe?'

'No, never, and do remember; Jeremy.'

'Of course. And . . . Mrs . . . Jemima, did you ever see Magda with a man?'

'With a *man*?' She looked down her nose at him. 'No, never.'

'I see.' Again, there was a hidden level in what she said, but he doubted he could dig it out with her in this mood.

'Can you think of anyone who disliked her? I must tell you,

that her injury was severe and Mr Batchelor and I suspect it was made with an axe. It is also unlikely, I have to say, that a woman could have done the murder. So, we are looking at men who would hate her.'

'Was it . . . was she interfered with?' Even Jeremy Zzerbe baulked at making it plainer.

'As far as we could tell, no,' Grand said. 'Of course, we could only go by what was clear in the room, but it didn't seem that her clothing was disarranged. A doctor will be able to tell us, but we are waiting for the police to come to arrange that. We are a little hamstrung at the moment as to how to proceed. But we also assumed that most people here would rather talk to us than the police.'

Jemima's eyes had been getting wider. 'Police?' she screeched. '*Police?*'

Zzerbe didn't even look at her, but let his head fall back and his eyes close. 'Of course, the police,' he murmured, as though to himself. 'A woman is dead, you stupid, brainless waste of breath. A woman, more to the point, who dressed you, bathed you, did your every bidding.' Suddenly, he sat upright, pointing at her with a trembling finger. 'You make me *tired!*' he yelled. 'It's "Jeremy, don't do that!" "Jeremy, don't get that out!" "Jeremy, how dare you try and put that there!"' He subsided again and looked at Grand, tears in his eyes. 'Would you believe, Matthew, that your little childhood friend here has never once let me into her bed?'

Grand tried to look noncommittal.

'Jeremy Zzerbe!' she cried. 'That is a lie!'

'Oh, forgive me, my dear,' he said, sketching a bow as he sat in the wingback chair. 'I forgot. On our wedding night, Matthew, she did allow me to capture the kingdom. Once. Briefly. So, you can perhaps see that if Magda snatched a chance of happiness from time to time, my wife of all people is not really cut out to judge her.' He sighed and got up from the chair, wiping his eyes. 'I am going now to find Josiah and possibly even Ira. And then, when I have found them, I propose to get drunk.' He paused. 'Drunker.' At the door, he paused. 'All this, of course, totally confidential. If I hear it from anyone else, I'll sue.'

And with that, he swept out.

Jemima sat there for a minute more and then, with as much dignity as she could muster, followed him, without a word.

Grand stayed where he was for a moment, digesting. It wasn't quite how he had expected the interview to go, but he now wondered if he was closer to finding out who Magda's afternoon visitor had been. He would note it down and wait and see – Zzerbe didn't look like a philanderer, but still waters sometimes ran deep.

Grand went quietly along the landing to his mother's room and tapped gently on the door. There was no reply, so he peeped in. What he saw warmed his heart. His mother was asleep against the snowy pillows piled around her, her pink and white skin unlined and soft in the spring sunshine. Annie was asleep in the chair by her bedside, a piece of knitting abandoned on her lap. Every now and then, one of the women would give a little sigh, but they seemed content, so he left them there. There was little enough rest in this house, without waking those who had found some. Shutting the door quietly, he tiptoed away.

Batchelor had to admit that he had rather glazed over with the catalogue of circumstance that had brought the Norwegian women to Smuttynose. They were relatives of the Hontvet and the Hontvet had a fishing smack. Life had been hard in Norway but it was harder still on the islands. When they couldn't quite make ends meet, they hired themselves out to wealthy families like the Grands. It was cash in hand and a lot easier than gutting fish all day. They had arrived at the Grand house on the morning of the dinner, about ten. Johann Hontvet had dropped them off in his boat before heading out to sea and they had reported to Mr Hart for their assignment. Mrs Stallybrass had first call – Anethe was known for the lightness of her Fastelavnsboller – and they were soon up to their eyebrows in flour and sugar in the kitchen.

Yes, they had worked for the Grands before, but they didn't know the dead girl. Polish, wasn't she? They didn't know if Mr Batchelor knew it, but back in the old country, there had been some trouble between the Norwegians and the Poles, over the centuries. You don't forget a thing like that, even in America, the land of the free.

'Smuttynose,' Batchelor chuckled when they had gone. He looked out to sea, to Appledore, bathed in light. And Smuttynose, suddenly dark under a gathering cloud.

'Contrary to what some folks'll tell you, Mr Batchelor,' a voice made him turn, 'I do not have all day.' Old Mrs S had come calling and made sure Batchelor knew it. To be fair, she wasn't actually all that old. But fearsome; she was certainly that. Batchelor was just glad he wasn't a maid in her kitchen. Come to think of it, he was glad he wasn't a maid at all.

'I had nothing to do with the maids, upstairs or down,' Mrs Stallybrass assured him. 'The kitchen is my domain, sir. Anything else is by the way.'

Batchelor sighed. So far, having encountered four people, he had learned precisely nothing.

'Of course,' Mrs Stallybrass had plonked herself down, 'I hear things.'

'Hear things?' Grand repeated. 'You mean voices? In her head?'

Batchelor threw his spare pillow at his colleague. Now that Ira had turned up and Edward Latham seemed to be staying, rooms had become fewer at the Grand house and the enquiry agents had been asked if they minded doubling up. After the *Frisia*, the accommodation was positively palatial. The pillow only just made it across the room. 'No, Matthew,' he said. 'I mean she hears tittle-tattle.'

'Lost the battle, they say.' Grand threw the pillow back.

'Maybe,' Batchelor caught it and put it back behind his head. 'But it can also catch murderers.' Both men had been busy all day, asking questions, noting answers, watching for the little telltale signs that someone was lying. For Grand, it had not been easy. For Batchelor, it had been a nightmare. 'I want you to know,' he said, 'that Mrs Stallybrass had nothing but praise for your mother and father.'

'Well, there's a comfort.'

'For God's sake, Matthew,' Batchelor snapped. 'Don't be so proprietorial. Nobody's accusing your parents of anything, at least not directly.'

'Meaning?' Grand sat up in bed.

'I'll get to that. Mrs Stallybrass had an interesting take on the dead girl.'

'She did? What?'

'Magda was a tea leaf. Only little things, but they were noticed. She had only got here the day before the dinner, but already the maids had missed the odd item – a hair clip, that kind of thing. But these girls don't have much – they don't like it when one of their own steals from them. There were other things too.'

'Oh?'

'Men. Note the plural.'

Grand knew this; it was his experience that when a story came from more than one source, it was often true. But Jemima had said nothing about any thefts and he was sure she would be the kind of mistress who would dismiss a servant if so much as a sugar lump was unaccounted for. 'The Zzerbes suggested as much.'

'Yes. And one of the kitchen maids had seen her on the beach with a local. She – the kitchen maid – didn't know him, but she knew where he had his hands.'

'If she didn't know him,' Grand asked reasonably, 'how did she know he was a local?'

Batchelor shrugged. 'Clothes, I suppose. Anyhow, Mrs Stallybrass assured me that she, Mrs Stallybrass, that is, was too much of a lady to repeat the precise details. Apparently, the maid had not been so delicate and at least one of the footmen had come over unnecessary, just hearing it.'

'So, the late ladies' maid was a woman of ill-repute.'

'As far as Mrs Stallybrass is concerned, yes. But I got the distinct impression that the minister from yesterday's ceremony would be Beelzebub in her eyes. She's a daughter of the Pilgrim Fathers all right.'

'Anything else?'

'Jackieboy Thornton, the groom.'

'Shifty?'

'Like quicksand. Drinks like a fish and has a temper.'

'Don't tell me – doesn't suffer ladies' maids gladly.'

'Doesn't suffer anybody gladly,' Batchelor said. He was silent for a while. 'Then she started talking about somebody else. Somebody outside the household.'

'Oh? Who?'

'Well, she can't be right.' Batchelor was rechecking his notes.

'Who?' Grand repeated.

'Miss Thaxter. Celia Thaxter.'

'Sorry to drag you away from your bride, Mr Chauncey-Wolsey.' Batchelor was sitting opposite the man as the spring sunshine flooded the Grand's drawing room.

'Are you married, Mr Batchelor?' the groom asked.

'No,' Batchelor told him. 'I never seem to have the time, somehow.'

'You must make time, sir,' Chauncey-Wolsey laughed. 'Believe me, as a married man of twenty-four hours' standing, I can recommend it.'

Grand and Batchelor laughed too, though Grand was secretly thinking that, give him a few more weeks, when Martha had thrown a couple of her famous temperaments, and he might be singing a different tune.

'We need to know where people were when the maid, Magda, was killed.' Grand had to get this started or they would be making wedding small talk all day.

'Hell, you know that already,' Chauncey-Wolsey said, lighting up a cigar without offering one to his interrogators. 'I was with you guys at dinner, sitting at the head of the table, in fact.'

'And you never left the room?' Batchelor asked.

'No, I . . . actually, yes, I did. I took a leak. What do you call that in your country, Mr Batchelor? "Answering a call of nature"?'

'That's what polite society calls it,' Batchelor said. 'I call it having a piss.'

Chauncey-Wolsey's face fell. Harvard Business School had not prepared him for this. 'Oh, yes; I see.'

'Where did you go?' Grand asked. There were offices aplenty in the Grand establishment, none particularly near the dining room, for some bizarre reason best known to the architect.

'I used the servants' offices.'

'Downstairs?'

'That's right.'

'How did you know where that was?' Batchelor asked.

'I didn't,' Chauncey-Wolsey said, puffing at his cheroot. 'I asked somebody.'

'Who?'

'I don't know. One of the waiters, footmen, whatever they are. They all look alike after a while. Boiled shirt. Blank expression. I had to wait a while until one came by . . . you don't ask females that kind of question, even if they are staff.'

'Did you know the dead girl, Hamilton?' Grand asked. There were things about his brother-in-law that didn't quite add up in Matthew Grand's estimation.

'Good God, no. Why should I know the maid of my wife's friend? I hadn't even met Jemima before the wedding dinner. Martha and I have had a lightning courtship.'

'Had to be, I suppose,' Batchelor murmured.

Chauncey-Wolsey pulled the cigar from his mouth and leaned forward, his handsome face disfigured briefly by anger. 'Just what the hell does that mean?'

'So, you had no idea where Magda's room was?' Grand decided to defuse the situation, as much as it could be defused, bearing in mind he was asking his new brother-in-law to prove he wasn't a murderer.

'No.' He sat back, but his face was drawn now, his eyes wary. 'I didn't know the woman, I tell you. Look, am I being railroaded here?'

'Just trying to get the facts straight while we wait for the police to arrive,' Grand said, soothingly. 'I haven't been in too much touch with the family. My fault; I am a very bad letter writer, as James will vouch. How did you meet my sister?'

'I'm a business partner with her . . . er . . . your father.'

'What sort of business, Mr Chauncey-Wolsey?' Batchelor wanted to know.

'Real-estate. Railways.' Chauncey-Wolsey spread his arms. 'Trust me, it's where the money's at these days. Your Uncle Josiah is thinking of investing. In a smaller way than your father, of course.' He had decided to speak exclusively to Grand; it was simpler that way. 'It was when I was working with your father that I first met Martha.'

'Love at first sight?' Batchelor asked.

Chauncey-Wolsey gnawed his lip, fighting his instinct to punch the man on the nose. 'You know, Matthew,' he turned even more pointedly to his brother-in-law, 'I always check out my business associates before I get to work with them. Pity you didn't do the same.'

Grand ignored him. 'I will be speaking to my sister later, Hamilton,' he said, evenly. 'So, if you want to change anything you have said to us today, now is the time.'

'No. I stand by everything. And yes, Mr Batchelor, it was love at first sight. And, before you make any grubby insinuations about the length of our courtship, I didn't know about the child being on the way until *after* the wedding. There was no shotgun at my head. And if you are looking for any skeletons in the closet about me and a maid, then you are barking up the wrong tree. That's all I am prepared to say.' He ground out his cigar in the ashtray on the table between them and got up, tweaking his already perfect waistcoat and jacket into line. 'I am now going,' he said, 'to speak to my business partner, if that's perfectly in order?' He looked at them until they nodded. 'Then, I'll wish you good day. Mr Batchelor. Matthew.' And he left, too much of a gentleman to slam the door.

There was a silence for a moment.

'Well, that's us told.' It was such a perfect Mrs Rackstraw from Batchelor that it made Grand quite homesick.

ELEVEN

'What we are trying to establish, Mr Latham, is exactly where everybody was when the maid died.'

The *New York Times* man looked at James Batchelor. Then he looked at Matthew Grand. 'Grand and Batchelor,' he said. 'No, it's no good. I've been thinking it over and I've still never heard of you. I've been away from London for a while now, I'll grant you, but I keep abreast of what's happening over there. I'm fairly sure your names have never cropped up.'

'Answer the question, Latham,' Grand scowled at the man. He could do without the pomposity of *The Times* at the moment.

Latham sighed. 'Well, it all depends on when exactly the wretched girl died, doesn't it? Do you have a time of death, even an approximate one?'

'Half past seven, give or take,' Batchelor ventured. He had seen plenty of doctors give opinions on time of death, flexing fingers, taking temperatures; in one memorable case, licking a finger and holding it up to check wind direction. But he had never managed to get any of them to explain to him what it was that made them solemnly pronounce the time of death.

'Well, let's see.' Latham closed his eyes and placed his fingers together on the bridge of his nose. 'I would have been on the fish course about then. No . . . I tell a lie . . .'

Neither Grand nor Batchelor doubted that.

'. . . I'd finished. I was looking forward to the brandy, the port and the after-dinner cigars. I had that awful woman, Celia Thaxter, sitting next to me, boring me to death with what a marvellous writer Mark Twain was and did I know him. I said, "Look, dear . . ." I hope I didn't patronize too much, but I said, "Look, dear, he's sitting just over there. Why don't you go and talk to him?" She faddled around, blushing like a school-girl and saying she couldn't possibly. And, do you know, the groom's dratted sister apparently scribbles away at novels, would you believe? God save me from would-be literary women!'

'Did you leave the table at any point?' Batchelor decided it was time to cut to the chase.

'No, I . . . wait a minute. Yes, I did. I realized I'd left my cigars in my coat and I went to get them.'

'Where had you left them?' Grand asked.

'The cloakroom.'

'On the way to the west wing.' Grand knew the house like the back of his hand.

'If you say so,' Latham smiled, realizing the way this conversation was going, 'but two floors below where you found the dead girl. I never left the ground floor, I assure you.'

'How long were you gone?' Batchelor asked.

Latham sighed again. 'If you're implying that I had time to mount two flights of stairs – oh, having obtained a suitable weapon – find the girl, smash in her head, hide said weapon somewhere and join Miss Thaxter for the start of the meat course or whatever came next in that interminable junket, then I think you'll have a very hard time proving it.'

The three sat staring at nothing for a moment. Latham was breathing a little heavily, with the effort of not completely losing his temper. Batchelor broke out of his brown study and made a few desultory notes. This interview had taken them no further than the rest.

'Matthew . . .' Andrew Grand had hurtled into the drawing room, his face flushed. 'Oh, I'm sorry, Mr Latham. I didn't realize . . .'

'What's the matter, Pa?' The younger Grand was on his feet.

'Could I have a word?'

'Of course; Latham, James,' and the Grands left.

Latham was not happy that he, staffer on the *New York Times*, was to be interviewed by an ex-journalist on the *Telegraph*, but looked helpfully at Batchelor, trying to make it look as though it was all his own idea. 'Can I help you with anything else?'

There was no irony so deep that James Batchelor could not ignore it. Without another glance, he bent to his notes again, underlining judiciously whilst biting his lip and humming to himself. It never failed to disconcert and it was one of his favourite stocks in trade. But Latham was made of sterner stuff and sat calmly, waiting for the younger man to come to order.

'Pa?' Grand stopped his father in his headlong scurry down the passage leading to his study. The old man looked drawn and worried. And Matthew Grand couldn't remember a time when the old man had needed his help. 'What's the matter? What's going on?'

For a moment, Andrew Grand hesitated. He looked left towards the drawing room, to the right towards his study. Finally, because he had to, he looked at his son. 'I've been robbed, Matthew. Someone has broken into my safe.'

Andrew Grand's safe, a large, old-fashioned Diebold, was intact. The only signs of damage were scratch marks on the oak of the cabinet door, behind which the safe was fitted.

'What's gone?' his son asked.

'Papers,' Andrew told him. 'Business stuff. Not very important, but that's hardly the point.'

'When did you realize they'd gone?'

'Just now.' Andrew was irritated with the boy; he'd told him he was an enquiry agent, yet all he could do was stand there asking damn-fool questions.

'No, I mean, when did you see them last?'

'Er . . . I don't know. A couple of days ago, I suppose. I was in the safe when I was having a talk with Josiah. Before the wedding, you know. Sorting out Martha's allowance, that kind of thing.'

'I see. And who, besides yourself, has the combination?'

'Your mother.'

Matthew waited. 'Is that it?'

'Yes. Oh, I suppose Martha might know it, from your mother. I haven't told her, at any rate. But you know how those two gossip together. Like two hens.'

'Open it up.'

The door swung open on well-oiled hinges. Even the wards dropping into place as Andrew Grand swung the dial were silent. This was the safe of a man who liked secrets, but Grand knew that, without using his intuition. There were documents there. Deeds. Wills. Securities. Two very expensive watches and an ivory-butted Derringer. As well as a substantial wad of cash.

'A *very* discerning burglar,' Matthew murmured. He was thinking back to the burglar who *might* have been disturbed by Magda Galatski. 'Tell me, Pa, the missing documents—'

'They're nothing,' his father snapped. 'Nothing at all. It's the principle of the thing. A woman killed under my roof. Your sister . . .' he dropped his head into his hands for a moment, and recovered himself, '. . . married at least, but . . . well, your mother is distraught, Matthew, distraught. And now this. You inhabit this kind of murky world, Matthew. You tell me, what the hell is happening?'

'You see,' Edward Latham was sitting back in Andrew Grand's library. 'I feel I am intruding somewhat. I must get back to my hotel.'

'You don't row, Mr Latham?' Batchelor asked.

The journalist might have turned a little pale, but it might just have been the oil lamp's flare. 'Row?' he repeated. 'My dear fellow, one has *people* for that.'

'Celia Thaxter,' Batchelor said.

Grand crept back into the library; without knowing what had gone on between his colleague and the *New York Times* man, he could tell the interview was not going well.

'In this particular instance, yes, but I fear I have literally missed the boat. Miss Thaxter has gone without me.'

'Wasn't that the plan?' Grand asked.

Latham frowned. As a journalist, he was not used to *answering* questions, only asking them. 'Plan?' he requested.

'You've already told us my sister's wedding was by the by,' Grand said. 'You're looking for . . . what did you call him, the painter?'

'I was hoping to start the odd hare the other night,' Latham admitted, 'but they're a close-lipped lot, New Englanders. Besides, I believe I have an even juicier story now. The maid.'

'Which is why we're here,' Batchelor said.

Latham sighed. '*Do* put away the notebook, sonny,' he patronized. 'You're not working for the *Telegraph* now, you know.'

'No,' Batchelor felt his hackles rising. 'I'm trying to find out who killed an innocent girl.'

'Innocent?' Latham raised an eyebrow. 'Come on!'

'What have you heard?' Grand asked.

'Aha!' Latham tapped the side of his nose. 'A good journalist never reveals his sources, as I'm sure Batchelor will have told you.'

'Repeatedly,' Grand assured him, 'but, as Batchelor just told you, we are trying to solve a murder here, Latham. We're not competing for a story.'

Latham looked at them both. 'Very well,' he said, 'what do you want to know?'

'First, what precisely brings you to Rye?' Batchelor asked. 'This wedding. This house.'

'I told you,' Latham smiled. 'The painter. One of Boss Tweed's cronies, the bag-man. By my estimation, thirty-one railway lines that don't actually exist, into which the good people of New York and Boston have sunk considerable capital.'

'A fraud?' Grand checked.

'Unmitigated,' Latham nodded. 'It'll be a feather in the *Times*'s cap, not to mention mine when I expose him.'

'And you know who it is?' Batchelor checked.

'Let's just say I'm ninety-nine per cent certain,' Latham nodded.

'Who?' Grand asked.

Latham chuckled and wagged a finger, 'No, no, Grand – that's a professionalism too far. Let's just say the painter has nothing to do with this wretched murder.'

'Really?' Batchelor raised an eyebrow. 'Are you ninety-nine per cent sure of that too?'

But Edward Latham had no time to answer before a scream shattered the night. The men rushed to the window and peered out. The rain had stopped; the leaves dripped wet and shiny nearest the glass and they could all make out a white shape in the stable yard beyond the gate. Suddenly, the dogs were barking and there were lanterns swinging in the outbuildings.

The three made for the stairs, joined at the bottom by Ira and Sam.

'What the hell . . .?' Clemens had dropped his lighted cigar on to his chest when he heard the scream and was still trying to tamp out the sparks glowing like fireflies on his waistcoat. Hart, the perfect butler, even in a crisis, swept past him and flicked the ash off the young man's sleeve.

'Came from outside,' Matthew Grand said. 'The stables.'

People were coming from the house, the servants' quarters, everywhere, some with lanterns, some groping in the dark. The bulk of Mrs Stallybrass, her hand shielding her eyes as she peered into the gloom, blocked much of the light from the kitchen door. Andrew Grand snapped at his dogs and they fell silent, cowering on their haunches, whimpering in their throats and looking up at him with trusting eyes.

'Jackieboy?' The master of the house saw his groom first, standing in his shirtsleeves like an ox in the furrow. 'What's amiss here? Who's that screaming?'

The groom crouched over something lying to one side of the yard, in the shadow of the stable. 'It's Mr Josiah, sir,' Thornton called out. 'Miss Thaxter tripped over him in the dark. It's her screaming.' He pulled her to her feet and gave her a shake, something not every man could manage.

Andrew Grand gave a grunt of annoyance. 'Drunk again,' he said, disgusted. 'Get him into the house, Jackieboy,' he said. 'Into the library where he can sober up.'

'Can't.' The groom was a man of few words.

'Well, get some help if you have to. Miss Thaxter,' he called out across the yard, 'my wife will find you some sal volatile, or whatever it is you need.' The woman was standing, her knuckles to her mouth, her breath coming in ragged gulps.

'Don't need help,' Thornton said, kicking the bundle at his feet lightly. 'I c'n carry him all right. But not to the library, sir; somebody's stove in his head.'

Celia Thaxter gave another piercing scream and fled for the house, looking for James Batchelor for preference, but landed on the whale-reeking, pea-jacketed chest of Ira Grand, where she clung, weeping; any old port in a storm.

Panic and chaos is what Grand and Batchelor did. Not cause it, but help it subside. With Jackieboy Thornton's help, they carried Uncle Josiah into the stable and laid him down on the straw.

Andrew Grand and Sam Clemens shooed the women away. Nobody wanted a repetition of two days ago and some sights were not for the fairer sex. The exception to that was Celia Thaxter. She had disentangled herself from Ira and stood now, trembling in her off-white cloak, in the stable, looking down at the bloody mess that was old Josiah Grand's head.

On Matthew Grand's orders, Thornton had cleared the other men into the yard, despite protests from his father and Edward Latham. Of Hamilton Chauncey-Wolsey and Jeremy Zzerbe there was no sign, despite the hullabaloo.

'Are you all right, Miss Thaxter?' Batchelor asked her as he crouched over the body. She was glad it was the Englishman who had asked her. Had it been Mattie Grand, the years would have faded away and she would have cried, melting into his arms as she had wanted to do since they were children, rowing out to Appledore and Smuttynose through an eternal summer.

'As anyone can be who has just stumbled over a dead body,' she said, a touch on her dignity.

Batchelor got up and helped her to a bale of straw and sat her down. 'What were you doing out here?' he asked her.

'I felt guilty,' she said, trying to compose herself. 'I'd rowed away without Mr Latham and I came back for him.'

'In this weather?' Grand spoke to her for the first time.

'You know the weather means nothing to me, Mattie,' she said, staring into his eyes. How could he not remember? 'Unless it's a nor'nor'wester and a mean one at that, I can make it.'

'Where's your boat?' Batchelor asked.

'Down at the jetty,' she told him, waving her arm in the vague direction. 'I thought I'd cut through the stable yard as the fastest way up. It wasn't raining on the way over, but a body can get soaked coming through the shrubbery.'

'Did you see anybody?' Grand asked. 'Apart from Josiah, I mean.'

'Nobody.' She shook her head. 'I thought . . . I thought Josiah was a tarpaulin at first, something Jackieboy had left out for the morning. I had no idea . . .'

Batchelor came closer to her and put a friendly hand on her shoulder. She leaned in briefly and closed her eyes. 'Look, Miss Thaxter . . . Celia . . . you've had a shock. Get yourself over to the house. The ladies are there and there'll be a fire and brandy. Go on, now. We'll join you later.'

She hesitated, her eyes flitting from face to face. But, in the end, it was the face of Josiah that led her towards the door. The old boy's eyes were wide open with shock and his mouth was creased in a rictus grin. There would be no more hair of the dog for him.

When Celia had gone and the enquiry agents were finally alone with a dead man, Grand examined the corpse of his late uncle with the aid of Thornton's lantern. 'Same as Magda,' he said. 'Look. Single blow to the back of the skull.' Batchelor peered closer. His colleague was right. Old Josiah's blood and brain had spattered his collar and the shoulders of his coat.

'Helluva rider in his day,' Grand said. 'Anyhow, that's how the story goes. Did a stint with the Pony Express in the early days. Of course, that was rather a long time ago. He claimed to come to the stables to see the horses. My view; he had a stash of liquor out here somewhere, for emergencies such as Hart removing the decanters.'

'Another inside job, then?' Batchelor methodically checked the old boy's pockets for any clues.

'You think?' Grand was looking around the stable. His father's greys were still there, chomping their hay and flicking their tails without a care in the world. The bay saddle horse was there too, in a stall by itself, the tack gleaming in the lantern's beams. The faint smell of Josiah's blood mingled with the warm scent of horse, hay and leather.

'Don't you?' Batchelor asked. 'Did you hear a dog barking? Before the scream, I mean.'

'Dogs in the night time,' Grand chuckled. 'You know as well as I do what a myth that is, James. Old Rollo is as deaf as a poker. I know. I chose him as a puppy and got him free on account of his disability. As for that other mutt, from what I've seen of him, he's as mad as a tree; follows Rollo round like his shadow. If Rollo doesn't bark, he doesn't bark. I guess that's how it is in the doggie world.'

'So . . . what are you saying?'

'If somebody in the house wanted Josiah dead, why not kill him in the house? It's not as if it hasn't happened already.'

'Why, though?' Batchelor frowned, leaning back against a bale. 'What's the link between Josiah and the maid?'

Grand sighed. 'For all I know, he could have been her grand-father. Anything more . . . I'd rather not think about. Anyway, Maisie would have named him, surely, not just called Magda's visitor "the other fella".'

Batchelor nodded, but wasn't sure. It would take a maid with rather more about her than Maisie to name the master's brother as a Lothario. He decided a change of subject might be wise. 'How long, would you say?' he asked.

Grand looked again at the blood, the deep gash, the swollen, bruised face. 'Maybe an hour,' he said.

Batchelor nodded. 'That's what I thought,' he said. '*Before* we started talking to Latham. Which means, unless I miss my guess, that there are only two people in this house with cast-iron alibis – me and you.'

Grand nodded.

'And, what a coincidence,' Batchelor was thinking aloud, 'that Celia Thaxter should have a fit of the consciences and come back for Latham just in time to trip over dear old Josiah.'

Grand shook his head. 'You have a nasty, suspicious mind, James Batchelor,' he said, 'just like mine. And I thought you were kind of sweet on Celia.'

Batchelor ignored him. 'I don't know the system,' Batchelor said, 'from these country places. But do you think it might be time to send another telegram to the police in Boston?'

'We don't know whether they got the last one,' Grand pointed out.

'True. But we have to try. We already have a maid stiff and stark under the eaves. We can't leave Uncle Josiah here. People will talk.'

'True. I'll find Hart and he can roust out the boot boy.' He felt in his pockets. 'Do you have a spare dollar?'

TWELVE

'**N**ow, Lulu.' Sergeant O'Farrell was not a patient man, but Father Rafferty had had a word with him that Sunday and wondered whether the sergeant couldn't perhaps be a little less draconian in his approach. Sergeant O'Farrell had protested that he'd been a good Catholic all his life, so Father Rafferty had been more specific.

'Ease up,' the saintly man had said, 'on the drunks, the layabouts, the sisters of sin.'

'What about the Protestants, Father?' O'Farrell had asked the priest.

'Ah, do what you like with them,' Rafferty had told him, 'the Godless bunch of no-hopers.'

O'Farrell had no idea what church, if any, Lulu Luscious belonged to, but there was no doubting she was a sister of sin, so, this morning, the desk man was being extra nice. 'Lulu,' he repeated, 'what are we going to do with you, huh?'

'You're gonna let me go with a caution,' the girl sneered. 'And that's Miss Luscious to you, copper.'

O'Farrell shook his head. 'You're not making this easy,' he said.

'Telegram for you, Chief.' It was that boy again, the irritating one with the speech impediment.

'I'll take it.' Tadeusz Berlowski helped himself to the paper. 'The sergeant's busy right now.'

'Well, he said you did.' O'Farrell was trying to reason with the girl. 'And would you mind buttoning up your bodice? Officer Berlowski is a single man.'

Lulu took a sideways look at him. 'I'm not surprised,' she said.

'Sarge.' Berlowski's attention was elsewhere. 'There's been another one, at Rye.'

'Another one what?'

'Murder, Sarge.'

'Where?' O'Farrell straightened, his fatherly moment with Lulu clearly over.

'Rye, Sarge. Maine.'

'Out of state,' O'Farrell said. He looked down the line of miscreants, each accompanied by a disgruntled and bored-looking policeman. 'Who's next?'

'But it's Mr Josiah Grand, Sarge.'

'Who?' The desk man held his finger up to silence the next lady of ill-repute with a story to tell.

'Josiah Grand, Sarge. You know. The Grands. Own half of Boston, some of Washington and a little bit of New York.'

O'Farrell grabbed the telegram. 'The chief'll need to know about this, Berlowski, while you're dithering about. Here.' He threw the officer a bunch of keys. 'Show Miss Luscious into the lock-up. She's going down this time.'

He would apologize to Father Rafferty in the confessional the next time he saw him. Again.

If truth were told, John Savage didn't like leaving Boston. He'd lived there all his life, police chief and boy, and it was in his blood. He knew its parks, its squares, its alleyways and brothels. He knew the Irish gangs of Battery Wharf and the Italian bloods who were trying to turn the place into New York. He knew the rich gentlemen of Harvard too, the young men who could buy

him ten times over. And he knew all thirty-six of the buildings
that claimed to have been General Washington's headquarters
back in the Revolution.

Yet here he was, rattling north in the Pullman with Sergeant
Roscoe at his elbow. A good man to have in a crisis, was Roscoe.
Calm, thorough, if a little morose. Handy with a night stick,
too, if things got a little rough. But now they were on their way
to Rye. How rough could it get?

'Did you know the decedent, Chief?' Roscoe asked, lighting
his boss's cigar.

'Personally, no. I know *of* him, of course. Read me the
telegram again.'

Roscoe ferreted in his inside pocket. '"Josiah Grand. Stop.
Bludgeoned to death. Stop. Come at once. Stop. How many
more? Stop."'

'How many more?' Savage repeated. 'What do you suppose
that means, Bill?'

Bill Roscoe had not been a detective for the last nine years
for nothing. His rise had been meteoric, from the horse troughs
to the chief's blue-eyed boy, and he was nobody's fool. 'I'd say
there's been at least one other bludgeoning, sir,' he said. 'Maybe
more.'

'Hmm,' Savage nodded. 'My thoughts exactly. You don't
think . . .? No, it would be stretching coincidence too far.'

Roscoe knew exactly what his chief was talking about. A
year ago, the body parts of a man had been found in two barrels
floating in the Charles River. His head had been smashed in
with a blunt instrument. Savage had a man in the frame within
days, but the evidence was thin and the thick-headed Irish-
Italian jury had let him go. It was one of those cases that
policemen can't let go of. It would haunt them both, long
beyond retirement and perhaps to their dying day. Unless, by
the merest chance . . .

'What do we know about this place?' Savage asked. 'Rye?'

'Not much more than a fishing village, apparently. Hasn't
even got a police force.'

'Shocking.' Savage shook his head as the locomotive snorted
and whistled in agreement.

'Lots of summer lets there. Rich folks move in by May or

June and stay until the weather turns. Artists, writers, oddballs like that. Locals are farmers or fishermen.'

'Ah, yes,' Savage suddenly remembered a distant lesson in geography. 'The Isles of Shoals.'

'Smuttynose.' Roscoe was proud of his superior geographical grasp, though he rarely had a chance to shine, stuck in Boston with a boss who knew every crack in every sidewalk. 'Appledore. Star. White. Malaga and a couple more. In the summer, you can't move for painters, they say. Biggest hazard is tripping over easel legs. 'Course, it's different in winter.'

'It is?'

'Wild place, they say. Hostile. The weather turns on a dime and God help you if you're out on the water when a squall comes up. There are more wrecks on those rocks than O'Farrell's had Hail Marys. Haunted, they say – all that stretch of coast.'

Savage looked at his man through the cigar smoke. 'I had no idea you were such a sensitive soul, Bill,' he said.

Roscoe bridled a little. 'No, no, it's not that. It's just . . . well, like you, Chief, I'm a city slicker. Wide open spaces, rolling sea, black rocks . . .' He felt himself shudder a little and hoped his chief hadn't noticed.

But of course, his chief had. You don't get to be Chief of Police of Boston without noticing little things like that.

They lay in the tack room, side by side, united in death as they had never been in life. The spring sunshine filtered through the cobwebbed window and shone on buckles and stirrups hanging against the whitewashed wall.

'What the hell is that?' Chief Savage had to ask.

'That is . . . was . . . my uncle, Chief,' Matthew Grand told him.

'No . . . Sorry, Mr Grand, I meant no disrespect. That,' he was pointing to the second body, or should it have been the first? Under Annie's watchful eyes, the maids had stripped the dead girl's clothes, washed her body and laid her in her shroud. Her hands were clasped around a bunch of dying lilies, culled from the tons of floral decorations which still bedecked the house. Her eyes, black in the greyness of her skin, were closed.

'That,' Grand said, 'was Magda Galatski. Mrs Jeremy Zzerbe's maid.'

'Known to some as Alice.' James Batchelor didn't intend to muddy any waters; but he was not about to leave a stone unturned either. Nobody mixed a metaphor like an old *Telegraph* man.

'Did we know about this?' Savage asked Roscoe.

'*I* didn't,' the sergeant said.

'We sent a telegram when we discovered the body. That was . . .' the time had gone very strange here in Rye and Grand had to think, '. . . three days ago. Two, I suppose, depending on when it reached you. It was late at night when it left here, you see. It was very simple and clear, just telling you a murder had been committed, where and who the victim was.'

'It didn't reach my office,' Savage said.

'Would you have come if it had?' Batchelor asked. He had read Karl Marx. He knew how the world wagged in places like Boston and sometimes he just had to speak up. 'Just for a ladies' maid?'

Savage rounded on him. As a Boston man through and through, he had always disliked Limeys, on principle. He'd always liked to think that there had been a Savage with the Minutemen at Concorde all those years ago, giving the Redcoats a bloody nose. 'Remind me who you are again,' Savage said.

'James Batchelor,' Batchelor told him, standing up to his full height. 'My card.'

'Enquiry agent,' Savage read aloud. 'Just what we need.'

'I think you'll find it's all here, Superintendent.' Batchelor held out his notebook.

'What the hell's this?' Savage asked. 'And that's Chief, by the way.'

'In the absence of the police,' Batchelor said pointedly, 'my associate Mr Grand and I took the opportunity to investigate.'

'You did?' Savage asked, flicking through the book.

'We did,' Grand told him. 'Batchelor talked to the staff. I talked to my family. We both talked to the wedding guests.'

'There was a wedding?' Roscoe was trying to make notes of his own.

'Two days ago,' Grand explained. 'My sister Martha and Mr Chauncey-Wolsey.'

'*Hamilton* Chauncey-Wolsey?' Savage asked.

'Yes,' Batchelor said. 'Do you know him?'

'Oh, one of those names that crops up now and again,' Savage said. 'I had expected to meet Mr Andrew Grand by now.'

'My father, you can imagine, is under rather a lot of strain at the moment, Mr Savage,' Grand said. 'What with Magda and now Josiah. I thought it best if we talked to you first.'

'On account of you both being enquiry agents?' Savage checked.

'We *have* done this sort of thing before,' Batchelor assured him.

'Sure,' Savage smiled. 'Sure you have. Well, thank you, gentlemen, for your co-operation. We'll need to talk again. Mind if I keep this, Mr Batchelor?' He was talking about the notebook.

'Of course,' Batchelor said.

'We'll leave you to it.' Grand strode for the door.

'I presume there's paperwork for these two.' Savage stopped him. 'Death certificates.'

'The local doctor signed them,' Grand told him. 'They are in the house.'

'But he wasn't much older than the backstairs maid,' Batchelor said. 'Seemed to be a little out of his depth with sudden death.'

'Yes,' sighed Savage. 'It's amazing how many people are. Tell me, Mr Grand, is there a plan of the house? Blueprints of some kind?'

'I don't know,' Grand said. 'I can find out. I know my father had a lot of changes made when he bought it, but that was when I was still in dresses.'

'If you could find out,' the chief nodded, trying to stifle his amusement; these nobs – the things they put their children through. He waited until they had gone, clicking the tack room door quietly behind them, respectful of the dead.

Savage swept off his wideawake and threw his topcoat on to a rail. Then he went to work. In moments like this, Bill Roscoe left his boss to it. The man liked to work in silence, with no distractions and while he did it Roscoe was reading Batchelor's notes. Savage began with the dead woman, untying the shroud and peeling it back. He unlaced her fingers and removed the lilies. Putrefaction had not quite started in the chill of this room, but the whole of the back, legs and arms were purple with bruising where Magda's blood had pooled. Someone had cleaned the head wound and clipped the tangle of hair around it. There was one gaping hole that couldn't be hidden, black and dry now, at the base of the skull, a sliver of white bone showing through.

Savage was looking at the rest of the body. 'No sign of rape,' he said. 'No bruising to the thighs or anywhere else.' He checked the dead girl's fingernails. 'Nothing here,' he said. 'She was hit from behind. Axe, if I don't miss my guess. Short-handled type you'd use for firewood. Remind me to ask Grand if they've found a murder weapon.'

'"Fully clothed", it says here.' Roscoe was reading. '"Blow from behind. Probably didn't know what hit her."'

'Does it?' Savage cocked a professional eyebrow. 'Does it really?'

He closed the shroud again and replaced the lilies in the pale, cold hands. Then he turned to Josiah. The chief had no way of knowing that most of the old man's blood was a hundred per cent proof and *his* skin colour was very different from Magda's. Even so, it told the same story. No signs of a fight, no struggle. The look of horror that Grand and Batchelor had seen on the old man's face had gone now. His bloodshot eyes were bloodshot no more and his lids were closed. His mouth, which had been stretched to the horrible grin as the axe blade severed his spine, was closed too and peaceful. The maids had done that, typical of women the world over who served below stairs. They brought babies screaming and kicking into the world and they carried the dead out, decent and clean, into the silence of eternity.

'Same hand?' Savage was asking himself. 'Same killer, Bill? A lone mad axeman?'

'"Almost certainly done by the same hand",' Roscoe was quoting Batchelor again. '"Same modus operandi." Hey, that's Latin, Chief.'

'Yes,' Savage sighed. 'I know it is. Look, Roscoe, don't take this amiss, but that notebook . . . if you find yourself taken short in the woods around here, you can use it to wipe your ass!'

*   *   *

'So, who haven't we talked to?' Grand poured the last of the coffee from the pot that Hart kept bubbling over the spirit burner on the sideboard. He made a mental note to get one for the London house, if Mrs Rackstraw could be trusted not to burn the place down with it.

Batchelor sighed. 'If I never talk to another maid again, I'll be happy,' he said. 'Good of Hart to employ the three wise monkeys – well, technically, eight of them, but they all exhibit the same tendencies. They're blind, deaf and mute. So . . . Jackieboy Thornton, the groom. He's last on my list. If I still had a list.'

'Yes.' Grand was stirring the coffee thoughtfully. 'It might have been a *little* rash of you to give that to Chief Savage.'

'It was only a loan,' Batchelor said. 'I didn't want to be accused of hindering the police in the pursuance of their enquiries.'

'No, indeed.'

'Right.' Batchelor was on his feet. 'I'll be in the stables. You?'

'Ira,' Grand said. 'I talked to him briefly after Josiah, but he was three sheets in the wind. He was very fond of the old man. Even so, there are some things that don't quite add up.'

Batchelor had never quite got used to the smell of ammonia and horse liniment that filled every stable in the world. He trod carefully past the temporary charnel house where the bodies of Magda and Josiah lay. One of the greys lifted its head at Batchelor's approach and the enquiry agent patted the soft, warm muzzle. Not for the first time, Batchelor thought how silly this was. In the human world, stroking somebody's nose was probably not the first thing you would do to somebody in greeting, unless you were an Eskimo, of course, in which case—

'Can I help you?' From nowhere, Jackieboy Thornton was at Batchelor's elbow. The man was half a head taller, with a lean muscular frame from years hauling tack and rein for the Grands. Batchelor tried not to show how startled he was and turned the involuntary falsetto shriek into a manly cough.

'You know Master Matthew and I are conducting enquiries,' he said, surprising himself by dropping so easily into the feudal address.

Thornton brushed past him, saddlery dangling over his shoulder. 'I thought all that was done now the real cops are here,' he grunted. He sat down on an upended tub and started to work the greasy yellow soap into the leather.

'Ah, we never sleep,' Batchelor smiled, finding a stool to sit on.

'That's the Pinkertons,' Thornton murmured. He stopped polishing. 'And you, sure as Hell, ain't no Pinkerton.'

'Same line of work, though,' Batchelor pointed out. 'Same devotion to duty.'

'Happy for you,' Thornton commented.

'How long have you worked for the Grands, Jackieboy? Er . . . you don't mind if I call you Jackieboy?'

'Yes, I do,' the groom said. 'You can make it Mr Thornton. That'll do 'er.'

'Right.' Batchelor sighed. This was going well. He had met men like Thornton before – a chip on the shoulder you could see a mile away. 'But the question still stands.'

'Always,' Thornton said. 'I was born on the Boston estate, moved with them to Washington. Then come here.'

'So you know them well – the family, I mean.'

'Right enough.' Thornton was spitting on to the leather now, watching the surface shine develop under his fingers.

Jackieboy Thornton wasn't so much a man of few words; it was just that the ones he used were either offensive or futile. 'Where were you, exactly, on the night Mr Josiah Grand died?' Batchelor was on his dignity; if Thornton insisted on the proprieties, he could go further.

'Right here, in the stable.'

'And you didn't hear or see anything?'

'Not 'til that Thaxter biddie screamed, no.'

'What do you think Josiah was out here for?' Batchelor asked. 'If I remember right, it was a wet, windy night.'

'Wetter than some, windier than others,' Thornton nodded. He was working on the brassware now, burnishing buckles to further order. Marvellous, thought Batchelor. Even something as mundane as the weather can be stopped in its tracks by this bastard. Suddenly, the sun shone out of Jackieboy Thornton and Batchelor couldn't quite see where it came from. 'Old Josiah'd often come out to the stables, for a jar and a talk.'

'Really?'

Thornton put the tack aside and crossed to a stack of straw bales. He thrust an arm between two of them and pulled out a bottle. 'His secret stash,' he said. For a moment he cradled the thing, brushing off the straw. Then he put it back. 'I'm gonna miss the old fella,' he said, and was back to polishing again.

'You liked him.' Batchelor could see that.

'Reckon I did,' Thornton said, 'seeing he was my pa.'

One of the greys whinnied softly, turning its head and rolling an eye at Thornton. Without the whinny, Batchelor did something similar. 'He was?' he said.

'Him and Annie,' Thornton said. 'They was different days back then, but I've seen the photographs. She was a looker, was Annie. I never dared call her Ma. She made up some story about me being her sister's boy and how she – the sister – died in childbirth, so's the other Grands wouldn't find out. It would never do in Boston society for Josiah to be seen in bed with a servant, hence the sister, like. Like I said, "different days".'

'And Josiah knew?'

'Oh, he never said nothing, but I knew. Why else would he take me under his wing if we wasn't related? I wouldn't have wished it this way, but I reckon I'll be a rich man once the legal is all sorted. Always wanted a coach and four. And this brass?' He held up the gleaming buckles. 'It'll be solid gold. Stands to reason; he's got no other sons but me.'

Batchelor got up. Revelations aplenty for one day and now he looked at Jackieboy in a very different light. 'Well, thank you, Mr Thornton. We'll be in touch.'

'Doubtless.' The groom was polishing again. 'By the way,' he stopped Batchelor at the wicket door, 'I don't care who catches Josiah's killer – you or the cops. All I ask is just five minutes with the sonofabitch in a room alone. You catch my drift?'

Batchelor nodded. He caught it all right. And he hadn't even asked Thornton about the maid.

'Bad business, cousin,' Matthew Grand was walking along the seashore with Ira.

'It is,' the whaler nodded. 'Look yonder.' He pointed out beyond the breakers where the Isles of Shoals loomed out of the water. 'Storm coming.'

Grand couldn't help chuckling. 'According to James Batchelor, that's what the Christensens said too.'

'Who?' Ira looked at him.

'Ladies from Smuttynose. They helped at the wedding.'

'If they're from Smuttynose, they can sense these things.' He looked his cousin up and down. 'You're a landlubber, Mattie,' he said, thrusting his hands into his pockets and walking on. 'You haven't got the salt-sea in your veins.'

'What brought you back, Ira?' Grand asked. 'I wouldn't have said there were many bowheads in Boston.'

Ira chuckled. 'Maybe I've had my fill of all that,' he said. 'The blood. The burning stench. Ever been on a whaler, Mattie?'

The enquiry agent shook his head. Unlike Batchelor, he had never even read *Moby Dick*. 'Man, it's a charnel house. From the time the boy in the tops'l calls out a sighting, until the bitch rolls over in her dying circle, it's pure hell. See this?' He pulled back his sleeve to show livid white scars. 'That's the ropes. You lash one end around the boathead while the other's taut along the harpoon line and you pray.' Ira laughed softly at the memory of it. '"All astern",' he said, mimicking some long-lost comrade. '"All astern for your lives."'

'You were a harpooner?' Grand checked.

'I was,' Ira said. 'And, if I say so myself, a damned good one. Ended up first mate. I'd never make master – you need money for that.'

Grand frowned and Ira saw it.

'Oh, I know what you're thinking,' he said. 'The family money. When I split with my pa, I turned my back on all that. He cut me off without a penny, I think is the phrase. So I made my way. Oh, I've got a little put by.' He paused, looking out to sea. 'Maybe I'll settle on an island somewhere. I've always had a soft spot for Smuttynose. A man can live there in peace and quiet. No sound but the sea.' He nodded to himself. 'I can live with that.'

'Just that?' Grand asked.

Ira laughed. 'Well, a man needs some female company,

I'll grant you. Take that Celia Thaxter, now . . .' and his voice tailed away.

'I never did,' Grand admitted. 'Back in the day. Though it wasn't for want of her trying.'

'How old were you?' Ira asked.

'Sixteen or so,' Grand said. 'She was a handful, even then.'

'And you were the scion of a noble house,' Ira laughed. 'The other day I'm afraid I wasn't so genteel with the maid.'

'You weren't?'

'On a whaler, you get rum aplenty, hard tack and whale meat. Baccy and bonuses. What you don't get is women. I've just come off a two-year hunt.'

For Grand, it all fell into place. The dead maid had been seen on the beach – *this* beach, it must have been, in clear view of the house – with a local 'by his clothes'. But a whaler's clothes would look local in this setting, at that distance.

'So . . . you and Magda . . .?'

Ira nodded. 'I haven't been quite straight with you all,' he said. 'As far as anybody knew, I turned up on the night Magda was killed. And that's true as far as the house and the family are concerned. But I'd been in Rye for a full day and I met the girl up the coast aways. She was pretty enough and willing . . . and, like I said, two years before the mast. But that's not all.'

'It's not?' Grand kept walking. He didn't really know his cousin Ira, even less than he knew Uncle Sam. The man was older than he was and had suddenly disappeared before Grand had gone to West Point. There was a darkness about Ira that he couldn't quite fathom.

The whaler stopped walking. He was looking out to sea again, towards Smuttynose. 'I killed a man.'

'You did?'

'It was a fair fight,' Ira assured him. 'On board ship. It was one of those stupid, pointless things that should never have happened. He accused me of cheating at cards one night. Things got out of hand and we went at it.'

'And he lost,' Grand nodded.

'He did, and he took it badly. Later, in my cabin, he pulled a knife on me. Thought I was asleep.'

'Were there witnesses?'

'No. And that was the point. It was self-defence, Mattie, I swear. But he had his friends and I had mine. It could have turned ugly but the master was a kind man. He put me off in Valparaíso and made me promise never to work on a whaler again. It's a promise I've kept – will keep.'

Grand turned Ira to face him. 'Is there a price on your head?' he asked.

'Not as such, no. But there are places it's safer for me not to be. New Bedford. Nantucket. Anywhere where whalers meet. Somebody will know somebody who knows. That's why,' he looked across again at Smuttynose, crouching underneath the darkening sky, 'that's why I want an island. Solitude, Mattie. And I can put all that blood behind me forever. Besides,' and he gave a shudder, 'all this countryside gets a man like me down. I'm not used to all this . . .' he waved his arm inland, 'all this. All these critters, these birds chirping away. I heard a bear coughing not a ship's length from the house last night. Did you hear it?'

Grand shook his head.

'Just give me waves. Gulls. Whale song sometimes, if the wind's right. That's all I want to hear.'

Matthew Grand patted his cousin's shoulder, 'I must get back to the house,' he said. 'Are you coming?'

'No,' Ira sighed. 'I reckon I'll stay here awhile. Look at those thunderheads. I like to watch the sky now I know it can't kill me.'

Grand looked out to sea. The clouds rolled huge and menacing to the horizon on all sides, yet the sun still sparkled on the wavelets at their feet. Behind the house, the trees were wreathed in mist as they marched over the hill into the next valley. He turned and made for the dunes.

THIRTEEN

'**M**r Grand,' Sergeant Roscoe was staring out to sea, trying to light his pipe in the skittering gusts of wind. 'God damn it,' he muttered. 'When a lovely flame dies, sand gets in your eyes.'

Grand smiled. 'Do I get the impression you're not at one with the great outdoors, Sergeant?'

'You got that right,' Roscoe muttered, giving it up as a bad job and, tapping the ash from his pipe, he stowed it away in a pocket. 'I'm a Boston man, through and through. Oh, I've taken the ferry once or twice, you know, across the harbour. But give me the sidewalks every time.'

'My associate would agree with you,' Grand said, 'except that he'd call them pavements.'

'London, England, huh?' Roscoe chuckled. 'Never been.'

'Ah, it's a great city.' Grand was allowing himself to get a little nostalgic. 'Although even there we don't get two murders in as many days.' He thought for a moment. 'At least, not in one house.'

'This is all about the city, you know.' Roscoe tapped the side of his nose.

'It is?'

'Was that Ira Grand you were talking to down there on the beach?' Roscoe was watching the whaler walk away, blurring to a dark blob below the curve of the bay.

'Yes,' Grand said. 'What do you mean, "this is all about the city"?'

Roscoe looked at him. Perhaps he'd given too much away. And certainly the chief would have broken him to the horse troughs for the throwaway comment he'd just made. Still, James Batchelor's notebook had not been consigned to the use the chief had suggested; Roscoe had found it damn useful. So, he felt he owed the private detectives something. 'I cut my teeth on a City of Boston night stick,' he said. 'Know every inch of that place like the back of my hand. Know its lowlife, too.'

'Goes with the territory, I guess,' Grand said.

'It does,' Roscoe nodded. 'And right away when I saw the maid Magda, I thought, "I know this woman." You know how it is, Mr Grand, you meet so many people in our walk of life.'

'You do.' Grand offered the man a cigar. Seeing as how his pipe had died and he was clearly about to spill some beans, it seemed the gentlemanly thing to do. Roscoe accepted gratefully and sheltered behind the larger bulk of Matthew Grand so that the cheroot had a chance to catch the flame. He puffed on it like a man facing the gallows.

'I couldn't place her at first, but then I remembered. It came to me in a flash. She's a whore, Mr Grand. Or she was when I locked her up. And her name's not Magda, either. Well, it might be, I suppose,' he took another long draw at the cheroot and blew out smoke which was whipped away by the wind. 'But we knew her as Michalina. Worked out of Madame Tinkerbelle's in Summer Street before the fire.'

'The fire?'

'Sure. You must have . . . Oh, no, you'd have been over in London then, I guess. Last November—'

'Yes,' Grand interrupted. 'I know about the fire.'

'Arson, of course.'

'Hand of God, I'd heard,' Grand countered.

Roscoe chuckled, then stifled it, suddenly unsure where Grand's religious sensibilities lay. 'That's one way of putting it.'

'But you never caught anybody.' It was a statement, not a question.

'Nope.' Roscoe took another drag of the cigar. 'And I doubt we will now. Thirteen people died – for all we know, the arsonist could be one of them. They often are; no one said they were clever. We just look at it, some you lose, some you lose.'

'And Magda . . . er . . . Michalina?' How many names could one woman have?

'Madame Tinkerbelle was in a bind. She couldn't exactly claim insurance money, seeing as how she was using her premises for illegal purposes. So she had to let her girls go. She didn't run a very classy house. Most of the business was done on the street anyway, but at least with her up and running the girls had somewhere to lay their heads. That's why we didn't come down too hard on them; apart from the usual, they were no trouble. But, after the fire, most of them took to the streets in the regular sense; even sleeping out, some of them. We got a desk man, back at the station, name of O'Farrell. I thought I knew my street people, but against him, I'm a beginner. He could give you Michalina's date of birth, her speciality and her tittie measurements. Then she disappeared. I didn't see her no more.'

'That's because,' Grand nodded, 'she forged her references and became a lady's maid. With possibly a little business on the side.'

'That's very true,' Roscoe agreed. 'You can take the girl out of the street. It ain't so easy to take the street out of the girl. I don't expect Mrs Jeremy Zzerbe suspected; what do you think?'

Grand gave it a moment's thought. He doubted that Jemima Zzerbe was unaware of Magda/Michalina/Alice's habits, but Mima was a past mistress at turning a blind eye to anything not quite nice.

'I don't think all this helps us much, though, does it?'

'I don't think it does, no,' Grand said. 'But anything that can shine a light on to the dark corners of this case is pretty welcome about now. Thanks, Sergeant.'

'Any time,' Roscoe said, 'and, by the way, Mr Grand, you didn't hear any of this from me, all right?'

'Any of what, Sergeant?'

Jemima Zzerbe spent her life at the end of her tether. She had stormed out of the house, regardless of the worsening wind and the threat of rain. If she stayed in a moment longer, she would scream and she knew she couldn't do that; so impolite. She had vague memories of being a carefree girl, but they seemed very long ago. The only friend she still had from her childhood was in an interesting condition approximately five months too soon. She also seemed to be as happy as a June bug about it; so was her unfeasibly handsome and socially acceptable husband. She called her parents Mom and Pa and they lapped it up like kittens in the cream, whereas she, Jemima,

Mrs Jeremy Zzerbe, with a houseful of servants and everything a woman could want, called her parents Mama and Papa and hadn't spoken to either of them in months. She gave her maids every advantage. Only a fifteen-hour day and a whole afternoon off every six weeks – and how did they repay her? Oh yes, she knew how they repaid her. They died on her or they got themselves brutally murdered. And now, the police would be poking around in her, Mrs Jeremy Zzerbe's life and . . . she was suddenly aware she wasn't alone and looked around.

For once in her life, she let herself go and screamed like a steam whistle. The man at her elbow flinched as the noise ripped through his eardrums and put out a hand to quieten her. This was a mistake, as anyone but he would have known. Anyone's hand uninvited on her arm would have been unwelcome. His simply increased the volume of the screams.

It was unfortunate that Wagner the handyman had chosen this very moment to accost Jemima. Her nerves were on the brink of giving way and he had just given them the tiny extra push they needed. He was never an attractive sight, but with all the coming and going over the last few days, he was even more unkempt than ever. The slight aroma that hung in the air around him, even on this blustery day, could be partly traced to the dead seal on the beach a few days before, but was mainly due to his complete avoidance of soap and water. Sometimes, when the smell got very bad, the ladies of Smuttynose would silently hand him a bar of rough lye soap and point him to the pump. He would sometimes appeal to Karen's husband, Ivan, but he was a weak man in Wagner's opinion, always doing what the women told him. But just now, he needed work and hadn't had the time to wash up or even brush his hair. He knew this made him look like the kind of man who put work before womanly things like keeping clean. He hadn't yet noticed that he was the only person in Rye, or for miles along the coast, or even out to sea, who saw it quite like that.

'Missus, missus,' he said, pulling at her sleeve. 'Missus, quit the yelling. All I want is to ask if you have any odd jobs here. Any wood wants chopping. Any trees need lopping. Missus? Missus?'

Jemima had finally worn herself out and the screams subsided.

She looked at him dumbly. He seemed to be asking her something. He still had hold of her arm and was looking at her, his head on one side. In the tangle of hair falling over his forehead, something moved. She opened her mouth to scream again. If she had to be raped and murdered, please let it be by someone clean.

The scene was complicated further by the appearance of Grand from the direction of the beach and Batchelor from round behind the house. Roscoe was not far behind, his cheroot still firmly clamped between his teeth.

Wagner looked frantically this way and that, his eyes wild. All he had wanted to do was get himself a job for the afternoon, give himself a dime or two for a drink in town. He wasn't going to bother rowing out to Smuttynose tonight, not just to sleep in the barn. He could sleep just as well in a barn on the mainland, save the time and the effort for drinking. There was a widder in the town as well – old, crabby, but she hadn't had a man beside her for a good while. She didn't mind Wagner's smell. He was young beneath the grime and virile; he might go see her.

But now the men were shouting. One of them, the fancy one, something or other Grand, he didn't rightly remember what, had the stupid screaming woman by the arm and was quieting her down. The little one, the Limey, who didn't know a seal from a pottwal, had his hand on one of Wagner's arms, the cop from Boston had the other. The cop was smiling, his cheroot wagging in his teeth.

'Mr Grand,' he was saying, 'Mr Batchelor, I think we've got us a murderer, what do you say?'

'Roscoe,' the Limey said, 'can it be that simple?' He turned to Wagner and asked him a really dumb question. 'Where have you been since I saw you on the beach with that dead seal?'

Wagner opened his eyes wide and laughed. 'Well,' he said, 'I only come over to bring the girls to wait on the weddin'. Soon as I done that, I was back over to Smuttynose. I got my chores.'

Batchelor looked at Roscoe, whose cheroot drooped disconsolately.

'And when did you come back?'

'Just now. I rowed over yesterday, took the girls back, come back over today. Just looking for a job, mister. Just wanted some money for a drink. They keeps short rations on Smuttynose.' He looked anxiously round at the men's faces. They were hard to read.

'Sorry, Roscoe,' Grand said. 'I don't think you've got your man this time.'

'You believe him?' Roscoe said. In Boston they would have had the shackles on this lowlife soon as look at him.

'He doesn't look much like a cunning criminal mastermind to me,' Grand said, 'who could sneak into a house full of people and bludgeon a maid to death without making a sound.' Jemima gave a groan and sagged against him. 'Sorry, Jemima. I think he's telling the truth. I think it's just his bad luck he chose Mrs Zzerbe here to ask for a job. She is . . . a bit nervy.'

Roscoe spat out the remains of his cheroot and stomped it out in the grass of the sloping lawn. 'A bit nervy?' he repeated. 'The woman's as mad as a coyote with a cactus up its ass.' Another groan from Jemima. Roscoe looked at Wagner, cringing in Batchelor's loosened grip. The handyman tried a smile, which didn't help. After a moment, Roscoe nodded. 'You're right, I guess,' he said to Grand. He foraged in a vest pocket and pulled out a half-dollar. 'Here you go,' he said, handing it over. It disappeared into Wagner's pocket in a flash. 'Don't leave the area without telling me. Now, make yourself scarce and don't go bothering the ladies.'

Wagner was off like a racoon up a pipe. He knew when he had had a lucky escape and he wasn't hanging around to meet another crazy woman like that one. Next time you see a woman with one of they frilly umbrellas when it's blowing a hoolie, he told himself, don't wait to talk to her, just run.

Grand and Batchelor, with suitable warnings as to their intentions, took Jemima Zzerbe by an arm each and led her into the house. Roscoe watched them go; it was his nature to trust no one anyway, but this crowd just about beat the band. He wanted sidewalks. He wanted Boston's vice area that men called the Black Sea. He wanted straightforward old street crime, stuff he could understand. Next time they asked him to leave Boston, he would tell them what to do; it wouldn't be easy or even physically possible, but he'd tell 'em, just the same.

'That was a little bit odd,' Batchelor remarked as they were having a well-deserved sit-down in the library, after delivering a still mute and quivering Jemima into the care of a wandering upstairs maid.

'Odd?' Grand had known Mima a long time. Nothing had struck him as odd at all.

'Well, I know the man Wagner is a bit smelly. Socially awkward, perhaps. But I wouldn't have thought he would cause that kind of hysteria.'

Grand waved the question away. 'Mima will go into hysterics at the drop of a pin,' he said. 'She was always like it, and that was before Jeremy got something out of his pants that gave her the heebie-jeebies. I don't think we need worry our heads over Mima and her little outbursts. I learned something from Ira which *was* a little disturbing.'

'I bet you anything you like that what *I* learned from Jackieboy Thornton beats your information by a head and a length.'

Grand looked across at his colleague, who was clearly bursting to share his news. He had held it in well when dealing with the whimpering Jemima, but now almost had steam coming out of his ears. He considered pulling rank; his turf; his seniority; hell, why not bring up his money? But he smiled and extended a hand. 'After you,' he said, affably.

Batchelor took a deep breath. 'Well . . .' he wanted to build up the tension, he was still a story teller at heart, but knew Grand's tolerance for such drama was limited. 'Jackieboy Thornton is the illegitimate son of Annie and Uncle Josiah!' He leaned back in his deep buttoned chair, conscious of a punchline well delivered.

Grand could usually shrug off Batchelor's more histrionic deliveries, but this one had him poleaxed. After a moment, he spoke. 'I beg your pardon?'

'Jackie—'

'Yes, yes, I heard what you said. I just need a minute to . . . are you *sure?*'

'Well, I am just repeating what Jackieboy told me. He may

be lying. But there was something about it . . . he genuinely loved Josiah. And I suppose it makes sense. In the house together, thrown into each other's company. And, pain me though it does to say it, Matthew, you Grands are a good-looking bunch. I expect Josiah has had his moments.'

Grand chuckled. 'Yes, indeed. In fact, I believe Boston and all points north, south and west are littered with hearts he broke, back in the day.'

'Not east?' Batchelor liked to check his facts.

'Ocean.'

'Ah.'

'But even so . . . *Annie?* She was our nannie, for heaven's sake. She slept in the nursery with us! When would they . . . oh! No. Tell me it isn't so!' A thought struck him. 'How old is Thornton, anyway? It's hard to tell with those leathery, horsey types.'

'I don't know,' Batchelor had to concede. 'He could be anything. Your age? Older? Younger? I really have no idea. You could ask him, I suppose.'

'I think I'll ask his mother; we will need to talk anyway. I . . . I'm sorry, James. You have no idea what this means to me. Annie is like a second mother, to me and to Martha.' He sat tensely on the edge of his chair, almost poised for flight.

'What about your news?' Batchelor did need to know, after all, being an enquiry agent on the case.

'What? Oh, nothing much. Ira killed a man and is on the run.'

'But . . .' That did seem to make a difference to who might be a suspect, at least in James Batchelor's opinion.

'No, no, it was in a fight. No clandestine bludgeoning or anything . . . oh, and one other thing. He and Magda had a brief dalliance on the beach.'

'Did they?' Batchelor's eyes widened. 'A bit breezy, I would have thought. When did this happen?'

'Well, that's just it. *Before* he turned up at the end of the dinner.'

'I see.' Batchelor was chewing it over. 'So, black sheep of family who has disappeared for fourteen years pops up unexpectedly at niece's wedding, just as a woman is brutally murdered – a woman of whom he has had carnal knowledge.'

'What?' Grand blinked.

'Sorry,' Batchelor apologized. 'It's how we had to put it in the *Telegraph*, back in the day.'

Grand shrugged. 'Yes, well, we're a bugger of a family, but we *are* the Grands.' He sprang to his feet. 'Look, James, you're going to have to excuse me. I must go and see Annie. Ring for Hart, why don't you? Have him bring you a drink. Have one for me while you're at it.'

Batchelor reached out for the bell-pull. He was rather thirsty, now he came to think of it. But before he could touch it, the door opened and the butler entered, pushing a trolley, with tea kettle about to sing above its spirit burner, a pile of English muffins oozing butter, and a pot of gentleman's relish. If it had not been for the man's perfect timing, silent entry and elegant manoeuvring of the sugar, cream and silverware, he could have been Mrs Rackstraw's twin.

'That was . . . quick.' Grand couldn't think of another way to put it. Did the man wait outside doors on the off-chance, or was he psychic?

'My pleasure, sir,' Hart said, proffering a plate. 'Muffin?'

'Um . . . tempting, Hart, very tempting. But I must go up and see Annie. Do you happen to know where she is?'

'I believe she is in the sewing room, sir,' Hart said. 'Preparing for the . . . new arrival.'

Grand could not suppress a chuckle. Of course she was; another baby. She would be in her element. He nodded to Batchelor and left him to his feast. They really would have to get one of those kettle things and trust in providence that they wouldn't all burn in their beds.

FOURTEEN

Grand took the right-hand rather than the left-hand turn at the head of the stairs and made his way to the sewing room at the very end. It faced north, into the trees which marched down the hill towards the house and the sea, but they didn't obstruct the light and it was always as bright as the day could make it. On this spring afternoon, it was almost sparking with the sunshine streaming in, picked up by the polished lenses that Annie still liked to use in front of her candle in the evening to focus the light. The over-mantel was packed with foggy pictures of the family, frozen in time for Annie to love all over again. The old Singer sewing machine still had pride of place. Grand could remember the day it was delivered, to the Washington house, and how Annie and all the women in the square, it seemed to him, had gathered around to watch the salesman demonstrate its wonders. It was looking a little the worse for wear now, but Annie flatly refused to replace it. It did everything she wanted it to, she said; all the added refinements of the new machines were just so much new-fangled trumpery.

Today, though, she was not at the machine, but sitting in a low chair by the fire, smocking a tiny garment and singing quietly to herself. It was a moment before she looked up – she had reached a difficult tuck and couldn't stop just because Master Mattie had come in – but when she did, the naked love on her face made Grand's heart turn over. How could he ask this woman what he must ask? What if Thornton had made it up, was as mad as a tree? What if Batchelor had misunderstood? What if Annie never spoke to him again? What if . . .?

'Mattie,' she said, 'will you sit yourself down? I'm getting a crick in my neck looking up at you.'

He folded up on the rug in front of the fire. He might have been ten again, coming to tell Annie his woes. She reached out and stroked his cheek.

'My land, Mattie,' she said. 'You Grands are a good-looking family.'

Grand felt his heart lurch again. Batchelor had used almost those very words minutes ago. Was this some kind of conspiracy? He smiled at his old nurse. 'You're too good to me, Annie,' he said. He wrinkled his face up at her. 'I've got Great-Grandma Waterford's nose and that's no prize.'

'It suits you,' she said, bending back to her embroidery. He watched the needle flash in and out a few times without speaking. 'What's on your mind?' she asked him, putting the little garment down and smoothing it absently with a soft hand.

'Nothing,' he said. 'I just came to have a chat. We haven't had a word since . . . well, since it all.'

She smiled at him and sat back. 'You could always say a lot in a few words,' she said. 'Do you know, you didn't say a single thing until you were nearly two? They were all beginning to think you were a bit short in the top storey, but I knew different. "You just wait," I'd tell your Ma. "Master Mattie is just biding his time." And then, you started jabbering away and we all wished you'd stop. You weren't at all like . . .' She stopped and patted his cheek again. 'Never compare, that's what my ma told me. And I don't.'

'Not at all like Martha?'

Annie picked up her sewing again, still smiling, but didn't answer.

'Or like your son?'

'Ah.' This time she folded her sewing carefully in a white cloth and put it away in her workbasket. She laced her fingers together in her lap and looked her erstwhile charge in the eye. 'So, you've been speaking to John, I assume.'

'John?' Grand was confused.

'Jackieboy, they call him here. And in the bars. I call him John, his given name. Although we don't see too much of each other these days.'

Grand felt as though the stone he had carried in his throat since he had heard the news had shifted to his chest. 'So, it's true, then.'

'It's true that John Thornton is my son, yes. Is that what you mean, Mattie?'

'I . . . James interviewed Ja . . . John, and he told him that . . .'
He didn't know how to go on.

'He told him that Josiah was his father, I expect. That was
his favourite version of events and of course it did give Josiah
a lot of pleasure. But let me tell you the facts, Mattie, and you
can do with them what you will. I am leaving here when Martha
and Hamilton are allowed to go to their new home. I knew
about Martha's baby almost before she knew herself. I may be
getting on, but I am not deaf or stupid. Footsteps along the
corridor. I won't go further, it isn't seemly, but there were signs.
So, it doesn't matter to me what is spoken about when I'm
gone. Josiah had every reason to believe that John is his. He
certainly visited me often at about the time, always at dead of
night, me blowing out the candle, waiting in the dark. But he
isn't Josiah's. He looks just like his father, does John, though
even a mother must allow that he is no painting. But his father
made up for it in being the kindest, best man in the world. He
made me laugh. He hadn't got much, but what he had he shared,
with anyone in the whole world.'

She patted Grand's hand. 'I want you to understand, Mattie,
these were different days. We didn't have a horrible war to take
our men, but jobs were few and my Johnnie had to go looking
for work. We were married, don't you worry, so John's revelling
in being a bastard hurts me terribly, but there's no talking to
him. I . . . well, I was starving, not to sugar it, Mattie, and I
was pretty in those days. Josiah . . . he was good to me. When
John came along, he found me a job in Washington, with your
ma. And you.'

'So . . . you brought John with you?' Grand had no recol-
lection of another child in the nursery.

'Yes, I did indeed. But he had to go out to a wet nurse, so
I could be yours.' Annie laughed at the irony of it. 'I could
have fed you both, but your pa wouldn't hear of it. Nothing but
the best for his boy.'

'So . . . where did John go?'

'There was a family down the block had slaves. Oh, don't
look at me like that. Your ma and pa wouldn't do such a thing,
no. Nobody in the North had slaves by then, but this family,
they'd come up from West Virginia and didn't know any better.

One of those slaves took in John and fed him. I could see him every other Sunday afternoon.'

'Do you hate us?' Grand blurted out.

'Land sakes, Mattie,' she said. 'Of course I don't hate you! My Johnnie never came back, though I heard later he had taken up with a widow in Charleston, so he didn't get far.'

'And Josiah?'

Annie's face closed in a little. 'He was betrothed to your Aunt Nell for a while.' Her face fell for a moment. 'That was hard. But it wasn't my place to be jealous and, of course, nothing came of it. Well; you know your aunt Nell!' She gave a shout of laughter, and Grand had the feeling that another family skeleton had peeked briefly out of its closet, for the first and final time. 'We stayed friends, Josiah and I,' she said. 'It was hard not to be friends with your uncle Josiah – you know that, Mattie.'

'He was certainly friendly,' Grand said with a grin.

'If you had a drink by you, Josiah wouldn't be far away,' Annie agreed. 'But then he met that woman he nearly married . . .'

'I don't think I know that story.' Grand settled down for a gossip, his back against Annie's chair.

'Oh, yes,' she said, stroking his hair. 'You'd have been about, oh, four, five? I can't rightly recall. He came to me one afternoon when you were out for a walk with your pa . . .'

'Pa took me for walks?'

'Land sakes, Mattie. Your pa idolized you. Still does.' She tapped his head with her knuckles, gently. 'You Grands aren't just good lookers, you're as stubborn as a mule in a thicket. Now, do you want this story, or do you not?'

And Matthew Grand, four going on thirty-two, settled down to listen.

If truth were told, there wasn't much that was deluxe about the Hotel de Luxe in Rye. It was the only such establishment in town and, whereas no one outside Boston would have expected an elevator, staff to carry luggage up the four flights of stairs would have helped. As it was, Savage and Roscoe had to do that themselves, the sergeant, as the younger and junior man, bearing most of the burden. There was nowhere to eat in the building, so they availed themselves of a restaurant across the road. It was also the only such establishment in town, and the waitress's thumb in Roscoe's eggs-over-easy did not bode well for the haute of the cuisine. But there it was; Andrew Grand would not permit the police to sleep under his roof – he claimed there was no room – and the stable was a morgue. So the de Luxe it had to be.

After supper, Roscoe was trying to ignore the thinness of the single pillow behind his head. He was sprawled on the narrowest of beds, his notebook in his hand, the dim beams of the oil lamp lighting his way. Savage had two pillows, as befitted his rank and, even though the hotel room was damp and squalid, had thrown caution to the wind and had put on his night shirt. He had even placed his boots outside the door in the fond hope that, come morning, some hotel fairy would have cleaned them. Roscoe, hoping to God they would not be here long, stripped down to his necessaries and then replaced his boots, for fear of the cockroaches.

'Are you sitting comfortably, Sergeant?' the chief asked.

Roscoe nodded. He was going to have to talk in a minute and there was still something indescribable caught in his teeth from supper. 'Ready, Chief,' he managed at last.

'First,' Savage began, savouring a cigar that Sam Clemens had given him, 'and I've been giving this considerable thought, I don't think the maid and Josiah Grand died by the same hand.'

Roscoe's eyelids flickered as he looked up at his boss. It was going to be a long night. 'I know what you're thinking,' Savage went on, 'same house, same single blow to the back of the head. What are the odds? But think of the differences, Bill. She, thirtyish, female, skivvy. He, loaded old soak. Where's the common ground?'

'The Grand household, sir.' Roscoe held *his* ground.

Savage watched the smoke rings rise to the brown of the ceiling, where they added to the discolouration of the ages. 'No,' he shook his head. 'I think what we're looking at is a copycat situation. Somebody kills the maid – I'll come back to that. And then somebody kills old Josiah – same method, suggested by the first one; different motive.'

'But—'

'Now, the maid. One of our own denizens of the night, you tell me.'

'One of Madame Tinkerbelle's, Chief.'

'Wants a fresh start,' Savage was thinking ahead. 'Make her mother proud of her. Becomes a lady's maid. Nothing wrong with that; I think the Save the Sisterhood for Sainthood of Boston would welcome it.'

'Except it may have led to her murder.' Roscoe felt he had to remind the chief.

'It's an irrelevance, Roscoe,' Savage shook his head. 'Trust me, I've been doing this a lot longer than you have; I've got a nose for these things. No, we should focus on old Josiah. What do we know?'

'He'd have been sixty-nine next birthday, Chief.'

'Really?' Savage's eyes widened. 'He looked a hundred in the stable. Still, I suppose an axe in the head'll do that to a man.'

'He's one of three Grand brothers. Andrew's the other. Third deceased. All of them made their pile – and it's a sizeable one, by all accounts – out of property and railways.'

'The deceased brother?' Savage wanted to leave no stone unturned.

'Died of cholera, Andrew Grand says. They had it bad in Washington during the war. Place was crawling with soldiers. Philip Grand was a do-gooder, doing his bit for the war effort. He'd been out there serving soup to the wounded, that kinda thing.'

'And Josiah? Don't tell me he was a Quaker during the war.'

Roscoe shrugged. 'Don't have anything on that. Probably saw it all through a haze of booze, anyhow. I wouldn't want to be the doctor who does the autopsy, coming face to face with a liver like that.'

'All right,' Savage was screwing up his face, wrestling with the case in his mind. 'There's the table, Roscoe. Show me how it looked on the night the old man died.'

Roscoe got off the bed and did the honours. 'Here,' he put his notebook down, 'is the stable.'

'One groom,' Savage was adding the detail. 'Thornton.'

'Surly cuss,' Roscoe remembered, 'but strangely fond of the deceased.'

Savage raised an eyebrow. 'Anything . . . unnatural?'

'Don't think so, Chief,' Roscoe frowned. Just how much deviance could there be in the state of Maine in the year of their Lord 1873?

'Say on.'

'Here,' Roscoe placed an empty plant pot alongside the notebook, 'is the house.'

'Side on to the stable,' Savage said. 'Doors at all points of the compass. What about lights?'

'Chief?'

'Well, the old man's body was found after dark. This here,' he pointed to the stained tablecloth, 'the yard where he was found. Was it lit?'

'There was a torch bracket over the stable door,' Roscoe remembered. 'Unlit, according to Thornton.'

'But there were lights from the house.' Savage was thinking it through.

'And from the stable,' Roscoe added. 'Thornton was there.'

'Right,' the chief said. 'Time for the people.' He crossed the room – it didn't take him long – and fished a silver box from his coat pocket. He spilled out its contents, bone toothpicks, and placed them accordingly. 'Thornton,' he put him down on Roscoe's notebook. 'In the stable. Who else?'

'So, that's a bit sad, really,' Batchelor said, when Grand had told him the story of Jackieboy's parentage.

'I almost feel guilty,' Grand said, cradling his post-prandial brandy.

'Hardly your fault, Matthew,' Batchelor pointed out. 'You weren't given much choice in the matter, I wouldn't think.'

'No . . . my mother was ill, apparently, after I was born, so . . . but still. Jackieboy, kicked out to a neighbour's house. And not even Josiah's son, in the end.'

'Did he find out, do you think? Lose his temper?'

'Who?' Grand had lost track of the personal pronouns. 'Josiah? I don't think Jackieboy would be the one he would lose his temper with. It would be Annie, surely? Are you suggesting self-defence?'

'No, no, no. I mean, *Thornton* found out and lost his temper.'

'Again, it would be Annie he would be angry with. No, I think that this is a red herring. I don't think Jackieboy would hurt Josiah.'

'But he thinks he's in the will.' Batchelor had seen people killed for a lot less than Josiah Grand had to leave. He had seen men killed for a worn-out pair of shoes, back home.

'He may well be. I haven't seen it.'

'That might be a starting point. Who knows who's in it? Ira could be in it, for example. Martha. People do strange things for money.'

Grand was not sure whether to be appalled or amused. 'Are you saying Martha stove in her uncle Josiah's head? And, don't let's forget, it is hardly likely that we have two mad axe murderers here in the house; why should Martha kill Magda?'

'Was Hamilton the other fella?' Batchelor was clutching at straws and he knew it.

'Don't be ridiculous. Hamilton wasn't even in the house when Magda was alive. So, long story short, is the killer Jackieboy Thornton?'

'Umm . . .' Batchelor hated to let a good suspect go. 'No.'

'Better put the corpse . . .'

'In situ, yes, you're right. They'd moved him, of course, but this seems to be about right.' The hand hovered, the toothpick that was Josiah Grand fell into place on the tablecloth.

'Now, the house.'

'Well, that's complicated. The staff . . .'

'Forget 'em,' Savage said.

'Chief?' Roscoe couldn't believe his ears.

'Come on, Bill,' Savage patronized. 'Think, man. Josiah Grand didn't actually live in the Rye house. He lived in Boston. None of the servants worked for him, so there's no room for a grudge, or anything like that. As far as we know, nothing was taken from the old man's clothing, so we can rule robbery out. Unless he'd seriously crossed one of 'em in the couple of days he was here, I don't see a motive.'

'Unless our axeman's just plain mad,' Roscoe ventured.

'No such thing as *plain* mad,' Savage told him. 'There's

always method in madness, Roscoe – William Shakespeare could've told you that.'

'Criminologist, was he?' the sergeant felt obliged to ask, 'Shakespeare?'

Savage ignored him. 'The family.' He tapped the table, waiting with his handful of toothpicks. 'Where were the family?'

'Mrs Liza Grand was in bed. Been there on and off since the wedding.'

'Nervous indisposition.' Savage nodded. He'd seen it before. 'Two funerals and a wedding. Yes, it would take its toll.' He didn't have enough room on the plant pot to place his toothpicks accurately, so he had to improvise, putting them vaguely where he remembered the various rooms were. It was at best an imprecise science, even with the rough sketch that Andrew Grand had made for him in lieu of a blueprint.

'Andrew Grand was with her.'

'In bed?'

'No, Reading in a chair. Er . . .' With his notebook doubling for the stable, Roscoe had to dredge his memory. '*Every Man His Own Accountant.*'

'Gripping,' Savage nodded, rolling the cigar-end around in his mouth. 'Who else?'

'Matthew Grand, that fella Batchelor and the journalist Latham were all in the drawing room . . .'

'They say,' Savage said. 'Who else?'

'Ira Grand was in his room.'

'Reading a book on accountancy?'

'No. Darning his socks.'

Savage frowned.

'He's the poor relation, Chief. Been on a whaler for fourteen years. I guess you learn to be self-sufficient.'

'So,' Batchelor had to move on, 'I suppose we have to consider Ira. The only man we know to have a record.'

'He has no record,' Grand pointed out. 'He was just put off the ship at Valparaíso.'

'Before we move on, where exactly *is* Valparaíso? I can't say I have often wondered, but I am wondering now.'

'It's in Chile, isn't it?' Grand had not covered much international geography at West Point – possibly a serious omission, but not one that had ever worried him much.

'Oh. Is that the fat one at the top on the right as you look at it?' Batchelor had an encyclopaedic knowledge of London; it was unreasonable to ask for more.

'I think it's the skinny one on the left. But anyway, wherever it is, he was put off there with his wages and he made his way back here. It must have taken him a while.'

'In that case,' Batchelor pointed out, 'why was he so anxious to . . . make Magda's acquaintance on the beach?'

'Well . . .' Grand was embarrassed. Surely this wasn't the moment for The Talk.

'I know what he *said*,' Batchelor flapped a hand at his colleague. 'But what I am saying is, he had thousands of miles in which to make the acquaintance of as many ladies as he wanted. Why wait for a beach in Rye?'

'That's a good question. It didn't occur to me to ask. Perhaps he was looking for that special someone.'

'That's what I'm saying. Was that special someone Magda Galatski?'

'I don't think we can push coincidence quite that far, James. He didn't know that Martha was getting married this week. If by some wild chance he did, he certainly wouldn't know that Mima was her matron of honour. And if he knew *that* – and by now we're in the odds of millions to one, I guess you know that – then he wouldn't know that Magda was her maid.'

Batchelor took over. 'Yes, I know. And even if he knew *that*, why travel across continents to bash her brains in?'

'Especially after the beach. It went well, as far as these things do. He had no scratches on his face or anything I could see. And he was being so *honest*, James. I don't know him well. He was gone really before I grew up, and the age gap that doesn't count when you are men is everything to children. But even so, he just seemed to be telling the truth.'

Batchelor couldn't forget the financial angle – after all, more people got murdered for money than love, no matter what the novelists said. 'Why is he so poor? Wasn't he left anything in his father's will? In trust, perhaps.'

'His father, my uncle Philip, was a great philanthropist. It's how he died, doing good. When Ira left home, he didn't wait to see what would happen. He changed his will then and there, to benefit the poor. In the end, I think it went to war orphans, something like that. My father would know; he is a trustee.'

Batchelor was unwilling to let go of a good idea. 'You said he might be in Uncle Josiah's will, though.'

'Indeed he may. But the family at large don't know how much Josiah had to leave. Even the house he lived in wasn't his own, don't forget.'

'Oh, yes, I remember,' Batchelor said, a little archly. 'It's yours.'

'Correct.' Grand still found it hard to bear in mind that Batchelor didn't own so much as a stick of furniture, let alone a house. 'So, I vote that we cross Ira off our list of suspects. Agreed?'

Batchelor poised his pencil over the first page in his brand-new notebook, lent to him, reluctantly, by the recluse writer Sarah Chauncey-Wolsey. Then he nodded. 'Yes.' He drew a thick line. 'There. He's gone. Who else?'

'Who else?'

'Samuel Clemens. He was in the library.'

'Of course he was; he's Mark Twain. Don't tell me *he* was reading a book on accountancy.'

Roscoe chuckled. 'No, Chief. And he wasn't reading himself, either, although he did look. Apparently he was a bit put out that there wasn't a single Twain on the bookshelves.'

'Ah,' smiled Savage. 'What's a family for, other than to give love, admiration and support? The Zzerbes?'

'She was in her room . . .'

'The women don't count.' The chief was sure on this point at least.

'They don't?' Roscoe wasn't.

'You saw the man's head, Roscoe,' Savage reminded him. 'A blow like that. No woman could do it. No woman would want to.'

'Celia Thaxter, Chief?' Roscoe raised an eyebrow.

'Ah, yes.' Savage placed her toothpick alongside that of Josiah Grand. 'The finder of the body.'

'Did you get a good look at her?' the sergeant asked.

'As good as is decent in a married man,' Savage said, a little on his dignity. Mrs Savage was clear on that point, as on so many others.

'Muscles, Chief,' Roscoe winked. 'Her old man keeps the light on the island of Appledore. She rows across the open sea like you and I pick up a newspaper. She could do it.'

'Now, don't rush your fences, Bill,' Savage wagged a finger at him. 'The night is young and we'll get to motive in a minute. For the moment,' he checked the toothpicks, 'that's everybody accounted for.'

Roscoe smiled. He knew that Savage had ignored over half the inhabitants of the house. Still, he *was* the chief . . .

Grand took the initiative. 'I hate to bring this up, James, but we have to consider Celia.'

Batchelor bridled a little. It was true he found her a very nice woman, but since their first walk on the beach he had spent less than no time with her. She always seemed to be rowing somewhere, a pastime with which he had little affinity. 'Please don't try and spare my feelings,' he said, his throat a little tight. 'If you think Celia bashed in the heads of a maid who was no better than she might be, and your Uncle Josiah, then please, don't let me stop you.'

Grand got up and refilled their glasses. 'There you are, you see,' he said, gesturing with the decanter. 'On your high horse straight away. I wasn't accusing the woman. I agree with you that she had no motive that makes any sense. But you have to allow that all that thing about her marriage was a little bit strange. They say the man has never been seen from that day to this. It's only a matter of time, surely, before the police ferret that out.'

'Pardon?' Batchelor felt as though his lips had frozen to his teeth.

'It's only a matter of time . . .'

'No, not that bit. The bit about the man never having been seen.'

Grand sat back down, handing Batchelor his drink as he did so. 'I had no idea you had no idea,' he said. 'I felt sure it would have cropped up.'

'Cropped up?' Batchelor took a swig of brandy. '*Cropped up*? How does a missing husband – I assume the man in question was her husband?'

Grand nodded.

'How does a missing husband crop up? Where did he go missing from?' His eyes widened. 'Not lost at sea, please God.'

'James,' Grand laughed, 'you are so melodramatic. No, what happened was that some snake-oil salesman came to town one Fall, ooh, I don't know how long ago. Ten years? A dozen? Anyway, he swept our Celia off her feet and they got married and moved down to Boston. They say it nearly killed her father, to lose his little girl like that, so suddenly and to a stranger. She wrote him regularly but she never came back. Then, one day, or so I'm told, she *was* back, as if nothing had happened. No tribe of little Celias or little snake-oil salesman clinging to her skirts, just plain old Celia, large as life. And she never spoke of him, nor used his name again. Folks from here who had moved back to Boston told stories of how they would be seen about together and then not so often and then suddenly,' he clicked his fingers and made Batchelor, who had been rapt, jump, 'he was gone. He left not a sign behind to say where he'd gone to.'

'But surely, someone knows what happened?' Batchelor, as either an enquiry agent or a journalist, couldn't let it rest there.

'Yes. Celia does. For all we know, she whacked him on the back of the head with an axe and buried him in the cellar.'

'Do you think so?' Batchelor was giving it due consideration.

'Of course she didn't, James. Use your sense. I expect he just ran off with another woman, or went back to his wife and six children in Spokane. But it makes you think.' Grand swirled his brandy and mused on its amber depths. 'It makes you think.'

'All right.' Savage returned to his position on the bed and rear-ranged his pillows. His cigar had gone out and he relit it. 'Motive. Andrew Grand. How did he strike you?'

'It's whether he struck his brother that's important, Chief,' Roscoe said.

'Yes, yes, very amusing, Sergeant, but we *do* have a murderer to put away.'

'Yes, Chief.' Roscoe's smile vanished and he cleared his throat, ever the professional policeman, even when lying on a bed in his necessaries. 'They got on, as far as I could tell. Josiah was a bit of a trial to everybody but nobody had a bad word for him. I guess he was drinking Andrew out of house and home.'

'And I guess he was probably used to that.'

'Right. So I just don't see a motive.'

'Neither do I. Rule him out.'

FIFTEEN

B atchelor had an ace up his sleeve and he played it now. 'I hate to say this, Matthew, but have you considered it might be your father?'

'Yes.'

Batchelor sat up, slopping his drink. 'Really? Your *father*?' That was a turn-up for the book.

'I have considered it. It isn't my father.'

'Why not?' It was no good just ruling people out; there had to be a reason.

'He's my father.' Grand didn't really see the point in pursuing this.

'That isn't a reason, though, is it?' Batchelor was like a dog with a bone sometimes.

'It's reason enough for me, but if you want another, here it is. I have never seen my father in any mood other than suppressed dissatisfaction. That covers my sister marrying a man none of us likes. It covers my mother's dressmaker's bill. It covers me leaving the army and going to London instead of into his business. It covers the toast being cold. But it isn't a mood to ever cause him to beat in the back of the head of his only surviving sibling.'

As a reason, it was hard to refute. A black line through his name seemed to be the only way forward.

* * *

'Matthew Grand.'

'Bit of a black sheep in some ways,' Roscoe said. 'Nice enough cuss, but he ran away to England soon after the war.'

'Why?'

'Some case he was on. He wouldn't tell us what.'

'No,' Savage remembered Grand's polite, smiling but implacable refusal. 'He wouldn't, would he?'

'He came back for his sister's wedding with that Batchelor fella in tow.'

'Anything . . . unnatural?' The chief was raising eyebrows again.

'I don't know, sir,' Roscoe said. 'I didn't like to enquire.'

Savage removed the cigar from his lips. 'Didn't like to enquire, Roscoe?' he said. 'Good God, man, it's what they pay you for! We'll come back to Batchelor in a minute. Tell me about Ira.'

'Ah, now this is where the maid comes in,' Roscoe began.

'Now, Bill . . .'

'I know, I know. But remember what the maid, Maisie, said about the "other fella" going into Magda's room. Stands to reason, Chief,' Roscoe said. 'Been on a whaler. Looking for female company. Maybe she gave him the come-on.'

'Maybe she did at that,' Savage agreed. 'But why kill her? She was hardly going to make a complaint, now, was she? What's his relationship with the family?'

'Estranged. He quarrelled with his old man before running away to sea. No love lost, I'd say.'

'They seemed happy enough to see him back, though,' Savage commented. 'Let bygones be bygones, that sort of thing. What about Samuel Clemens?'

'How many famous authors do we know who are also axe murderers, Chief? I don't know about you, but I would have said the man hadn't a violent bone in his body. And again, why kill the old man? They were second cousins, somewhat removed by the sound of it. Hadn't seen each other for years as far as anybody can recall.'

'And as you say; he's a famous author.'

If Savage was being ironic, Roscoe couldn't tell for sure, so he moved on hurriedly, lining up his toothpicks to cover his confusion.

*   *   *

'It could always be Uncle Sam,' Grand said, reminded of the author as he lit a cheroot.

'Mark Twain?' Batchelor struck an extra thick line through the man's name. 'Don't be insane.'

Grand tossed his head, shrugged and blew a perfect smoke ring to the ceiling. 'Just saying.'

'All right,' Savage said. He was looking at the murder scene as laid out on the table, wrestling with what they knew, wondering what they didn't. 'Let's get to the people at the edges. Jeremy Zzerbe.'

'Ah, now, if it was Jemima Zzerbe on the barn door in the stable, I'd have slapped the bracelets on him already.'

'You would?' Savage asked. 'Go on.'

'He clearly can't stand his wife. And she clearly can't stand him. Mind you, the way she was carrying on this morning, I'm not surprised.'

'Carrying on?' This was news to Savage. 'What happened?'

'Some vagrant came calling, looking for work. She screamed the place down. Didn't you hear it?'

'No.' Savage didn't care to explain to his sergeant that he'd been down in the kitchen enjoying Mrs Stallybrass's apple dumplings at the time and his mind had clearly been elsewhere. 'What're you saying? This Mrs Zzerbe is deranged?'

'Well, I don't know about that, Chief. Highly strung, shall we say? Did you notice how they didn't touch at all – Mr and Mrs Zzerbe? Like there was an invisible wall between them.'

'So, Maisie's "other fella" could have been Jeremy Zzerbe.' The Chief was thinking aloud.

'I guess so,' Roscoe said. 'But I thought we weren't looking at the maid.'

'No, no.' Savage was back on track. 'We're not. We're not. Any known link between this Zzerbe and old Josiah?'

'None we know of,' the sergeant admitted, 'unless you count the fact that Zzerbe will *be* Josiah in a few years' time if he doesn't cut back on the liquor.'

'And then, of course, there is Mr Jemima Zzerbe, as I can't help but think of him,' Grand offered.

'He is a strange one,' Batchelor agreed. 'Hates his wife, but is how he is because of her. What a horrible life.'

'Yes. If it does turn out to be him by some strange quirk, she should be in the dock with him. No man could stay quite sane when shackled to Jemima.'

'You knew her when you were children, didn't you?' Batchelor checked. 'What was she like then?'

Grand thought for a moment. 'Well, she was very nervy, scared of mice, spiders, snakes, bears.'

'Bears? That's an odd thing to be scared of, surely?'

Grand gave him an odd look. Who wasn't afraid of bears? Meet one when it was in a bad mood and you could say goodbye to your face. 'I seem to remember she was afraid of jelly at some point.'

'Jam,' Batchelor automatically corrected him.

'No, jelly. I was speaking English there. Who in hell is afraid of jam? Anyway, yes, she was nervy. And I guess whatever . . . well, we'll think wedding night . . . poor old Jeremy must have spooked her. A bit like putting up a pheasant without your gun cocked.'

They both mulled over the analogy for a moment.

'As it were,' Batchelor finished the thought.

'Yes. So, I don't think it was Jeremy, though I do have much more than a slight suspicion he is the other fella. What I *don't* think is that he would bash in the head of his . . . let's call her his antidote to Jemima. Why would he?'

'Jealous. If he saw her with Ira on the beach.'

'Hmm. No, I think that's unlikely. For a start, I don't know if he had even joined the party at that point. Don't forget, he came up from Boston later than Mima did. But second, I just don't see Jeremy doing anything out of passion.'

'Except drinking.'

'Always excepting that,' Grand agreed. 'So, I think, cross him out.'

Batchelor did so with a flourish.

'Edward Latham,' Savage said. 'The other Limey. Suddenly we're awash with the bastards.'

'I don't like him, Chief,' Roscoe conceded. 'You know my views on newshounds.'

'One up from rapists and child-killers,' Savage nodded. 'Mine too. What's he doing here in the first place?'

'Covering the Grand wedding, he said,' Roscoe reminded him.

'Yeah, and I'm the next President of the United States when President Grant has the goodness to step down. *New York Times* men don't get out of bed for anything less than . . .'

'. . . a juicy murder,' Roscoe finished the sentence for him.

'You're not telling me this Latham bludgeoned the old man just to get an exclusive?' Savage asked.

'It had crossed my mind,' Roscoe said, 'but, no.'

'What do you think of Edward Latham as a suspect?' It didn't come naturally to Batchelor to accuse a fellow journalist of murder, but Latham had not lived up to the pedestal that Batchelor had forced him to climb.

'That's unlike you, James. A fellow journalist in the frame?'

'We have to think of every eventuality.' Batchelor sounded prim.

'He is hiding something, that's for sure,' Grand said. 'But what?'

Behind them, the door clicked.

'Hiding something?' said Edward Latham. 'I didn't think my newshound's nose had deserted me in this godforsaken hole, begging your pardon, Mr Grand. Who's hiding something?'

'Is that how you get your exclusives, Mr Latham?' Grand asked. 'Snooping at keyholes?'

'I think you're confusing me with a *Telegraph* man,' Latham sneered, looking at Batchelor.

'For the last time,' Grand looked at him levelly, 'why are you really here? If you don't tell *us*, you'll have to tell Savage.'

'Will I?' Latham bridled.

'Let's put it this way,' Batchelor said. 'If we have a word in the chief's ear, Sergeant Roscoe will put the bracelets on you. You will be escorted to the Boston lock-up, where, unsurprisingly, you will be locked up.'

'The Boston police are an enlightened force, I understand,' Grand chipped in. 'You will be allowed to contact one person.'

'Who will be your editor at the *New York Times*,' Batchelor went on. 'Mr . . .?'

'Edward Delane,' Latham said.

'Now,' Batchelor was getting into his journalistic stride. 'I don't know what sort of relationship you have with Mr Delane, but I can't imagine him taking the news too well. I can see the *Times* headlines now, can't you, Matthew?'

'I can, James,' Grand smiled. '"Limey Journalist Axe Murderer".'

'"Guilty as hell, says Police Chief",' Batchelor added the subtitle.

'Don't be absurd,' Latham hissed, clearly rattled by now.

'Even when it's all sorted out,' Batchelor said, '*if* it's sorted out, you'll have caused no end of embarrassment to the paper, not to mention loss of earnings because they won't take your stories.'

'Hell,' Grand said, '*nobody* will take your stories.'

'That's right,' Batchelor said. 'Think of the shame, Edward – may I call you Edward?' He didn't wait for an answer. 'Turned down by the *Huish Episcopi Gazette*.' And he winked at Grand.

'All right!' Latham snapped. 'All right, you've made your point. I'll tell you why I'm here, but I promise you, Grand, you won't like it.'

'I tell you what, though, Chief. It's the groom that got up my nose.'

'Thornton?'

'No, the *bride*groom.'

'Ah, yes, Mr Chauncey-Wolsey. Too handsome that man – if you like 'em that way. I would imagine he would be a favourite with the ladies.'

Roscoe wasn't much of a judge of manly beauty; as a happily married man and father of six, he had never had the time to practise, but he knew a bad 'un when he met one, and Hamilton Chauncey-Wolsey was a bad 'un, with knobs on. 'He's shady, Chief. Don't ask me how or in what way, but he is. He was too slick with the answers, too sure of himself.'

'Money'll do that to a cuss,' Savage nodded. 'Let's face it, Bill, anybody upstairs in this house could buy you and me a dozen times over. That's what a police force is for – to keep the bastards in check. Do you see him as a murderer, though?'

'No,' the sergeant had to concede again. 'No, I don't. I can see him paying somebody else to do his dirty work but . . . why Josiah? There's no motive. He's out, I reckon.'

After sharing his news, the journalist, smug and worried in equal measure, excused himself. So did Grand.

'No, James,' Grand said as Batchelor got up with him. 'This is family. Wait here. I won't be long.'

Grand went through the house like a whirlwind, maids and boot boys clearing out of his way. Even Waldo Hart, who rarely stepped aside for anyone, took one look at the man's face and gave him a wide berth.

Hamilton Chauncey-Wolsey was in the drawing room when the whirlwind swept in.

'Matthew,' he nodded to his brother-in-law, 'I'm glad you're here. Martha and I will be leaving tomorrow.'

'Will you?' Grand asked.

'Well, you asked us to stay after the wedding and, what with the way things are, I agreed. But this whole business is nothing to do with us. We've got a honeymoon planned.'

'Oh, I don't think there'll be a honeymoon, Hamilton. Come to think of it, I don't think there'll be a marriage after today.'

Chauncey-Wolsey stood up, frowning. 'What are you talking about?'

'You said it yourself,' Grand faced him, 'a minute ago. "Business" you said. What and where are they?'

'What are what? Matthew, you're talking in riddles.'

'The letters you stole from my father's safe.'

'Letters?' Chauncey-Wolsey blinked. 'What letters?'

The banker from New York didn't see it coming. One moment he was chatting, albeit obliquely, with his brother-in-law. The next, he was looking down the muzzle of a .32 calibre pocket Colt, the butt of which was gripped firmly in the hand of said brother-in-law.

Chauncey-Wolsey gulped, but decided to brazen it out. 'I don't think you're going to use that,' he said. 'If only for Martha's sake.'

'You're right,' Grand said, sliding the hammer back gently and smiling as he did it. 'What *was* I thinking?'

His left fist thudded into Chauncey-Wolsey's stomach and the man jack-knifed, fighting for air. Grand slid the pistol away in his shoulder-holster and brought both hands, clasped, down on the man's neck. Chauncey-Wolsey suddenly had an excellent view of Andrew Grand's carpet. Not for long, though, because he felt his hair being pulled up by the roots and he was kneeling up, still trying to breathe, trying to stop the room from reeling. When he focused again, he saw Matthew Grand's raised fist. 'Not the face,' he gasped. 'Not the face.'

'No, of course not,' Grand said. 'We'll start with the fingers.' And he wrenched them back.

'What the hell do you *want*?' Chauncey-Wolsey shrieked.

Grand relaxed his grip and pulled the man to his feet. Then he pushed him backwards into a chair.

'I've just had a fascinating conversation with Edward Latham,' he said. 'The man thinks my father is a fraudster and thief. He thinks he's the one in the Tammany Hall case; that he's the one the papers call the painter.'

'Does he?' Chauncey-Wolsey was still looking wide-eyed. Then he saw Grand's fist again. 'All right, all right,' he said, his whole life flashing before him. 'Andrew's not the painter. I am.'

Grand sat down opposite the man. 'Tell me,' he said.

'We bankers always walk a fine line,' Chauncey-Wolsey told him, 'between honest investment and . . . shall we call it creative accountancy. I had the misfortune to meet William Tweed, ex-mayor. Well, they don't call him the Boss for nothing. He had such schemes, Matthew, it'd make your eyes water. Having laid them out in front of me, he asked me, was I in? Well, of course I was. But we needed investors.'

'My father,' Grand nodded, everything falling into place.

'Tweed got too greedy and somebody went to the law. I told him not to, but . . . well, you have to know the man. There's no stopping him once he smells money and power. Andrew sensed that something was wrong, but I strung him along, assuring him it would be fine.'

A thought suddenly crossed Grand's mind. 'Is that why you married Martha?' he asked, his jaw flexing, 'just to buy the old man? And . . . wait a minute. Was your best man involved? Was that why he didn't turn up?'

'Poindexter? Yes. He was the one who put me in the way of what he said was a sure-fire thing. He was in deeper than me and was arrested. He's a true friend, though; he didn't name either me or your father.' Chauncey-Wolsey was adamant. 'And as for all this having anything to do with Martha – whatever you think of me, Matthew, I really love your sister. If her father was a road-sweeper, it'd make no difference. I've got a chance, just an outside one, mind, to make this right. I got a letter the other day from New York. There *is* a way that won't see me and your father go to jail.'

'Or,' Grand said, 'you could do the decent thing and go to the cops.'

'I could,' Chauncey-Wolsey leaned back, his heart still pounding along with his head. 'But it'd mean a prison stretch for your father. Is that what you want?'

'I'd settle for the letters,' Grand said.

'I don't know what you're talking about?'

'Papers from my father's safe. I told you . . .'

'I don't have them. I've never broken into a safe in my life and I wouldn't know where to start.'

The door clicked open and Martha Chauncey-Wolsey stood there. 'Well, that's nice,' she smiled. 'Two of my favourite men in the whole world having a cosy chat.' She swept past Matthew, giving him a kiss on the forehead, before joining her husband on the arm of his chair. 'Uncle Mattie,' she said, smiling at her brother. 'Papa,' and she kissed Chauncey-Wolsey on the top of his immaculate head. 'What're you boys talking about?'

'Which brings us to the real culprit,' Savage said, biding his time and making the sergeant wait.

'Who?' he asked after a suitable interval – the silence was killing him.

'I'll humour you,' Savage said, 'and start with the maid.'

At last, Roscoe thought, but it was more than his job was worth to say so.

'The maid was killed by Ira Grand,' the chief said. 'Either she spurned his advances or maybe – just maybe – he knew her from before. Fourteen years on whaling ships, he says, but we've had no chance to verify that. What if he puts into Boston in Madame Tinkerbelle's glory days? What if he was the dead girl's client? Or even pimp, maybe – we don't know. No better disguise than a whaler's coat – who's going to wear one of those unless they have to, most people would say. So he follows her, or meets her again by accident, here at his niece's wedding. He threatens to tell all. They row. He kills her.'

'Noise, Chief,' Roscoe pointed out. 'Wouldn't there have been noise? Wouldn't somebody have heard it?'

'Place was full of guests for the pre-nuptial dinner,' Savage reasoned. 'Laughter, talking. Hell, singing and music, for all we know. I wouldn't put anything past these rich bastards.' Savage paused for a moment. He was letting his prejudices show. He coughed and resettled himself on the pillows. 'I'll wager Ira's strong enough to overpower the woman, stifle her noise until he lost it altogether and hit her with the axe.'

'So, he killed Josiah too, fond of him or not?'

'Ah, no.' Savage swung his feet off the bed, looking for one last time at the model murder scene. 'You see, Sergeant, the complexity of this case is that we have not one axe murderer, but two, like I've said all along, had you been listening. Sam Clemens and Ira Grand are the only two who have no alibis for the time Josiah was found.'

'So it's Clemens?' Roscoe's brain was whirling. That really would be a scoop for that sonofabitch newshound.

'No.' Savage blew rings into the air. 'Three men in the house have an alibi for the time the body was found.'

'Er . . . Matthew Grand, Batchelor and Latham.'

Savage nodded. 'All together in the drawing room,' he said, 'but that's for the time the body was *found*, not the time the axe actually fell, which we reckon was up to half an hour before.'

'So, it could have been any one of them?'

'It could,' Savage nodded. 'But I haven't been exactly straight with you, Bill, and I'm sorry about that.'

'Oh?'

'Remember I interviewed Andrew Grand alone?'

Roscoe did. He was trying to get some sense out of half a dozen giggling maids at the time; rank has its privileges.

'He let a little something slip.'

'Oh?'

'Brother Josiah, it turns out, is just a shade richer than God. You can forget the Rockefellers and the Vanderbilts. The cuss was loaded.'

'He was? How come?'

'Investments. Mainly through his brother. Living rent-free in a family house in Boston. Eating nothing, drinking cheap – I suppose money comes to money. But that's not it. Guess who his heir is?'

'Er . . .'

'Matthew Grand,' Savage said. 'That's who. And that gives the plausible bastard several thousand reasons to want to stove in his uncle's head. I don't know how he thought he could get away with it. How could he think we would be taken in by all this "enquiry agent" nonsense? How can anyone make a living at that?' He reached over and picked up the late, lamented Josiah Grand and picked a tooth with him. 'In the morning, we just need to wait until the wire comes from Boston, OK-ing the warrants, and then we'll have two birds with one stone.' Savage blew out the candle and punched his pillows into submission. Roscoe was left to sort out his bedclothes as best he could in the dark. 'Oh, and, Roscoe?'

'Yes, Chief?'

'When we go up to the house tomorrow, make sure you have your bracelets ready.'

By the time he got back to the library, Matthew Grand had calmed down. He'd made the briefest of small talk with his sister and the man whose face Grand still wanted to demolish and now he could pause awhile before he solved that particular problem.

Batchelor knuckled his eyes. He had done it when tired since he was a little boy, despite his mother's dire warnings that he would make his eyes pop out of their sockets. 'Is all well, Matthew?' he asked.

'Right as ninepence,' Grand told him. He was beginning to

miss London very much; things were simpler there with no family to muddy the waters.

'I've had enough,' Batchelor said, yawning. 'It's been a busy evening.'

'Busy day, James, old man,' Grand said, finding his chair again. He looked over at the list. 'Where were we? Anyone not crossed out?'

Batchelor held it to the lamp. 'Just two,' he said.

'Well, that's splendid,' Grand said, clapping his hands. 'They must be first in line for the murderer. Who are they?'

'Well,' Batchelor said, 'to start with, you.'

Grand sighed. 'Let me guess who the other one is? You?'

Batchelor nodded ruefully and leaned across to blow out the lamp.

SIXTEEN

B reakfast in any house with Andrew Grand resident was not a meal for the faint-hearted. Some time, long, long ago, he had been told it was the most important meal of the day and he had never forgotten that. So the buffets down the side of the dining room groaned with silver chafing dishes, filled with kidneys, sausages, bacon and eggs, along with a few delicacies he thought suitable for the ladies; sweetbreads, scrambled eggs and kedgeree. All of this had gone to feed the grateful staff for the last few mornings but today, by some kind of invisible consent, everyone finally felt up to it and every place was full. Martha, having had quite a few months on dry toast and hot water with a slice of lemon floating in it, had got her second wind and was eating for two at least; Hamilton looked at her speculatively, remembering that his mother was a twin. Did they run in families, like wall eyes and a wonky nose? Who knew?

Liza Grand had got up. She wasn't a woman to loll about in bed if she *could* get up and so here she was. Annie had insisted on taking over the preparation of her breakfast and the kitchen had an atmosphere you could cut with a knife. But Mrs Stallybrass had never had much of a hand with a boiled egg, usually producing something akin to a golf ball, so Annie had been in attendance. Mrs Grand's egg took three verses of 'Onward Christian Soldiers' at a rolling boil, then straight out of the water, on to the plate with a pile of thin cut toast and up to the dining room, spit spot. So, Liza Grand was the only person not sitting in front of a plate of food that could stun an ox.

Grand and Batchelor, still fairly fresh from the training that Mrs Rackstraw's gargantuan breakfasts provided, were tucking in to a bit of everything and then some. Although they were doing the food justice, they were taking the opportunity to watch the rest of the table. For this reason, they sat opposite each other, to give the better view. It was hard to decide just what would constitute unusual behaviour. Was it unusual to pick at a plateful? Did that mean guilt? Or was it even more unusual to eat like a starving person, with two bodies waiting in the stables for the attentions of the undertaker from Exeter, the one in Rye being considered a bit of a fly-by-night, being a slaughterman by trade when no burying was in the offing. The undertaker from Exeter had his own hearse and everything; he was coming over later in the day, to remove what he called the dear departed. When arranging it, Andrew Grand had asked for discretion but didn't expect it. Two murders up at the Grands' place were not going to go unremarked and, as it was, gardeners were kept fully occupied beating back sightseers at the boundary.

Jemima Zzerbe fell into the guilt-by-picking category. She had come into the room accompanied by her husband, an unusual enough occurrence to start the maids twittering in the servants' hall. He had carefully pulled out her chair, then had shoved it so far in towards the table that she was pinned like a butterfly on a collector's board. He had delivered to her a plate with everything on it but, so far, she had only picked one or two of the less threatening-looking Boston baked beans. Something in the dynamic of the relationship intrigued Grand. She looked beaten and he wasn't happy to see that. Although she was air-headed, stupid and hysterical, he had known her all her life, had pulled her pigtails, tied her by her apron strings to the gate and run away . . . he would always be on her side. Jeremy, on the other hand, was tucking in with a will. If he missed Magda, he showed no sign. Grand was not an enquiry agent for nothing; his eyes scanned the maids standing back against the wall, waiting to jump to attention when Hart gave them the slightest sign. Was one smirking? Yes; there she was. The rather buxom blonde on the end. No doubt about it, Jeremy had moved on. Did that make him a murderer? Who could tell?

Batchelor had a full-on view of Ira's table manners and it wasn't pretty. Chewing with your mouth open and swilling coffee round your mouth before swallowing some of it, the rest of it drooling down your front, might be acceptable on a whaler, but not so much in Rye in the state of New Hampshire. He showed no sign of guilt or remorse. He was, however, still swigging at his black bottle of hair of the dog, so it might not signify anything.

Gratefully, Batchelor moved his attention along to Ira's right, where Edward Latham was taking a slightly more abstemious breakfast. He was leaning as far across as he decently could, to avoid the spin-off from Ira's plate. Batchelor felt his pain; second-hand, half-masticated sausage is never a pleasant addition to any meal. Despite Latham's revelations of the night before – or perhaps because of them – Batchelor couldn't see him as a murderer. But then, he loathed the man so much he might easily become a victim.

Moving right one more space, he found himself looking into the cool blue eyes of Hamilton Chauncey-Wolsey. Batchelor was embarrassed; he didn't know quite why.

At the bottom of the table, flanked on his left by Sarah Chauncey-Wolsey, sat Sam Clemens, suited and booted for the road. His stay had been extended beyond his wildest expectations and he was needed at home. His wife had not sent word; she never bothered him when he was away, she was perfect in that regard, but he knew he should be with her with their little girl so new, and so he had made his excuses to the family and would be gone as soon as he had eaten. The police knew where to find him, after all; he was Mark Twain and a national treasure now that the States were a nation once again. Sometimes he wished that wasn't so. Especially now. Batchelor couldn't read lips with any fluency, but it wasn't hard to guess that Miss

Chauncey-Wolsey was bending the great man's ear about her latest opus. Listening as hard as he could for any gem from Clemens's lips, Batchelor was sure he heard him ask her if the book was about insects. She began explaining something in a very excited tone, tapping the table for emphasis. Clemens's coffee slopped into its saucer and Hart blew his whistle to alert the nearest maid and made everyone jump. He pulled his cuff down sharply and glowered at his people.

The interruption seemed to take Andrew Grand's attention off his food for the first time. He cleared his throat and looked meaningfully at Hart, who blew his whistle even more piercingly.

Andrew Grand waited until silence fell, by degrees. The last words which rang on the silence came from Martha's new sister-in-law, who was saying '. . . and my sequel will be about what she did at school. Isn't that just too thrilling?' It was the longest sentence anyone present had heard her say since she arrived and she almost got a round of applause.

'Ladies and gentlemen, if I may interrupt for a moment?'

Grand's head snapped up. He had never heard his father this conciliatory before. This man gave orders and knew they would be obeyed; he didn't ask, he *told*.

'I won't interrupt your breakfast for more than a minute. I know it is the most important meal of the day.'

Martha and Mattie caught each other's eye and had to stifle a giggle. They had heard that very phrase more often than any other, or so it seemed.

'I would like to thank you all for coming to our home to celebrate the wedding of my beautiful daughter, Martha, to Hamilton, here. I know you join me in wishing them every happiness.'

There was desultory applause and someone, Batchelor suspected Jeremy Zzerbe, muttered, 'Good luck with that, Hamilton, old chap.'

'I can't pretend that the last few days have gone according to plan.' Andrew Grand, as well as being a whizz at all things financial, was also something of an expert at the understatement. Sam Clemens doffed a metaphorical cap at the man, for his succinct summing up of events. 'I offer my condolences to Mr and Mrs Jeremy Zzerbe for the sad loss of Magda, a treasured member of their household, I am sure. My staff became very fond of her in the short time they knew her and I understand that they have made a donation to cover a floral tribute.'

Grand had heard rooms go silent before, many times. But, had it been the season, the katydids outside would have been deafening. After a pause, Hart said, 'Hear hear,' and led a smattering of applause.

'As for my dear brother, Josiah, my family and I have no words to express the depths of our loss.'

Aunt Nell brushed away a tear and blew her nose like a Charles River foghorn. If her sister was surprised to find her still in her house, she didn't show it. Nell had ceased to surprise her family back in the thirties.

Her brother-in-law went on. 'He was loved by all who knew him and the police, I am informed by message this morning, are close to making an arrest.' He looked round the table, a furrow in his brow. 'A vagrant of some kind, I would imagine. Yes.' He cleared his throat again. 'The funeral will be in Boston, from Josiah's house. I will let you know when that will be; the police have yet to apprise me.'

He raked his guests and family with a penetrating look. 'I think that's all, ladies and gentlemen. Please, if you are not ready to leave us just yet, you are very welcome to stay, but . . .' He let the sentence die away. Short of his throwing their luggage out into the garden, there could not have been a clearer message. Everyone shuffled their feet and pushed back their chairs. Hart's whistle blasted into their ears for one last time and they all dispersed to their rooms, to pack.

'Matthew.'

Grand looked round, to see his father beckoning him over. 'Yes, Pa?' It was hard to be quite the same with him, with what he now knew.

'I have some business to discuss with you, if you would step into the study.'

'I just need to go and—'

'Now, Matthew.'

'If I could just take mother up . . .'

'Your mother can manage the stairs, Matthew. In my study, if you please.'

Grand turned pointedly to Batchelor before he went out in his father's wake. 'I don't know whether we are included in the bum's rush,' he said, quietly. 'But I intend to stay, regardless. I need to know Martha is going to be all right, what Latham intends to do . . . we can't go yet.'

'I know,' Batchelor said. 'Do you know how long you are going to be?'

Grand smiled. 'It depends on whether he wants to give me the strap or a good talking-to. Either could take an hour, so if you could amuse yourself, James, that would be best. And by amuse yourself, of course I mean . . .'

'. . . find who did it.'

'If you would, old chap,' Grand put on an excruciating English accent, 'that would be absolutely splendid, old bean.'

Batchelor frowned. He didn't do faux American; he wished Grand would do him the same service and leave off the mimicry.

Sam Clemens clapped Grand on the back as he passed by on his way to the door, moving quickly to escape from Sarah Chauncey-Wolsey. 'Great accent you've got there, Mattie, me boy.'

Batchelor's Clemens pedestal rocked; could his hero have just attempted an Irish brogue? Please let it not be so!

The room emptied quickly. Latham had no packing to do, not this side of the water. All his things were still on Appledore. He strolled down the sloping lawn to the water's edge and took up a stout Cortés pose on the jetty, looking out to sea in the hope that Celia Thaxter and her rowing boat might appear on the horizon. Landlubber that he was, he didn't realize that lowering black clouds, a Force Six heading towards Seven from the east with a wicked cold spat of rain in it, would not entice even the most heroic of hostesses out in an open boat. Apart from anything else, though he could not have known it, her father's lumbago was playing him up again, and she was up in the lighthouse, trimming the wick. But hope sprang eternal and he stayed there until the cold drove him in.

Back at the house, all was light and warmth. No one walking through its rooms would guess that two dead bodies lay in the tack room outside, nor that a storm was building out to sea. The maids were busy setting, lighting and making up fires, putting out trays for morning coffee, making beds, dusting and sweeping, all under the eagle gaze of Hart, who, they whispered to themselves, had flannel feet and eyes in the back of his head. Not only that, but woe betide anyone taking a breather; it was as sure as eggs was eggs that the next person round the corner would be Hart; the man was everywhere.

In Andrew Grand's study, the atmosphere was solemn. It was hard not to regress back to the time Matthew had painted his sister's face with gentian violet, the day of the school concert when she was to have been playing the piano and singing in front of the whole school; Grand tried to shake off the feeling. His father had a sheaf of papers in front of him and he picked them up and tapped them square, before inviting Grand to sit.

'I don't know if you were aware of this, Matthew,' his father said, 'but your uncle Josiah was a very rich man. In terms of actual dollars and cents, richer than I am, in fact. He would never invest in property, that was his shortcoming, but his other investments are very sound and easy to access.'

'Good old Josiah,' Grand said, weakly. He wasn't sure what else to say.

'Of course, you probably know the scuttlebutt in the servants' hall that Jackieboy Thornton is Josiah's son?'

Grand shrugged and made a noncommittal noise. There was no need to let his father know how recently that piece of information had reached him.

'That isn't so, of course. Annie was a respectable married woman when she came to us. As you can imagine, we would have allowed nothing else for your nurse.'

Again, Grand managed to be noncommittal.

'So, Josiah had no children. And he thought Ira lost.'

Grand was waiting for the punchline.

'In a nutshell, Matthew, he has left all his money, apart from a few small legacies to servants, bar tenders and similar, to you.'

'Me?' Grand was a little nonplussed. 'But I haven't seen him in years until the other day.'

'Perhaps that's why he left it to you.' Andrew Grand gave his bark of laughter. 'It comes to somewhere in the region of . . .'

he shuffled his papers, '. . . ah, here we are . . . in the region of . . .' He looked up at his son. 'Now, I know the gossip is that he was richer than Cornelius Vanderbilt, but that wasn't so. No, indeed. So, don't be disappointed, Matthew, will you?'

'Pa.' Grand was getting frustrated, as he always did when his father was talking money. It sometimes seemed that all he wanted to do was spend little and gain much. 'Can you just tell me how much, please? We can discuss my disappointment or otherwise then, can't we?'

Andrew Grand frowned. He had had many disappointments in his life, but his son having not a financial bone in his body was probably the worst. 'You have been left . . . in the region of . . .'

'Pa!'

'Six hundred and twenty-four thousand, nine hundred and forty-two dollars and sixty-nine cents. As the markets stood yesterday, that is. Never forget an investment can go down as well as up.'

'Six hundred and twenty-five thousand dollars?' Grand had only expected a tenth of that sum, if that.

'No, Matthew, listen to me. Six hundred and twenty-four thousand, nine hundred and forty-two dollars and sixty-nine cents, as the markets . . .'

'Yes, I understand. I was rounding up.'

His father shook his head and tutted. 'Matthew, Matthew, Matthew. Whatever will we do with you?'

'Sorry, Pa.'

Andrew Grand was right. His only son had never appreciated money; never would. And anyway, Matthew's thoughts were elsewhere as he collided with Maisie outside the library. The woman had a feather duster in one hand and an ash bucket in the other.

'Sorry, sir,' she bobbed.

'My fault, Maisie,' he said. 'I should look where I'm going. Oh, Maisie . . .' The woman had scuttled away down the corridor, but stopped now and turned to face him.

'I have to ask,' he said. 'The "other fella" you saw going in to Magda's room that time.'

'What about him, sir?' Maisie asked.

'Now you've had time to reflect, do you remember who it was?'

She frowned at him. Master Mattie, who she had known almost all his life, was using the master's patronizing tone on her – the apple didn't fall far from the tree, she decided. ''Course I do, sir.' She almost stamped her foot. 'People think I'm stupid, but I ain't. It's just that I can't always make up my mind about things.'

'Well, who was it, Maisie?' Would Grand have to wring it out of the woman?

She looked backwards and forwards, checking that the coast was clear, if need be all the way out to Smuttynose. 'That Mr Zzerbe, sir. Always sniffing around the domestics. He's moved on to Mary-Ellen now, God help her.'

'Mr Zzerbe,' Grand nodded. That was interesting.

'I don't know why Mr Hart put up with it,' she said.

'Mr Hart?' Grand frowned.

'Well, he's particular about us all, sir. Oh, I know Magda wasn't actually one of us, but he takes it personal, sir, us below stairs. Truth be told, I think he carried a bit of a torch for her himself.'

'Why do you say that?' It was difficult to imagine Hart carrying a torch for anyone. He didn't look the lovelorn type.

'I saw them together. Standing real close, they were, but she wasn't having any. Well, he's a foreigner, ain't he? I know *she* was a foreigner as well, but not the same. Where was I?'

'Standing close together.'

Maisie blushed and then recovered herself. 'And as well as that, there's that horrible skin of his. Tell you the truth, I thought he carried a torch for Mrs Stallybrass. There's no accounting for taste, is there, sir? Now, if there's nothing else, sir, I've got to get on. Mr Hart is a stickler for his fires and I've got to get rid of this ash.'

James Batchelor always got on well with servants, but he was a little wary of Mrs Stallybrass. She clearly ran a tight ship and he wasn't at all sure how she would take to the question he was going to ask her. He imagined Mrs Rackstraw in the same position and he couldn't vouch for the outcome; in her case, a lot would depend on whether she had been cheeked by the butcher's boy or how her corns were. He didn't know Mrs Stallybrass's weak points, so he just had to brazen it out.

He poked his head around the door. The kitchen was at its most relaxed at this time in the morning. The pots and pans, plates and silverware were being dealt with in the scullery beyond and he could hear the echoing cries of the maids as they went about their hot and soapy work. Mrs Stallybrass and a few of the more senior maids were taking their ease around the kitchen table. One of them was reading the tea leaves in her friend's cup.

'Land sakes, Dolly,' she said, cuffing her friend on the arm. 'It says here you will meet a tall, dark foreigner. Be careful where you go; foreigners ain't always good news, even if they is tall and dark.'

'Does it say handsome?' Dolly asked, hopefully.

The first maid peered closer. 'Nope,' she said. 'Just tall, dark, foreign.'

Mrs Stallybrass groaned and leaned forward, her hands on her knees. 'I don't know, girls,' she said. 'I think it must be these new stays, but I've got the most consarnin' wind.'

Batchelor wasn't sure whether his timing was perfect but, even so, he coughed deprecatingly and waited. All three women jumped and clutched their breasts, as women round a kitchen table will do at intervals the world over.

Mrs Stallybrass was the first to respond. 'Oh, Mr Batchelor. You gave us a start. What can we do for you, sir?'

The maids had scuttled off to the scullery. This was that enquiry agent and they'd had enough of snooping and prying to last them a lifetime, even though Dolly noted, in passing, that he was foreign and, if not that tall, taller than her.

'I was wondering, Mrs Stallybrass, if I could have a packed lunch of some kind.'

She looked at him dubiously. She had literally no idea what he could possibly mean. 'Come again?'

'Packed lunch. Some food. Packed. For lunch.'

She still didn't quite seem to grasp his meaning.

Then, a distant memory came to him, of his only other visit

to America, five years before. 'Vittles,' he said. 'Vittles to take out on a hike.'

'Oh,' she flapped her teacloth at him before tucking it into the waistband of her apron. 'Why didn't you say so? Any vittles in particular?'

'Not really,' he said. 'A chicken leg, perhaps? Some cheese? Bread? Fruit? Something to drink?'

'You go and get yourself ready for your . . . what did you say you was doing?'

'Going on a hike.' He waited. 'A walk in the woods.'

She gave him an odd look. 'All right.' The excuses these youngsters came up with these days when they wanted to do a bit of spooning. 'Come back when you've got your . . . hiking . . . clothes on, and it'll all be packed up for you.'

Batchelor went up to the room he shared with Grand, hoping the man would be back, but he seemed to be still closeted with his father. Never mind. Probably Matthew wouldn't want to come for a walk, anyway. He probably knew every inch of these woods from when he was a boy. It would be nice to get out in the fresh air. He looked out of the window. The storm seemed set to stay out to sea. Beams of light shone down from the clouds, lighting the tips of the branches of the taller trees. It looked set for a fine afternoon. A nice picnic under a tree. Perhaps a snooze. He might even write a poem or something. He popped Sarah Chauncey-Wolsey's lent notebook into a pocket, along with a pencil. He changed his boots for something a little sturdier, borrowed one of Grand's tweedier coats – he knew he wouldn't mind – and, picking up his vittles on the way, strode out and was soon under the trees.

Mrs Stallybrass wiped down the table and put away the chicken, cheese and the loaf of bread. She got down to her puff pastry and the maids, one by one, gathered to watch. Mrs Stallybrass was a dab hand at puff pastry; rumour had it that it was this and this alone which had secured her all her places. So whenever the magic was happening, she gained an audience; every one of the scullery maids had in her apron pocket the wooden spoon of a head cook.

She rolled out the first level and put her softened butter across it in arcane patterns, folded, and rolled again. Everyone held their breath; it was at this point that the pastry was at its most vulnerable. Too warm, too heavy-handed and the whole thing could collapse in a mound of goo and butter. But, as always, Mrs Stallybrass had pulled another masterpiece out of the hat and, for the next two rollings-out, things got a little more relaxed.

'Mrs Stallybrass?' Maisie, having been almost in at the death, as it were, of Magda Galatski, had achieved a certain notoriety in the servants' hall and thought she should ask a question. 'Mr Batchelor, he went out into the woods, you said.'

'Mm hmm.' Mrs Stallybrass became a little monosyllabic, at best, when she was rolling out puff pastry.

'You know he comes from England?'

The cook couldn't stop rolling, so she nodded.

'They don't have bears in England.'

'Oh, course they do,' one of the other maids chimed in. 'This where we are is called New England, ain't it? That's because it's the same as *Old* England. They got bears, racoons, all them critters.'

Mrs Stallybrass rolled her eyes at the girl's passing acquaintance with grammar, but she agreed with her. Of course England had bears. Everywhere had bears. 'Everywhere's got bears, Maisie,' she said, as though to one simple-minded.

'Mr Batchelor lives in London, though,' Maisie said. 'He told Maggie when she was making up the fire. The fires in London burn so smoky that some days you can't see your hand in front of you out in the street.'

'Don't tell lies, now, Maisie,' Mrs Stallybrass said. 'Fires can't do that to a town.'

'London's a big city, Maggie said Mr Batchelor told her. Bigger than Rye. Bigger 'n Boston.'

Mrs Stallybrass risked her pastry and stopped rolling. 'Don't you talk so daft, Maisie,' she said. 'Nowhere's bigger than Boston. And England's got bears, and that's flat.'

She rolled in silence, then folded the pastry neatly and laid it to cool on a dish of ice, freshly crushed from the ice-house out in the yard. She leaned on her knuckles on the table and fixed Maisie with her best cook's glare. 'Why'd you ask?'

'Ask what?' Maisie had forgotten the beginning of the

conversation already. 'I didn't ask anything. I was just wondering, though, if you reminded him about leaving food about when you're in the woods. The bears are hungry with their young 'uns. Mean, as well. And if he's gonna go leaving chicken bones all over . . . well . . .'

'He knows about bears,' Mrs Stallybrass reassured her. 'England's full of bears. Known fact, that.' But as she turned into the pantry for the ham that needed marinating, she suddenly wasn't sure. Never mind; it would probably be all right in the end. Bigger than Boston! Ha!

SEVENTEEN

Grand was in a quandary. He was rich. He had always been rich, but not this rich and it took a little getting used to. Obviously, he would put some in trust for Martha's baby and, if things still went south, for Martha herself. He would give some to Jackieboy Thornton, because sometimes a man deserved to keep his dreams alive. Ira wouldn't want much, just enough to have a little shack somewhere where he could hear the whales singing . . . he realized that, since he had left his father's study, his new fortune had probably made enough interest to cover almost all of his plans. He didn't want the looking after of it, that much he knew; again, much would depend on the final outcome of the Tammany Hall investigation but, with a following wind and some tight lips, his father would live to invest another day. One thing he did know for certain, though, and that was that James Batchelor would not know, not now or ever, just how much money Matthew Grand was sitting on. When he was younger, he would have said that having enough money not to need to work would be heaven; but he had tried leisure, and he liked working more; the thrill of the chase, the air of mystery. So, a few hundred dollars from Uncle Josiah would fit the bill and enough said. But for now, he wanted to let his colleague know that Jeremy was confirmed as Magda's lover, not that there had ever been much doubt.

He started in the library. James Batchelor couldn't get enough of libraries. All this reading lark was all well and good, but too much of it sapped a man's strength, or so Matthew Grand had always believed, anyway. But he wasn't in there, even in the deep book nook that he had made his own, in the window-seat overlooking the beach. Nor was he in the drawing room, making small talk with the ladies. Nor in the conservatory, still a little brisk this early in spring, but an intriguing place for anyone interested in the flora of the Mid-West; cacti, mostly. It didn't matter that he couldn't put his finger on the man straight away. He was big enough, after all, to look after himself. But there had been two murders already in this house and who better for the next victim than someone who had been snooping around?

Bedroom? No. But Grand did notice that Batchelor had taken his notebook with him, so snooping was probably on the menu. Grand went down the stairs two at a time and swung round this time through the baize door, into the kitchen. Hart was alone, sitting by the range with a brimming cup of hot chocolate by his side, a hefty slice of Kuchen in the saucer. Mrs Stallybrass believed in keeping men well fed and, in the case of Hart, a nice dose of chocolate with as much whipped cream as she could balance on it could often mean the difference between a stand-up, knock-down argument about the accounts and a pleasant handshake and say no more about it. It wasn't just her puff pastry that had kept Mrs Stallybrass gainfully employed since she was fourteen.

'Hart?'

The butler turned his head, slowly. This was his morning break, but on the other hand, this was the young master. Hart was feeling mellow, full of chocolate and a good tablespoon of brandy for good measure. Without getting up, he said, 'Yes, sir. How can I help you?'

Used to Mrs Rackstraw, Grand was not as horrified as Jemima Zzerbe would have been, not by a country mile. He was also beginning to get a little concerned. 'Have you seen Mr Batchelor, Hart? I don't seem to be able to find him anywhere.'

Hart considered for a moment. 'He was at breakfast, Mr Grand,' he offered.

'Yes, yes. So was I. I was wondering if you had seen him since? He's taken his notebook and everything.'

This meant nothing to Hart, who shrugged.

'I'm afraid he's done something silly, gone off after the murderer or something. I . . . never mind. If you haven't seen him, you haven't. I'll keep on looking. Has Mr Clemens left, do you know?' It had suddenly occurred to Grand that perhaps Batchelor was getting in a last dose of hero worship before the Great Man left town.

'I believe Mr Clemens is on the beach with your father, sir. He is trying out the new Winchester repeating rifle which arrived last week; he has a small bet with Mr Grand that it isn't as good as his Sharps.'

Grand knew that once Clemens got down to some target practice, nothing would shift him short of an earthquake or fire. Olivia Clemens wouldn't be seeing him any time soon, at any rate. James would be there, watching his idol shoot cans off a log. 'Thank you, Hart. I'll see if Mr Batchelor is with them.'

A door opened from the scullery and Maisie's head peered around it. 'Master Mattie,' she said, and got a hiss from Hart for her pains. 'Mr Batchelor went for a walk in the woods, *sir.*' She laid heavy emphasis on the last word and tossed her head at Hart.

'Who with?' Grand said. He knew Batchelor wasn't one for the great outdoors, but they had been cooped up rather.

She stepped into the room and shrugged her shoulders. 'No one,' she said. 'He took some vittles in a pail, said he was going for a long walk.' She furrowed her brow. 'I asked Mrs Stallybrass if she told him about the bears . . .'

'And did she?' Grand said, urgently.

'No. She said she didn't on account of there being bears in England.' Maisie wanted to be proved right, but she didn't want Mr Batchelor to be eaten by no bear; he was a nice gentleman, when all was said and done.

'When did he go?' Grand could feel icy water down his spine. A walk in the woods out here was not a walk in the woods in England, even allowing for the bears probably – hopefully – being still higher up in the mountains. He tried to cast his mind back to when he had spent time here as a boy. When did the bears come down? It was no good trying, when all he could hear was Ira saying, 'I heard a bear coughing not a ship's length from the house last night.' Common sense told him that Ira probably didn't know a bear's cough from a pig's fart, but there was still no time to lose. One step off the path and it was easy to get lost. Two steps off the path and you had to hope those packed vittles would last a day or so. Three steps off the path and all that would be found of you would be your bleached bones, together or scattered, depending on which livestock had come your way.

Maisie looked vaguely at the clock. She had never really learned figuring. She relied on people shouting at her to tell her what she should be doing and when. 'A whiles ago,' she said, at last.

Batchelor turned to Hart, who was already draining his chocolate and getting to his feet. 'Get as many men together as you can. Everyone . . . on second thoughts, probably not Mr Zzerbe. He's still a little . . .'

'. . . he's as liquored up as it's possible to be and still be standin',' Maisie supplied.

'Yes. That. But everyone else. Are Mr Latham and Master Ira still around?'

'I believe Mr Latham is trying to arrange a boat to Appledore,' Hart said, shrugging on his coat. Grand noticed he leaned significantly to one side and Maisie helped him into the second sleeve, holding the collar with the very tips of her fingers, as if the man's back would bite. Grand wondered, with a spare bit of brain, just what the man's war wound could be, to make Maisie shy away like that. 'We suggested he ask a man who hangs around the dock. He would do it for a dollar.'

'He's already gone back, I think,' Maisie said. It was a shame she couldn't read or write; she was a gossip columnist to her fingers' ends. 'I saw him when I went out with the slops, down on the jetty.'

'And Ira?' Surely there were some able-bodied men around?

'I'm afraid I don't know, sir,' Hart said. 'But if you would like to fetch Mr Clemens, a handyman with a gun might be just what you need.'

'True.' Grand had to hand it to Hart; he knew how to organize people. It was just a matter of getting enough of them.

As a city boy born and bred, James Batchelor was not used to the silence that falls amongst trees. As he approached the edges of what he liked to think of as 'the wood', and anyone else in a five-hundred-mile radius would call Ragged Neck Forest, he could see the branches tossing in the increasing wind from off the ocean, but as soon as he was beneath them, walking on a springy carpet of pine needles and last year's shed leaves, there was a stillness which seemed to reach into his soul. He liked to think of himself as the sensitive one in Grand and Batchelor, Enquiry Agents, and that sensitivity now stretched his nerves to twanging point, as his ears pricked for any sound, his nostrils dilated to get the most of the smells around him. He had never known it before, not in London, but it really was possible, he realized, to smell the spring. There was a green smell in the air, the smell of sap on the rise, alongside the sound of buds creaking with the effort of bursting. He felt he could almost smell the warmth of the sun on the back of the red squirrel that leaned out from its frowsty winter dray and chittered at him as he walked beneath.

He had expected a path, preferably paved, but at least with a little fence with chains between the posts to mark the way, as he had seen so often in Green Park, his personal favourite because, with no water, it also had no goose droppings to nego-tiate. For this reason, he liked to walk there; if his mind wandered, he would still be at no risk of slipping. There were no horses there either, so he wouldn't be ridden down. But here, in these woods, the path was a path not so much because it was firm and dry underfoot, but because there was a narrow cutting through the trees, which otherwise crowded like importunate creditors, their hands out to catch at his clothing. The sun shone on the path, though, dust motes and small insects dancing in the light. He hummed to himself to beat back the silence; perhaps this walk was not such a good idea after all.

He had almost decided to sit and eat his lunch and then retrace his steps when he saw a flash of yellow ahead of him so vivid that he had to follow it. He felt like the hero of a fairy tale, following the magic to its source, and he increased his pace, to keep up with the sparkling yellow, white and black as it zigzagged through the trees, always keeping in the sun. Occasionally, it would pause on a low branch and let fall a liquid rill of sound, the notes tumbling over each other like water over mossy rocks. He was enchanted. Birds were London sparrows and pigeons to James Batchelor. This yellow marvel had stolen his heart.

Grand heard Sam Clemens before he saw him. He was standing back on the beach, almost at the waterline, his back to the lowering sky. He had lined up some cans on a piece of driftwood tucked close under the overhang of the surf-eroded bank and was sending them flying with every shot. Sam was as perfect a shot as Grand had ever seen; he had, or so the family legend went, never been known to miss. Andrew Grand stood back looking smug; clearly, his Winchester was knocking Clemens's Sharps out of the park. The new model was certainly impressive, its walnut stock sleek and contoured, its action crisp and reliable. But, to Grand's disappointment, there was no James Batchelor, looking on as his hero did his stuff.

'Sam!' Waiting until Clemens began reloading, Grand called and waved his arm.

'Have you come to take me on, Mattie?' Clemens asked as soon as he was near enough. 'Your father wouldn't take my bet.'

'I'm too old to make it fair,' the older man said. 'Mattie; have you kept your gun practice up in London?'

Grand didn't like to tell him that, though his gun had often been in his hand, it had always been a threat, not a weapon as these men would understand it. 'No call, Pa,' he said, quickly. 'Tell me; has either of you seen James Batchelor?'

They shrugged. 'He was at breakfast,' Clemens said, dubiously. 'I think.'

'He's gone into the woods, they say,' Grand said. 'I hoped they had it wrong.'

'Who's he with?' Clemens asked.

'He's by himself, or so I'm told. With vittles in a pail.'

'For the love of Mike, Mattie!' Clemens shouldered his gun

and started up the beach. 'That kid's from London! I guess he's looking for a park bench about now, planning to share his grub with the odd pigeon? Am I right?'

'I'm sure Mr Batchelor will be perfectly safe.' Andrew Grand was looking at both sides of the coin, as he always tried to do.

'No he won't, Pa!' Grand was hot on Clemens's heels. 'James doesn't know the first thing about being out in the woods. Sam's right. He'll be looking for the park keeper to show him the way to the nearest cab rank, by way of the public conveniences.'

Clemens was on the lawn now and calling to gardeners' boys as he walked. 'Fetch as many folks as you can. We have a man lost in the woods.'

'Lost?'

'In the woods?'

The boys looked at each other. A man lost in the woods just didn't make sense to them. Who in tarnation went out into the woods? Specially with a storm a-coming.

'Don't just stand there.' Grand was just a few steps behind. 'Find every able-bodied man you can and come to the stable yard. We have no time to waste.'

One of the boys, bolder than the rest, stepped forward. 'It ain't real safe, Mr Grand,' he said. 'The bears have come down early this year. I seen one just last night, on my way home.'

Grand's breath froze in his throat. 'Where? Where did you see one?'

The lad pointed. 'He was coming up from the jetty. They goes down there, you know, scavenge up the fish guts from where the boats come in.'

Clemens heard this and turned to Grand. 'This is bad, Mattie,' he said. 'We have no time to lose.'

James Batchelor lost sight of his magical bird when he fell over a tree root. By the time he was back on his feet, the goldfinch had flown, up through the trees on an up-draught of song. He looked around and found he was in a clearing. A nice spot to eat his food, and then he could just retrace the path and he would be back at the house in no time. He found a tree with a handy root sticking out above the fallen leaves. It even had deep moss on it, cushiony and soft. He opened his pail and took out the napkin that Mrs Stallybrass had tucked over the food. This fresh air had made him hungry and he set to with a will. Chicken, a cold veal and ham pie, cheese wrapped up in another napkin with a hunk of bread spread with sharp, salty butter. He sighed happily. So much nicer than a stuffy six-course meal with no one talking to anyone else.

By the time he got to the apple at the bottom of the pail, all that was left of the rest was a piece of lardy pastry, the veal jelly still sticking to it and some chicken bones. Batchelor dimly remembered something from his newspaper days, in a column written by Old Tobias, the Gardeners' Friend, about keeping the countryside neat by burying any waste you may leave behind. But for heaven's sake, Old Tobias lived in Coptic Street, just by the British Museum and would hardly know a tree if one reared up in front of him and bit him on the leg. So, he left the bones and the pastry where he had been sitting and set off around the clearing, looking for the way he had come.

By the time Matthew Grand had changed into some boots more suitable for looking for his friend in the woods, a small crowd had gathered in the stable yard. He had no idea his father kept so many servants here, but he was glad he did. They all looked able-bodied enough, quick on their feet and used to the terrain. Hart looked a little out of place, still wearing his indoor clothes, but he seemed keen enough so Grand forbore to send him away.

Grand climbed up on to the mounting block which was built into the stable wall and whistled to attract everyone's attention.

'Gentlemen,' he said, causing a wave of grunts of approval from the gardeners and their lads, 'thank you all for dropping what you were doing and coming here to help. Mr Batchelor has been gone for about an hour and a half now, which for one of you would be no time to be in the woods, but for him, coming from England, where there are no woods like these, it is too long. We need to find him before he wanders off the path, or worse. He's also taken his notebook. Now, I know you don't know Mr Batchelor, but I do; this means he has got an idea of who might have committed these dreadful murders . . .' more nodding from the assembly '. . . and he will be thinking hard. And when he thinks hard, he doesn't always look where he's going, so he will wander off the path more easily than we might do.'

Each man looked at his neighbour and nodded sagely. They all knew someone, or at least knew someone who knew someone who had wandered off the path and had never been seen again.

'I don't need to tell you how this works,' Grand continued. 'Spread out, but make sure you always have the man to your right and to your left in sight. Don't holler out unless you see Mr Batchelor. We have just the one gun with us, I hope – Mr Clemens is a crack shot and we'll leave it to him, if it should become necessary. We don't want people hauling off and shooting left and right; somebody's gonna get hurt that way.' Grand heard himself descending to the vernacular, but felt sure Batchelor would forgive the lapse in the circumstances. 'So, spread out, men. Let's find Mr Batchelor.'

There was one rebel yell from the crowd, but he ignored it. He knew it was Sam Clemens, trying to get a rise out of him and lighten the mood, so he let it go. Soon, the line of men were disappearing into the trees, some silently, others crashing through the underbrush; a little more woodcraft would have been nice, Grand mused, but this wasn't perhaps the time to train them in the ways of the Micmac.

Batchelor struck off down his chosen path with confidence. He certainly recognized that tree from before. He remembered that odd, bent branch and the streak of moss down one side. He swung his empty pail and tried a few verses of 'Little Maid of Arcadee', but had to admit after a while that Mr Sullivan, though undoubtedly destined for great things, didn't write for men with Batchelor's limited range of four or five notes in no particular order. After that, he was alone with the thud of his footfall and a growing certainty that, in actual fact, he had mistaken the tree and was now heading in a totally unknown direction.

The bear was hungry, the bear was ravenous. The bear's big mouth was cruel and cavernous. She was looking for something – anything – to eat, and although the chicken bones and lardy pastry were mere hors d'oeuvres, experience had taught her, deep in her hot, bear brain, that where there were picnic leavings, the picnicker was probably not far away. She bent her nose to the ground, snuffling around until she picked up the scent. She lumbered leisurely away. Another thing that her experience had taught her was that, in a race between a bear and a picnicker, there was only one winner.

EIGHTEEN

G rand had placed himself in no permanent position in the line. He needed to keep in touch with everyone and at that moment was walking alongside Sam Clemens, although he knew he would have to move on soon, to prevent him punching the writer upside the head. Clemens was bounding forward and then bending dramatically, peering at the ground. He would then stop and gaze into the distance, a hand shading his eyes, although the dappled shade of the woods, getting deeper as afternoon and the storm dimmed the sun, scarcely warranted it. Eventually, Grand had to speak out.

'Sam,' he said, wearily. 'You are taking this seriously, aren't you?'

'Sure am, son,' Clemens drawled and it was almost possible to imagine the wad of chewing tobacco in his cheek. 'Man's life's at stake.'

Grand sighed. 'Well, as long as you bear that in mind . . .'

'Odd you should say that,' Clemens said, speaking out of the corner of his mouth.

'Say what?'

'Bear. Because . . .' Clemens pointed to a patch of muddy ground on the path ahead of them and there, plumb centre, was a bear's print. In itself that would have been nothing exciting; everyone knew there were bears in these woods. It was the fact that it was overlaid on a man's boot print. And they were both heading in the same direction.

'Sam,' Grand said, pleadingly, 'can you stop playing at being an Indian tracker, now and be a proper tracker. I know you know your woodcraft; can we just have it without the fancy stuff?'

'Sure thing.' Clemens couldn't resist one last moment in character. He picked up the pace and, after a minor wobble in the line as they realized what he was doing, the men of Rye moved forward, nothing but rescue on their minds.

Ahead, in the fast-gathering gloom, Batchelor saw a wall. A *wall*! He almost sobbed with relief. He had found, if not the Grands' house, then at least someone's dwelling, and they would be able to tell him the way back. A bright idea made him smile. They might even have a gig or at least a cart and could take him back. His boots were rubbing his heels and he could do with a proper sit-down. He quickened his pace, then stopped. He thought for a moment that there were footsteps behind him, but in this damned silence, he knew his ears could play tricks. He put his hands to his mouth as a funnel as he had seen others do and called. 'Halloooo! Hallooo the house!' There was no reply, but that didn't mean no one was there. He would go and knock; on second thoughts, a much more rational behaviour anyway.

The bear had lost interest in the picnicker. There were other trails to follow, although she knew that a chipmunk, thin from its winter fast, wouldn't come close to feeding her and her two cubs waiting back in her newly scraped den. And then she heard it, calling to her. 'Halloo! Halloo the house!' Her head came up. An early supper would be very welcome. She lumbered into a run.

Clemens stopped, holding up a finger. 'Did you hear that? Someone called.'

Grand frowned. 'You tell them not to and they forget in minutes. What's the point?'

'No, it wasn't one of us, it came from over there.' Along the line, other fingers were pointing, other heads were up and the line turned forty-five degrees to the northwest and picked up speed. 'Over there. Run.' There was no need to run, except that feeling at the base of a man's spine when he feels that urgency. Could it be, Clemens wondered as he jumped over a fallen log, that, despite all evidence to the contrary, man could smell panic on the wind as well as any woodland creature? Whatever was causing it, every man in the line was running now, converging on the spot.

Batchelor broke into the clearing and could have cried. The wall he had seen was just that, a single wall, all that was left of the house which once had stood there. He realized that the path he had been following had once been the road to this forgotten hovel. He recalled Celia Thaxter telling him something; what was it? About a family, or two families, was it, wiped out by an attack by Indians. The hairs on the back of his neck stood up. He hardly dare look round. The muscles of his shoulders had grown stiff with tension during the walk, but now they refused to work at all and so all he could do was turn his eyes this way and that. To his left, he could still see the outline of the house, blurred now by the encroaching wood. A larch had fallen and lay at an angle across the broken wall. To his right, he could see grey stones, regular, recognizable the world over. Graves. Then, stiff shoulders or no, a sound made him spin around.

Batchelor was no good at judging distances. He had always had a healthy respect for Grand, who would unhesitatingly jump over or from obstacles in his way, but Batchelor didn't have the skill. All he knew was that the bear in front of him – and although he was no zoologist, he knew a bear when he saw one – was much nearer than any bear had any right to be. It was looking for him, that much he knew. It was swinging its head from side to side but suddenly stopped. It raised its muzzle and snuffed the air, scenting him out. Then, it took two giant bounds forward and raised itself on its hind legs, paws in the air. He had seen bears do this in zoos and at the circus and noticed for the first time how the lack of chain made a big difference in a bear's threat. Bear with chain; no threat. Bear with no chain and so close he could feel and smell its breath; bowel-looseningly terrifying. He took a deep breath and leaned back. He hadn't wanted a bear with its mouth open and its eyes gleaming to be his last sight on earth. Accordingly, he closed his eyes, gritted his teeth and waited for the first bite. Or would it be claw? In the final analysis, did it matter?

Matthew Grand, along with most of the men of the line, held his breath as they came out of the trees. It was a picture that would be imprinted on his mind for the rest of his life, he knew. There stood James, annoying much of the time, it was true, but the most loyal friend a man could want, in front of a bear, her winter coat still hanging from her back in sheets, the sleek fur of summer showing through. Her forepaws were raised and he could hear her visceral growl of warning. Then, almost before he could process the scene, there was a sharp crack of Clemens's Winchester echoing off the trees and the bear threw up her head, dropped to all fours and ran for her life.

Batchelor didn't move but Grand did. He turned to Clemens, words on his lips he never thought he would say. 'Sam,' he whispered, 'you missed.'

'I missed because some cuss fired first and spooked her,' the author said, looking angrily along the line. 'Who did that?' he shouted. 'Who fired a gun? We said *no* guns!'

All along the line, shoulders shrugged, heads shook.

Grand patted Clemens on the back. 'You missed, Sam,' he said. 'Blame Pa's rifle.' He looked at the Winchester, gleaming in the man's hands. 'That'll never catch on,' he said.

'There was another shot. Didn't you hear it?'

'I heard an echo,' Grand admitted.

'Another shot,' grunted Clemens and beat through the brush to where Batchelor still stood, beginning now to tremble slightly from shock. 'C'mon, boy!' Clemens called to him. 'She's gone. Let's get you home for some brandy.'

'I have brandy, sir.' Miraculously, Hart was at Batchelor's elbow, a silver hip flask in his hand. 'If I may . . .' and he offered the open flask to Batchelor, who took it and drank greedily.

Grand joined them. 'Hart,' he said, laughing with relief, 'you certainly are the perfect butler.'

'Thank you, sir,' Hart said, with a small bow. 'I do aim to give satisfaction.'

Clemens jabbed a thumb at him. 'Is this cuss real?' he asked. 'I just thank the Lord that Livy hasn't met him; she'd want one just the same, for sure.'

'I'm not sure they still make them like Hart,' Grand chuckled.

Batchelor, parted from the hip flask with difficulty, was now shaking in earnest. 'We must get him back to the house,' Clemens said. 'The walk will calm him down anyway, but he needs a rest. Boys!' he gestured to a couple of gardeners' lads, 'walk ahead, willya, so Mr Batchelor can see there's no critters. And you two, do the same behind. Now, come on, James, let's be moving. Tell me, have you read *Roughing It*?'

Batchelor didn't like to admit it, but he tried not to lie to authors; it was so easy to be caught out. So he shook his head.

'Thought not,' Clemens said with a grin. 'Because if you had, you'd never have wandered off into these here woods. You thinking of writing a novel, I expect.' In Clemens's experience, most people were.

And so, by fits and starts, Mark Twain the storyteller took James Batchelor, the shivering enquiry agent, back to the sanity and sanctity of the stable yard at Rye.

There were two policemen in the yard when the party got back. Chief Savage was standing, arms folded and legs planted like an ox in the furrow. Sergeant Roscoe was leaning on the stable wall, swinging a pair of gleaming handcuffs from one hand.

'Andrew,' Liza Grand was there as well, an anxious look on her face, her fingers twirling. 'These gentlemen—'

'Have a duty to perform,' Savage finished the sentence for her. His eyes scanned the crowd of men. Servants. Two Grands. Sam Clemens. One Limey, looking a bit green around the gills. 'Where is Ira Grand?' he asked.

There were murmurs and turnings of heads. Ira was here a minute ago. Wasn't he?

'Why do you want him?' Andrew Grand asked.

'We'll get to that,' Savage said. He crossed the yard and his stare made the boot boys scatter. Even Jackieboy Thornton, not given to the skitters, decided he was in the way and stood aside.

'Matthew Grand,' Savage looked his man in the face, 'I have a warrant here for your arrest.' He half pulled a telegram form out of his pocket and then stuffed it back again. He knew he was on thin ice; there were plenty of bankers in this house but, mercifully, no lawyers.

'On what charge?' Grand asked him.

'The murder of Josiah Grand, not a spit's distance from where we are standing now. Sergeant, the cuffs, if you please.'

There was uproar, everybody shouting and gesticulating. In the end, it was Matthew Grand himself who silenced it, by raising his hand. Above the hubbub, he had heard the snick of the Winchester's lever arm and he didn't want the situation to get out of hand. 'It's all right,' he said. 'There's been a misunderstanding.'

'There certainly has,' Batchelor said. He had faced a bear already this morning; a Boston city cop held no terrors for him. 'Why do you want Ira?'

Grand looked at him. That hardly seemed the point. It was his old friend who had just been accused of murder, not . . .

'To arrest him for the murder of Magda Galatski, also known as . . .'

'Beggin' your pardon, sir.' All eyes turned to Maisie. She was sheltering in the lee of Mrs Stallybrass, standing near the kitchen door and safety. Suddenly aware that she was the centre of attention, she shrank back and the cook put a hefty arm around her shoulders.

'Out with it, girl,' Hart snapped. 'If you know anything . . .' His hands were firmly in his pockets, probably because he was fighting the instinct to throttle the wretched woman.

'I seen Mr Ira a-rowing away from the jetty, taking that Limey across to Appledore.'

'Latham?' Batchelor frowned. He was the only other Limey left.

'When?' Savage asked.

Maisie had no real concept of time, but hazarded a guess. 'Not ten minutes ago, sir,' she said, with every appearance of certainty.

'Right, Grand.' Savage was still facing Matthew. 'You're coming with us.'

'Where?' Grand asked.

'Appledore. I'm not leaving you here and I'm not letting your bastard of a cousin get away.'

'I'm coming too,' Batchelor insisted.

'Suit yourself,' Savage said. 'Do I need the cuffs, Mr Grand?'

'No, Chief,' Grand said. 'You don't.'

'Mr Hart, Mr Hart!' All eyes turned to Lottie, the youngest maid, her face flushed, her heart pounding. She had just run from the lawn and, realizing that her ankles were on display, let her skirts fall quickly.

'What?' All this dash and fire could rattle even the most perfect butler.

'There's a signal, sir. A distress call from Smuttynose.'

In a body, the men of the household and the guests, with little Lottie leading the way, dashed beyond the stable block and looked out to sea. The girl was right. Above the distant black rocks, a beacon flared. Once, twice. Again.

'Can anybody read it?' Batchelor asked.

'Sam?' Matthew Grand turned to the writer.

'Your eyes may not be as good as mine, Mattie, but my Morse is rustier, I'll wager.'

Grand narrowed his eyes. The flashes were erratic, disjointed. 'Help us,' he murmured, trying to make sense of it against the rolling black of the clouds. 'Murder. Wagner.'

'Who's that?' Savage asked.

'Handyman,' Batchelor told him.

'He's the cuss who gave Jemima Zzerbe the vapours, Chief,' Roscoe said. 'I thought she was overreacting.'

'You could still be right,' Savage said. 'There's nothing in that message to say he has done murder. He could be the victim. He could be the one sending the message.'

'That's unlikely,' Batchelor pointed out. 'I doubt he's literate on paper, let alone in Morse code.'

Savage looked the man up and down. Amateurs! 'Who else is on the island?' he asked the crowd in general.

'The Hontvets,' Andrew Grand told him. 'Norwegians. But the menfolk are fishermen – they're often away.'

'Can anybody row?' Savage asked.

'We all can,' Grand told him, ignoring the look of mute horror on Batchelor's face.

'We don't know what we're going to find over there,' Savage said. 'Grand, Batchelor, you're with me and Roscoe.'

'If it's Wagner,' Hart said, 'you'll need me.'

'Why?' Savage asked.

'When he's drunk – which is often – he only speaks German. How is *your* German, Chief Savage?'

The chief shrugged. 'All right. Let's get a couple of boats. Mr Clemens, if you can use that,' he pointed to the rifle, 'you might be useful.'

'Say,' Roscoe fell into step with Clemens as they made their way to the jetty. 'Is that the new Winchester I've been reading about?'

At the jetty, Batchelor looked dubiously out to sea. The dark clouds and rough sea of earlier were no more. Now, it was one maelstrom, the water seeming to rise up and meet the clouds halfway. The wind blew straight inland, whipping Clemens's moustache into a life of its own and taking Roscoe's hat and flinging it to the seabirds flailing their way to a cushier billet in the town. Two small boats tossed on their ropes at the jetty, the oars lashed in place in the rowlocks. Roscoe was already feeling sick, with the slight movement of the boards beneath his feet, and he hadn't stepped into a boat yet.

'So,' Savage said, looking at Grand, 'you can all row, eh?'

'Well,' Grand offered, '*I* can row. I expect Sam can row. Sam?'

Clemens couldn't hear over the wind, but nodded anyway. There wasn't much call on a Mississippi riverboat, but anything his old friend Tom Blankenship could do, Mark Twain could do better.

'James can't row, that I know for sure. And Hart has some kind of . . . I'm not sure. A war wound of some kind, or so I believe. So, he can't row either. Can either of you?'

Savage shook his head. 'Of course we can't,' he said, as though Grand were simple. 'Why should we be able to row?'

'Because you come from Boston,' Grand suggested. 'There's almost as much water as land in Boston.'

'Not the bit I have anything to do with,' Savage told him in no uncertain terms. 'Strictly sidewalks, Roscoe and me. Will one rower be enough in each boat?' He had done the maths and could see there was not room for all of them in just one.

'Of course it won't,' Grand said. 'Look at the water, man. We shouldn't be setting out at all. It's suicide, more or less.'

'It's water,' Savage said. 'And to get to an island, there is no choice, as far as I know. So . . . where do I get some more rowers, then?'

'There might be some over in the boat sheds,' Grand said, pointing. 'They'll be mending nets or something, waiting, like sane people, for this storm to pass over. You'll never get them to come.'

Savage reached inside his coat and pulled out his badge, gleaming dully in the dying light. 'This will get them to come,' he said, 'or they'll see the inside of a cell. Obstructing the police in the pursuance of their enquiries.'

Grand sighed and let him go. If he knew his Rye fishermen, Savage would get a dusty answer, but no; after just a few minutes, he came back, with four burly men in waterproofs behind him.

'I'm frankly astonished, Savage,' Grand admitted. 'I would have bet good money that you would have had no takers.'

'I'm glad you saved your loot,' Savage said, with a sudden grin, 'because you have kindly agreed to pay them fifty dollars each for this trip.'

'Return?' Grand asked, sardonically.

'With any luck,' Savage agreed. 'Now, let's get on. Is that light still flashing?'

Grand looked towards the island. Now, it just said 'Help. Help Us. Help,' over and over again. 'My father is rigging up a signal at the house,' he said. 'I think he has in mind a system of window blinds or something. He will let them know we're on the way.'

'Is that wise, Chief?' Roscoe butted in. 'What if it's a trap?'

Savage thought for a moment. 'Bit elaborate, Roscoe, isn't it?' he said at last. 'I don't think we can assume anything; we must just go out there and deal with whatever we find. Now,' he turned to the four fishermen, standing behind him waiting like automata. 'We need to divide up so the boats are equally laden. Roscoe and I must have Mr Grand with us. So that means that . . .'

'No,' Batchelor was adamant. 'I travel with Matthew. We're partners and that's that.'

Savage looked at the fishermen, their faces shaded by their

sou'westers. 'Does it make any difference, how many are in the boat?' he asked.

One stepped forward and spoke for the others. 'As long as everyone sits still, no funny business, no panicking, we'll be there in no time, no matter how many in the boat. O' course, another coupla dollars . . .'

Savage looked grim.

'No offence, just saying,' the fisherman said. 'But no matter how many's in each boat, every minute we're jawing here makes getting over to Smuttynose less likely. So everyone in a boat of your choosin', gentlemen, and we'll be away.'

The boat of Batchelor's choosing was in plain sight, pulled way up the beach and turned turtle, waiting out the storm. But he doubted that was the one the fisherman had in mind. So he stepped down into the bucking coffin tied loosely to the rickety jetty and sat down and closed his eyes. He grabbed the splintering seat so hard that his knuckles turned white, braced his feet against the keelson, though to him it was nothing of the sort, just being a solid piece of wood that he hoped would fool his terrified mind into believing he was on dry land.

Of all the men on the ocean that day, Batchelor was by far the most terrified, but on such a visceral level that he didn't think he would die; that would have been a very good outcome as far as he was concerned. At least it would make the pitching and tossing eventually stop. What he hated the most was that moment – only a second or even less, though it felt like a lifetime – when the boat would hang apparently motionless in the air as it crested a wave, which was immediately sucked from beneath the keel by the storm. Then the boat would crash down, jarring everyone in her from the heels to the top of the head. And then – and this was the bit that Batchelor could hardly bear – no sooner had every nerve in his body finally stopped jangling, but it would all happen again, and again, and again.

Silently, fervently, James Batchelor began to pray.

He had never been so glad to feel firm ground under his feet in his life. In fact, the ramshackle jetty at the island's hip was not as firm as all that – it creaked with every step – but at least it was not an open rowing boat.

On the headland above them, a man stood, soaked through with the rain and spray. He held a lantern in his hand, which he swung to welcome them. 'Thank God,' he said, his accent strong with the shock of what he had just seen, his voice battling with the wind.

'Who are you?' Savage breasted the rise from the beach and yelled as hard as he could. The wind was less fierce here, in the lee of the island's highest point, but still almost enough to blow a man over.

'I am Johann Hontvet,' the man said. 'My family . . .' and his voice tailed away.

Savage waited until the others from the boat joined him. The second boat was making fast on the jetty and that crew would be with them soon enough. The fishermen would pull their craft further up the beach when they could. This storm could go on for days or blow itself out in hours; not even men who made their living from the sea could tell.

Clemens and Hart joined them, puffing up the path from the beach. Hontvet was babbling, mostly in a tongue that none of the others understood, but the police and the enquiry agents had noticed the blood on his cuffs; no amount of rain was going to wash that off.

The house squatted low to the ground, to make the most of the shelter afforded by the hill behind it. The lighter sky out to the east was not the dawn, not yet, although the journey had taken longer than it would have in calm weather. It was the reflection of the sunset over the mainland to the west, pale pink and blue, as if there was not the storm out of hell tearing the skies apart over Smuttynose and the other Isles of Shoals.

Batchelor looked up, the rain stabbing his eyes and making him blink. There were no trees on this side of the hill, so that was a mercy; it would be a while before he could look at a tree without flinching. But that very lack made the island all the more unwelcoming. Even on a sunny day, no birds would sing on Smuttynose, no soft breeze would ruffle the petals of wild-flowers. All that Smuttynose would ever have to offer would be the whistle of the wind, the gulls' cry like that of a soul in torment and a bitter, hard life for all who lived there. With a shudder, Batchelor turned towards the house.

As they reached the back door, a figure half stumbled out into the yard. Clemens's Winchester came up to the level.

'It's all right!' Hontvet shouted, the rain streaming down his face and burning his eyes. 'It's Ivan, my brother-in-the-law.'

'In there,' Ivan pointed to the house, then turned and vomited over a wall that skirted the swimming yard.

Savage went in first, Roscoe at his elbow and Grand and Batchelor behind that. All of them caught their breath. The room had been ransacked, drawers pulled out, cupboard doors hanging open. One had been pulled off its hinges and hung down at a rakish angle across a window which was blind to the black, rain-lashed night. In one corner, a mattress had been ripped open, pillows slashed. Feathers still floated in the air at the men's entrance and more would have twisted in the chill, wet breeze, were it not for the fact that they lay, sodden and scarlet, in the blood that was everywhere. It puddled on the floorboards, seeping into the hand-made mats. It sprayed over the walls and the woodwork. The room was a slaughterhouse.

Roscoe crossed himself and muttered something under his breath. Savage crouched as clear of the blood as he could. Two women lay dead. The first was Karen Hontvet. Even with her skull battered to a pulp, Batchelor recognized the face. It was masked with blood and the eyes were closed. The lips were pursed, as though in mild rebuke. Her nightgown was drenched in her blood and one hand was extended, as though reaching for the sister-in-law who lay to her left. Anethe Christensen was half wedged in a corner and it was obvious that she had been rolled off the mattress by whoever it was who had ripped it. The shift was thrown up, revealing the woman's nakedness.

'Cover that,' Savage growled and Roscoe edged the material down. All four men in that room knew that this was anything but procedure, but somehow, it was the right thing to do.

Savage stood up. Apart from the wind howling outside and the rattle of the clapboard cladding of this little house, the only sound was the ticking of the clock, something the Hontvets had brought with them from the old country, as they sailed west to begin their new lives. 'Grand, Batchelor,' the chief said, as though each syllable cost him money, 'your thoughts?'

The enquiry agents looked at each other. Could this be right? The professional seeking advice from the amateurs?

'Our friend was looking for something,' Grand said.

'Money?' Batchelor was thinking aloud. 'Valuables?'

'He was disturbed,' Grand went on, 'in more ways than one.' He peered closer at what was left of Karen Hontvet's head. 'Axe,' he said. 'He used an axe.'

'And he went that way,' Batchelor said, noting the bloody boot-prints disappearing into the next room.

'Wagner,' a voice behind them whispered. Johann Hontvet had forced himself to enter the bedroom again, the little private world that had been his and Karen's. 'It was Wagner, the handyman.'

'You saw him?' Savage asked.

'I did.' Ivan Christensen had steeled himself too and was standing alongside his brother-in-law, pale and shaking. 'He must have thought we wouldn't be here.'

'We wouldn't have been,' Johann said, 'but the weather drove us back. The first thing we knew there was a problem, we saw Wagner's boat floating on the tide.'

'It must have broken its moorings in the harbour,' Ivan said.

'You mean, he's still around?' Savage asked. 'On the island?'

'Must be,' Hontvet said. 'Nobody could cross even to Appledore in seas like this without a boat.'

Savage looked into Christensen's face. 'You're *certain* it was this Wagner?' he asked.

Christensen nodded. 'I'd know that mad, drunk bastard anywhere.'

'Right. You come with us. Mr Hontvet, stay here. I know this is hard for you, but you must not touch anything in this room. Do you understand?'

Hontvet nodded.

'Do one thing more for us, Mr Hontvet,' Grand said. 'Send a message to the mainland. Let them know we've arrived safely, at least.'

Out in the rain, Clemens and Hart were waiting, pressed against the wall to gain as much shelter as was possible from the eaves which overhung from the low roof.

'Sam,' Grand said, tapping the Winchester. 'We're going hunting.'

NINETEEN

They spread out as they had in the woods, but this time the ground was open and, Batchelor hoped, there were no bears. Christensen set the pace, leaving Hart to keep up as best he could at the far end of the line.

Some scrubby bushes lined a farm track, which wound around the side of the hill. The men moved cautiously here. The bushes weren't that high, but a man with an axe and murder in his heart could hide there with ease. Christensen's mind was a blur and he felt himself trembling, glad for the rain so that the others couldn't see his tears. Grand was doubly sorry he had left his pocket Colt back at the house. Roscoe was regretting that neither he nor Savage was armed. Sergeant O'Farrell signed out the guns and the detectives rarely carried them. Roscoe couldn't remember the last time he had fired a shot in anger. So, Sam Clemens it was. Roscoe hoped that what he had read in the papers about the man was true, although the most crack of shots would be hard pressed in this wind, rain and murk. One firearm between the six of them, but at least there *were* six of them. And they were chasing just one man.

'There!' Christensen yelled, pointing to a rocky outcrop that jutted over the sea. 'He's making for the Point.'

Grand saw him now and so did Roscoe. Wagner was a ferret of a man, wiry and shrivelled, as though the driving rain were shrinking him like a prune. His forelock, complete with the livestock that so repelled Jemima Zzerbe, was plastered to his forehead and over one eye with the rain, though he dashed at it with a dripping hand as he ran, trying to clear his vision. He saw them too, turned and snarled, shouting something lost on the wind as he stumbled on.

'Shoot him!' Hart shouted at Clemens's elbow. The rifle came up level, but Wagner had disappeared below the rocky horizon and the others gave chase.

'Watch your step here,' Christensen warned. 'It's a sheer drop to the sea on the other side.'

It was. Batchelor saw it first, as his feet slithered on the wet surface of the stones. He steadied himself, flailing briefly with both arms before jumping on to the next rock and the next, like a rather amateur mountain goat.

'Wagner!' Savage bellowed, cupping his mouth with both hands. 'This is the police. Give it up, man, you don't have a chance.'

Again, the turn and the snarl and he ran on.

'James,' Grand grabbed his friend's sodden sleeve, 'can you head that way, down the slope? I'll take the high ground here and we can catch him in a pincer movement.'

'Ah, you old soldiers,' Batchelor tutted; but it made sense. Taken all in all, the grass looked less lethal than the rocks he had almost dived from headfirst and he dashed off. The others ignored him, Christensen keeping pace with Savage, Roscoe in their wake and Hart struggling to keep up.

Almost immediately, Batchelor realized the error of his ways. The ground was steeper than he had imagined, *far* steeper, and the grass was slippery and wet, without a single foothold. He found himself running headlong, taking huge bounds and screaming as he realized he couldn't stop himself. The ground bobbed in his vision as the wind and rain drove him on. He tried to dig in his heels, anything to slow his progress, but nothing worked. In the end, all he could see was a grey mist where the sea met the lowering sky somewhere ahead, lit by the eerie false sunset. The land was disappearing fast for the simple reason that James Batchelor was fast running out of land. And he leapt into the sky.

Grand's boots slid and clattered on the rocks and he gashed his cheek, scraping past the upright stones in a hurry. The rain washed the blood into his mouth and he tasted salt, from the spray as well as his injury. The stones jutted above him like giants, guarding Smuttynose from the whirling winds of the sea, standing like sentinels against the weather. He jumped down into a clearing and felt a sickening slap across his head. He rolled across the sodden moss and knelt upright, his vision reeling. He was in a pocket in a stone circle, with the sea below him to the right and the left. Over him stood Wagner, an axe in his hand, his eyes gleaming. Grand felt the blood trickling down his temple and was grateful, briefly, that it must have been the blunt side of the weapon that had caught him and not the blade itself. The detective in him realized at once that this two-handed axe could not have been the one that Wagner had used on Magda and Uncle Josiah; it was far too big. The damage done to the women of Smuttynose proved that.

'*Legen Sie!*' a clear voice carried over the wind.

Both men in the rock circle looked up, but only one understood it. Sam Clemens, like all good shots, had both eyes open along the Winchester's sight.

'Do it!' Hart hissed at his elbow. 'Drop the axe.' Clemens didn't flinch, but he didn't like the urgency in Hart's command. He'd heard it before and seen it, too – the thrill of the chase, the excitement of the hunt. It brought out monsters in even the best of men.

'The axe, Mr Wagner,' Clemens said, pleasantly. 'Let it go. Now.'

Only Grand heard it, but the handyman let out a giggle, like a naughty boy caught with his hand in the cookie jar. The next thing he knew, Wagner had swung the axe horizontally under the kneeling man's chin, pressing on his throat and forcing his head upright. At the same time, he pressed his knee into Grand's back. The detective was too groggy to resist, his hands trailing uselessly in the wet moss, his throat clicking and rasping as the pressure increased.

'You!' Wagner called. 'Drop the rifle. And step wide of that bastard; he's a killer.'

Clemens's eyes instinctively swivelled to his left, but the rifle hadn't moved.

'Shoot him!' Hart shrieked, 'For God's sake . . .'

There was the bark of a gun and a whiff of smoke drifting through the rain. Wagner let go of the axe as the bullet hit the iron blade and ricocheted into who knew where, the man's hands stinging with the impact on the metal. This was Grand's moment. Dripping with blood as he was, blurred though his vision, he flung himself sideways and Wagner toppled with him. Both men rolled sideways in the moss, grappling for the axe, until Savage and Roscoe separated them and the sergeant's cuffs clicked into position behind the axeman's back, pinning him to the ground with his knee.

'Good work, Grand,' Savage said. 'But don't think this lets you off any hooks. And you, Mr Clemens,' he called, 'nice shooting.'

'It was,' Clemens agreed, 'but it wasn't one of mine.' He felt the warm steel of Hart's revolver against his temple and let the perfect butler slide the Winchester from his grasp.

Grand frowned, forcing his eyes to focus. He slowly clambered to his feet. 'And I'll wager you weren't going for the axe-head, were you, Hart?'

'No,' the man said, 'I was aiming for that degenerate the nice policeman has placed in handcuffs.'

'Why?' Grand asked.

'Because he killed the ladies, of course,' Hart said. 'Because he murdered people in my house. Why wait for the hangman's rope?'

'You're an expert, Sam,' Grand said, 'when it comes to guns. When Hart fired just now, had you heard that sound before?'

'I had, Mattie,' Clemens said. 'It's an Adams, not unlike the piece that Mr Hart is holding against my head right now.'

'You weren't shooting at Wagner then, were you, Hart?'

'I was aiming for the bear,' Hart said.

'No,' Grand was moving forward, slowly, inexorably. 'You were aiming for Batchelor. Why was that, Hart? Did you think he knew something about you?'

'Don't come any closer,' Hart growled, his accent coming to the fore. 'This man may be a famous author, but I guarantee he will write nothing more if I pull this trigger.'

'Are you going to shoot us all, Hart?' Savage asked, creeping closer to the man too.

'Why not?' Hart said. 'After all, there are five of you and I have five shots left in the chamber. I can reload for Wagner. He's not going to cause me any trouble in his handcuffs, is he?'

All of them except Christensen were edging forward now, keeping their eyes fixed firmly on Hart.

'What did you mean, Wagner?' Grand asked. 'When you said, "He's a killer." Who did Hart kill?'

'Don't listen to him,' Hart hissed. 'He's a madman. He has

the blood of the women of Smuttynose on his hands. You can't believe a word he says.'

'Wagner?' Grand repeated.

'I heard about what happened at the Rye house,' the German said. 'Magda the maid and old Mr Grand. They both knew. That's why they had to die.'

Hart snarled something in German, guttural and harsh, and Wagner sneered at him.

'That's why you wanted to come with us to the island, isn't it?' Savage realized. 'You didn't want to talk sweetly to Wagner in his native tongue; you wanted to shut him up in case he talked.'

'What did they know, Wagner?' Grand asked. The man was still on his knees with Roscoe standing over him and Grand had no intention of turning round.

'About the fire. The one in Boston. Thirteen dead and God alone knows how much damage, all because Herr Hart here likes to play with matches!'

Hart growled in his throat and pressed the gun harder into Clemens's temple. 'Magda was Michalina in those days,' he said. 'A street harlot. She saw me in Summer Street that day, with the matches in my hand. There I was and it could have been so perfect; I had certainly planned it to perfection. Even better than Chicago.'

'Chicago?' Savage said. 'You set that one too?'

'Don't believe what they tell you about arsonists, Chief,' Hart said, as calmly as though he were planning the day's domestic arrangements. 'We don't all dribble and whimper. We don't have trouble with the ladies, either – in fact, that's how Michalina recognized me so fast: I had been a very regular and, if I may say so, popular client.' He preened a little, but never released the pressure of the gun. 'I am perfectly normal. I just like to watch things burn, that's all.'

'But you got yourself hurt, didn't you?' Grand asked. He was almost close enough to reach Hart now, but not quite and, even with the rain stinging his eyes, he could see the man's knuckles whiten on the pistol grip. 'That's why you can't fetch and carry. Why you keep your cuffs lowered. That's why Maisie couldn't bear to see . . . what did she call it? Your horrible skin?'

'Hello!' A voice from behind him made Hart's concentration flicker. Clemens threw himself sideways as Hart's gun barked again, the shot whistling harmlessly into the sky. Grand lunged for the man, knocking the pistol from his grip and pummelling him into the moss. Savage and Christensen were on him in a flash, pinioning his arms and hauling him upright. Grand grabbed the man's cuff and ripped upwards, revealing the shrivelled skin beneath, with the knobbed scars of the fire.

'But why Josiah?' Grand said quietly. 'Magda I can under-stand, though hardly condone. She caught you. What did she do? Threaten blackmail?'

'I never expected to see her again.' Hart was beaten; he didn't struggle or even raise his head. 'She knew me as soon as she came into the house, struggling under all the boxes and bags her fool of a mistress brought with her; I could see it in her eyes. As soon as she could get away, she found me, told me she recognized me. And no, she didn't blackmail me, not then. Don't forget, she had as much to lose as I. Believe it or not, she loved that souse of a master of hers. She didn't want to lose her place. But I knew that when he left her, as leave her he would, she would be back, demanding, threatening. What better time to kill her than when the house was full of suspects?' He shrugged as best he could, held fast by the two men.

'And Josiah?' Grand persisted. The old man had not been perfect, but hadn't deserved to die like that, or so soon. He still had a lot of drinking to do.

'I heard him,' the perfect butler said. 'Saying things. Hinting. Things he knew. Things he'd seen. How he knew many of the ladies of the night back in Boston. What if he'd known Magda? What if she'd told? I couldn't take that chance.'

Sam Clemens had been spoiling to hit someone for some time. Having a muzzle to his temple will do that to a man. With no warning, he hauled off and caught Hart under the chin with an uppercut that would have laid out a mule. The man went down like a poleaxed steer and lay insensible on the moss.

'That was a nice punch,' Savage said, admiringly. 'Especially for a famous author.'

Clemens smiled and flexed his hand. 'That hurt,' he remarked. 'I'm out of practice. Excuse me, Mattie, if I stole your thunder.

But Josiah didn't deserve to die of bragging, because that's all it was. He was feeling out of it, I could tell. He was no longer the gay blade, the heavy swell, the womanizer, the story teller. In that house, gathered for Martha's wedding, were men who could out-drink, out-whore, out-gab him and not even pause for breath. So he pretended he knew something. And it killed him.' He turned to Savage. 'If you need me for a witness,' he said, 'you'll need to be quick. I go on tour again in three weeks. But who am I kidding? I'll be there. I want to see this bastard swing.'

They all looked down at Hart, groaning now and struggling to get up.

'Look,' a voice said again, 'would someone mind telling me what the hell is going on?' James Batchelor was still standing by the rock circle, the sea at his back, his jacket ripped and his face bruised. 'So far today, I've met a bear, seen the most ghastly sight of my life and fallen halfway down a sheer cliff face. And I haven't even included the crossing to this dreadful island; I'm hoping to forget that, given time. Can it get any worse?'

'Cheer up, James,' Grand smiled in spite of it all. 'You've just helped solve two murders.' He glanced back at Wagner. 'Actually, make that four.'

'And there's more good news, gentlemen,' Roscoe said, raising a finger in the air. 'Listen.'

They all turned their faces to the sea.

'What?' Clemens said. 'I can't hear anything?'

'The wind is dropping,' the sergeant said. 'The journey back won't be too bad at all. We'll hardly notice the swell.'

'Speak for yourself,' Batchelor muttered and stood aside for the policemen to start the descent. He wasn't going to go first down a slope, not for a long, long time.

There was no question of drawing straws. In the scheme of things, such was the gulf between the chief of police and humble sergeant, it was inevitable that it should be Roscoe who stayed behind. Smuttynose, so curiously named, so black and wild, had become a murder scene, and somebody in authority had to take charge. Savage would send men, a doctor and all the paperwork as soon as he could. In the meantime, it was up to

Roscoe to cope with the distraught Norwegian fishermen as
best he could.

No one spoke on the return journey and, apart from the moaning
wind and the lapping water, the only sound was the grunting
of the oarsmen, breaking their backs against the rolling deep.
An army had gathered on the jetty, Andrew Grand at their
head. He scanned the boat party. Thank God, Matthew was all
right. Not that the old man had any intention of letting his boy
know how relieved he was. He could rely on his wife to do
that. Liza Grand was all over her boy, smothering him with
kisses and crying. And, though neither of them knew it, Annie
was crying too, looking out from her room under the eaves,
watching the strange light creep over the sea and bathe the
beach in gold. She shook her head. She had no idea what had
happened on Smuttynose; just that the sea had delivered two
of its sons over the last days – first Ira and now Mattie. Annie
had never doubted that there was a God. He spoke to her every
day. He was speaking to her now.
Andrew Grand came face to face with Savage, linked by the
wrist to Waldo Hart. 'What is the meaning of this?' he asked.
Help like Hart hardly grew on trees.
'It's a long story, Mr Grand,' Savage said. 'And it's not one
I care to repeat with ladies present.' He tugged on the cuffs and
dragged Hart with him. All the men were soaked through but
only Batchelor was shivering.
As Hart reached Mrs Stallybrass, prim and starched in
her apron, she instinctively reached out a hand. 'Waldo?' she
whispered. He looked at her, his face ashy grey, as a man will
when he is facing the gallows. She let her hand fall and watched
him as they trudged on up to the house.
'Land's sake!' a female voice said. Batchelor knew instinctively that the words were aimed at him. 'Mr Botched, you're
wet through. Look at how those pants are clinging! C'mon, let
me help you out of those clothes. I hope the fire's drawing in
the house.'
One by one, Matthew Grand, Chief Savage and Sam Clemens
turned to look at her. James Batchelor was looking at Helene
Waterford already, showing the whites of his eyes like a startled

gelding under fire for the first time. She smiled broadly and opened her arms wide. And deep in his sodden, shaking, exhausted soul, he heard his own words. He had met a bear. He had seen the most ghastly sight of his life, the dead of Smuttynose. He had fallen halfway down a sheer cliff. 'Can it get any worse?' he heard himself say. 'Yes,' his own voice answered, 'yes, it can.'

Hart and Wagner were locked in Andrew Grand's basement with their wrists handcuffed to the plumbing. There, they exchanged hostilities in German, each blaming the other for their predicament. Wagner had nothing but contempt for the ex-butler. The man had pompous written all over him, a smug, convicted martinet who couldn't keep his hands off matches. Hart, in return, loathed Wagner, a tramp and a drunkard who thought no more about hacking two women to death over a few measly dollars than he did about gutting fish. Savage had left them both in their wet clothes. Discomfort in this life was nothing in comparison with what they would meet in the next.

Three floors up, Grand and Batchelor, replacing the freezing waters of the Atlantic with the hot water of Andrew Grand's plumbing, soaked in their suds. Each of them, across the huge bathroom from each other, had a cigar in his mouth and a warming brandy at the bath-side. Batchelor had many reasons to be grateful to Matthew Grand, although his own timely arrival on the Smuttynose rocks earlier had, arguably, saved the man's life. No, Batchelor was grateful because, somehow, Grand had managed to extricate him from the clutches of Aunt Nell. Old Josiah's death had hit her hard, of course, but she was over that now. Life had to go on. It would soon be the Boston season and there were gowns to buy and young men to flirt with. It was a shame about the young man her talons had sunk into earlier – James Batchelor, the Limey. But Mattie had explained it to her when James was out of hearing; it was an unfortunate fact of modern life in this gilded age, but Mr Botched was not as other enquiry agents. He, Mattie, was not equally inclined, of course, and all he could do was shake his head sadly and warn members of the opposite gender that, no matter how alluring they may be, with Mr Botched, they were wasting their time.

Batchelor had no idea exactly what Grand had said to the predator in pearls, but it seemed to have done the trick. Helene Waterford had hardly given Batchelor a second glance as her brougham had finally lurched away from the front of the house.

'How will they cope, do you think?' Batchelor asked Grand. 'The family?'

Grand sighed. 'Pa will be extra careful who he selects to run the household next time,' he said. 'Mom will have her hands full with Martha's baby, always assuming Annie ever puts it down. As for Martha herself . . . who knows?'

'Chauncey-Wolsey,' Batchelor nodded, closing his eyes in the mingling steam and smoke. 'Did you ever get to the bottom of that? When I was . . . out for my walk?' They had decided without actually discussing it to keep mentions of Batchelor's bosky stroll to a minimum. Perhaps one day, in about a hundred years or so, he would be ready, but not yet. Not yet.

'I did, to an extent,' Grand told him. 'There's just one little bit of that to clear up.'

'Oh?' Batchelor opened his eyes and raised his head. Grand hadn't moved and Batchelor knew the signs. 'Leave well alone' was written in the swirling steam over his partner's head.

'Ira,' Grand had moved on. 'I guess he'll find his island somewhere, but I doubt it'll be Smuttynose now.'

'The Zzerbes,' Batchelor said. 'What of them?'

'Divorce court, I shouldn't wonder, James. You and I have seen plenty of examples of people like them.'

'And will Sam Clemens step up as a witness, do you think? He's a busy man.' Batchelor would not be the man who got in the way of the march of great American literature.

'I expect he will and then they won't need us. But anyway, I get the impression that Chief Savage is the Dolly Williamson of the Boston force. He won't want another stealing his thunder. No, he'll claim the collar was all his own work. We'd just be beetles on a shit-hill.'

'Elegantly put, Matthew,' Batchelor smiled. 'I bet Edward Latham wishes he could find a phrase like that.'

*   *   *

Grand looked out towards Smuttynose. The storm had gone and
there was no doom-laden flashing signal now. The rocks jutted
as black as ever over the purple-grey of the sea and the faint
light from Appledore flashed its reassuring sign. The light was
still turning. The world was still there. Little boats were rowing
out to Smuttynose, carrying policemen from Boston, a doctor
and several undertakers. Sergeant Roscoe would be pleased to
see them all so that he could go home and find the sidewalks
of Boston under his feet again.

But it wasn't the outgoing boats that Grand was watching;
it was the one coming towards him, curving in an arc towards
the jetty, its oars in the capable hands of Ira Grand and Celia
Thaxter. They hailed him as Ira scrambled noisily on to the
planking and hauled on the rope.

'Hello, Mattie,' Celia said.

'Celia,' he nodded to her, smiling. 'I see you've brought
Mr Latham back.'

'I have,' she said, buttoning her cape under her chin. 'I
believe he has a story he is itching to tell his readers of the
New York Times. But . . . Smuttynose. We saw the signals in
the storm but the weather meant we couldn't hail them. Or
get there, come to that. What happened?'

'Go up to the house, Celia,' Grand said. 'James Batchelor is
there. He'll be pleased to tell you.'

'James Batchelor,' she said, smiling back at him. She looked
at Grand. How typical. All her life, it seemed, she had loved
Matthew Grand. Even when she'd made the biggest mistake of
her life and married the waste of space whose name she never
mentioned. Grand didn't know that she had scanned every newspaper she could during the war, looking for his name, praying
it would not be on the Casualty Lists. And she thanked God it
never was. And now, here he was. At her elbow, but still so far
out of reach. And he was passing her on to James Batchelor.
The Limey was pleasant enough, for sure, but he was not Mattie
Grand. There could only ever be one Mattie Grand. She patted
his arm and marched away, up the sloping lawn.

'Mattie.' Ira, his knots fastened in New Bedford fashion,
came over to him. 'Smuttynose,' he said. 'What's going on?
Any news of Josiah's killer?'

'Up at the house,' Grand said. 'James Batchelor will tell you all. Or Uncle Sam; he still hasn't left.'

Ira shook his head. 'He would be a medal winner at Staying, that man,' he said, and walked off in Celia's wake.

'Mr Latham,' Grand stood in the Englishman's way. 'A word?'

'Make it a short one, Grand,' Latham said. 'I've wasted more than enough time in this hell-hole and I've got a story to write up.'

'What about?' Grand asked.

'You know perfectly well,' Latham said, lifting his cases, reduced to two now that he had had to negotiate the sea crossing in a rowing boat. 'The painter.'

'Ah, yes.' Grand dodged sideways, blocking the man's path again. 'About that . . .'

Latham sighed. 'If you're going to attempt to bribe me, Grand,' he said, putting his cases down again, 'let me advise you that you are wasting your time.'

'I am?'

'Indubitably,' Latham said. 'You see, I have hard evidence of your father's guilt.' Instinctively, he patted his coat pocket.

'Excellent,' Grand beamed. 'I'll take those, then. Make your trip back to New York all the lighter.'

'Take what?' Latham frowned.

'The letters you stole from my father's safe.'

'I?' Latham bridled. 'How dare you?'

Grand's reflexes were like lightning. He grabbed the news-paperman by his right lapel and thrust his hand into his inside left pocket. Two envelopes lay there and, suddenly, they were in the hands of an enquiry agent whose offices were three thousand miles away, in London's Strand.

'They're mine,' Latham shrieked, his voice high with irrita-tion. 'I'll sue!' Celia Thaxter was too far away to hear him. She had already turned into the yard where she had stumbled over Josiah's body an eternity before. Ira Grand heard the shout, though, and turned.

'Sue away,' Grand offered. 'They certainly don't belong to you. They're my father's. And the only way you could have them in your possession is if you took them from his safe. Rather an unusual skill, isn't it, in a journalist of your repute?'

'You bastard!' Latham hissed.

'No,' Grand said, levelly. 'I am my father's son. And without these, Mr Latham,' he tore the papers, envelopes and contents and watched them float away on the wind, twirling and eddying and finally landing on the still choppy waters of the little harbour before sinking forever beneath the waves. 'Without these, you have no evidence. And no story. Next time you want to batten on to a gullible but essentially honest old man, pick on somebody whose son doesn't do this.'

'Do what?' Latham asked, fury etched in every contour of his face.

Grand drew back his fist and swung a powerful right to Latham's jaw. The newspaperman dropped like a stone and lay still. The last shreds of Andrew Grand's incriminating evidence danced across the sands of Rye beach, to be captured by the foam-flecked fingers of the incoming tide.

Up on the ridge of the lawn, Ira Grand smiled. He had no idea what that was all about. But he had wanted to do something similar to Edward Latham ever since he had clapped eyes on him.

'My God!' Celia Thaxter found herself shaking. James Batchelor had told her all he knew, sitting alongside her on a bench in the lee of the house. He had kept his voice low and level. He had checked from time to time to make sure no one was listening. Gossip could kill in a house like this. 'That's awful,' she said. 'Just awful. Poor Josiah. Poor Magda, too, come to that.' A sudden thought struck her. 'Do you think Mark Twain will write about this? A novel, perhaps?'

'No, Miss Thaxter,' a voice made them look up. A wild-haired man with a huge moustache stood there, on his way to a waiting gig. Jackieboy Thornton was up on the perch.

'Mr Twain,' she said, eyes wide with admiration. She had met her hero at last.

'I'm sorry we didn't get a chance to become acquainted,' he said, 'what with one thing and another. James,' he shook the man's hand, 'it's been an honour, sir. And next time you're in the States, make sure you and Mattie come over to Hartford. There are two ladies in my household who'd be delighted to meet you.'

'The honour has been mine, Sam,' Batchelor said. 'And, rest assured, I will. So, you're really not going to write about the Rye murders, then? And Smuttynose?'

'Hell, no,' Clemens said. He climbed into the gig and lit a cigar. 'No,' he smiled. 'I think that title will need another name on the jacket. How about Celia Thaxter?'

Jackieboy cracked the whip and they were gone.

Celia sat without speaking for a moment, then got to her feet. Despite the time that had passed since Batchelor had last added a word to his novel, he could recognize the signs. Her fingers were twitching, feeling the pen between them. Her eyes were vague, imagining that vital first line. He smiled and patted her arm.

'Celia?' He spoke quietly, unwilling to break her mood.

She looked out to sea, her lips moving.

'Celia?' He shook her lightly.

'James. I am *so* sorry. Did you speak?'

He shook his head. 'No. I know you are anxious to get back to . . . your hotel, your father.' He knew writing was a private vice. 'One thing, though, if you would. May I ask . . . what *did* happen to your husband?'

Her eyebrows rose into her hair. 'What an extraordinary question,' she said, but she was smiling. 'Even my father never asked me that.'

Batchelor waited, but she said no more. 'So . . .?'

'What the hell,' she said, turning away towards the jetty. 'The sonofabitch went back to his wife and six children in Spokane.' She leaned in and kissed the enquiry agent's cheek and trotted off down the lawn. The last thing he heard of her was her laughter over the water above the creak of the oars and the cries of the gulls, wheeling again over the Isles of Shoals.

TWENTY

'Matthew?'

'Yes?'

'Are we there yet?'

Lying in the dark, on the top bunk, Grand sighed. 'No. Not yet. We've got another day to go, or so the steward says. We've made good time, though. We may have to wait out in Beaufort's Dyke until our berth is ready.'

As this meant almost nothing to Batchelor, there was a silence. 'Is that rough, do you think?' he asked at last.

'I don't see why it should be,' Grand said. He knew no more about the shipping lanes of the Irish Sea than his colleague did, but he liked to stay informed. 'It hasn't been rough so far. You've got to almost every meal, James. I'm proud of you.'

In his lower bunk, James Batchelor smiled to himself. He was getting quite good at this international travel lark. Another thought occurred to him. 'Did you wire Mrs Rackstraw before we left?'

'I thought I could do that from Liverpool. After all, she only needs to get a few basic provisions in. I assumed she would use the time to spring-clean the house so it should be all ready for us.'

'True.' Batchelor had no illusions about Mrs Rackstraw's basic housekeeping skills, but a man can dream. 'Well, goodnight, Matthew. Home tomorrow.' And he turned on his side in his narrow little bed and let the sea lull him to sleep.

Grand was also sleepy but fought it for a while. He hadn't really known how much he loved his family until disaster had struck them. But once everything was back on an even keel, his father gone back to Washington, Martha and her husband off to make a little nest of her own, he had realized that his place among them had healed over, the scar tissue resilient enough to mean that though they would never forget him or cease to love him, they didn't need him there any more, in their back yard. He fell asleep with a memory of his mother's kiss on his cheek.

'Auntie?'

Mrs Rackstraw loved her niece. She really did. But over the last weeks she had come to realize that loving a niece who lived in Plaistow and loving her and her three horrible children when they were under the same roof were two very different things. She had never worked so hard in her life, keeping the little horrors from swinging on the curtains, drawing on the walls and generally creating havoc and mayhem. She no longer felt quite so badly towards their poor, benighted father. 'Yes, lovie?' She tried her best not to sound frayed.

'When do you expect your gentlemen back?'

'Ooh, lovie . . .' Mrs Rackstraw's brain whirled. This was her chance to get rid of the unlovely brood, but she was too good an aunt to take advantage. 'Not for a while.' She managed to hide her sigh.

'Well . . .' the woman said, coming into the room on a waft of tobacco smoke and gin, 'I don't read too well, I know, but this telegram says . . .' She held it at arm's length and squinted at it. 'It says . . .'

Mrs Rackstraw's patience broke. 'Give it here,' she said, snatching the flimsy sheet. 'Oh, my Lord!' She spun round in a circle, arms flailing, apron strings awhirl. 'They are back tomorrow.' She looked at the date and gave a little scream. 'I'll swing for that telegram boy! This was sent yesterday. They're back today!'

Her niece, never the brightest apple in the barrel, stood there like a lump of lard. Mrs Rackstraw could have hit her, but blood in the Rackstraw family was thicker than water – just – so she managed to restrain herself. Finally, the light dawned and the woman lumbered into action. 'I'll get my traps together, Auntie. I'll call the boys.' She wandered out into the hall, calling random names until she hit on the right ones.

Mrs Rackstraw had to lean on the table to collect herself. Her heart was thumping to beat the band and she felt quite faint. She had pushed her luck so many times with her gentlemen, but she somehow knew in her bones that this would be a push too far. She swept fluttering hands over her hair and tucked errant strands under her cap. A nice cup of tea would sort it out but, before she ever even reached the kettle, the door knocker was beaten in a mad tattoo and her heart leapt into her mouth again. It wasn't Mr Grand's nor Mr Batchelor's knock, but who could tell what they might have learned in foreign parts? You heard such things.

Listening out with half an ear for the welcome sounds of her niece and the three boys scurrying out of the back door, she crossed the hall, arranging her face into a smile of welcome. She threw open the door.

'Mr Gr . . . Who in the world are you?' Surprise had made Mrs Rackstraw almost polite.

The man on the step raised his hat politely. 'Could I speak to Mr Grand or Mr Batchelor?' he asked. 'This *is* the right place for them, is it? The enquiry agents.'

'Yes. But they are away at the moment,' she remembered the script imposed on her some time ago by Grand, finally exasperated by her showing people in at all hours of the day and night without a by-your-leave. 'May I help you?'

'Well . . .' The man was a little uncertain. Dolly Williamson had told him to take the message to Grand and Batchelor, but hadn't really clarified whether it had to be delivered to them personally or not. It certainly didn't *sound* too important, but with the guv'nor you never could tell.

Mrs Rackstraw had recovered herself now and had also pegged this visitor as both a bit of a geezer and also, clearly, a plod. 'Come on, come on,' she said, starting to close the door. 'I got work to do even if you haven't.'

The man bridled. As far as he could recall, he had done nothing to cause her to be so cantankerous, but you never could tell with women her age; his wife was living proof of that. He made a decision and Dolly Williamson would have to lump it. 'I suppose I can leave a message,' he said.

'Do you want to write it down?' A bit more of her training rose to the surface.

'It's very simple,' he said. 'Can you tell them—'

'Hush!' She held up a hand. 'Is that a cab?'

He listened obediently. Sure enough, there was the sound of

wheels, hoofs and the usual incoherent cries of a cabbie coming nearer. But London was full of noises like that, so he turned back to the woman, who already seemed to have forgotten him, as she was leaning back into the hall, a hand cupped round her ear.

He coughed and she turned back to him. 'Yes, it's a cab,' he said, 'but the message is very simple; tell them not to worry about that case Sergeant Jonas came to see them about because . . .'

The cab had drawn up outside the house and the cabbie had jumped down to open the door for two dishevelled-looking, travel-stained passengers, one tow-haired and muscular, the other darker and slender. Mrs Rackstraw let out a sigh of relief. If she had no squeaks narrower than this in her life, she would be happy. All she needed to do now was to shut up this gabbling police idiot. The young masters mustn't know she had stopped an important message from getting through. She turned to the man.

'Case?' she asked, acidly.

'Yes.' He was puzzled. She had seemed to understand him a moment ago. 'The Carberry case. The butler . . .'

Mrs Rackstraw nodded to him, smiling and turning him down the steps as she did so. 'Thank you so much for coming with the message. A little girl, you say. Do give Sergeant Jonas our best.'

The policeman gathered speed as he was half pushed down the steps. 'It was a boy,' he muttered. 'And he said to tell you that the . . .'

Grand and Batchelor took the steps two at a time, passing the policemen in their hurry to get back to their own chairs and a plate of Mrs Rackstraw's toast and bone marrow. Grand had been dreaming of it every night since the ship had cleared Manhattan.

'Mrs Rackstraw!' Grand gave her a peck on the cheek as he smelled that savoury smell coming up from the kitchen. He would discover later it was the dishcloths in their monthly boiling, but everything in its season. 'Have you missed us?'

The policeman watched as the door was slammed behind the returning wanderers. If they didn't want to know who did it, it was up to them.

AUTHOR'S NOTE

The Island was inspired by the murders on Smuttynose Island on 6 March 1873. It is not intended as an actual reconstruction of the case.